THE ONE DATE RULE

TAKAYLLA L. GORDON

Hyde
&
Seek
Press

Published by Hyde & Seek Press

Copyright © 2018 TaKaylla Gordon

ISBN-13:978-1-7322203-0-0

FIC027210 FICTION / Romance / LGBT / Lesbian

FIC018000 FICTION / LGBT / Lesbian

Illustration by Vincent Gordon

www.takayllagordon.com

This book is dedicated to all of the late bloomers. It's never too late to go after your dreams.

1

Quinn Kendall was exhausted by the time she climbed into bed. Teaching at the university all day and then trying to fit into Chicago's thriving night life left little time for rest and relaxation. But she wouldn't have it any other way. She loved her new lifestyle. At forty-four, she was young at heart, five years single and free. Who could ask for anything more? Although being a tenured English professor was a rewarding and fulfilling profession, it didn't hold all the thrills and excitement she craved. It was what she called a safe profession and provided her a very comfortable living. However, teaching did not check all the boxes of her life, it was only one aspect. She reached for the satin head scarf that she kept on her nightstand and tied up her loosely curled locks.

In her spare time, Quinn was an accomplished author, a talented cook, a connoisseur of fine wine, a travel junkie and an incurable romantic. She loved love. Yet on her new journey as a single woman, she didn't have time for love. In fact having been in love a few times and with her last relationship ending after eleven years, Quinn decided to reclaim her freedom and leave love to the tried and true professional; love was no longer on her wish list. Been there, done that, she thought.

While she was not looking for love anymore, that didn't mean she had to crawl into a hollow log and die. There was dating, and lots of it—and she had taken it to a new art form, she called it the art of "no strings attached." Since she was not in search of the perfect mate, only a good time, i.e. nice dinner, listening to music, maybe dancing and of course good conversation, she was free to enjoy herself without the burden of love, sex and marriage. She lived her life to suit herself, and it worked.

Things weren't always perfect. There had been a few flaws in her plan in the very beginning as some of the women she dated wanted more from her than she was willing to give. To them, multiple dates added up to forever, let's set a date and when should we rent the U-Haul? They totally misread her intentions. She decided that she had to assume much of the blame for their thinking because she never put a disclaimer on any of her dates. Naturally after several promising dates and frequent communication, one would assume that it was leading to commitment. Needless to say, she had broken some hearts along the way.

Now after some fine-tuning to avoid hurt feelings, her improved plan was foolproof in its simplicity. The trick was to go only on one date with any woman—also known as 'The One Date Rule.' The One Date Rule freed her from unwanted entanglements and as an added benefit, enriched the fun level immensely, giving the term 'seize the day' new meaning.

By the end of the date, she'd be exhausted and filled with satisfaction. Then there were evenings like this one, when the date was so dull and agonizing, that Quinn found herself praying for a speedy death. Anything would have been better than listening to that woman going on and on about one reality television show after the next or why she refuses to buy hair weave from one country as opposed to another, etcetera and so on. The high point of the evening came when the waiter arrived with the check.

All she could think about on the drive home was getting into her bed and how she was going to read Jerry, her best friend, colleague and confidant, the riot act for setting her up on this date in the first place. If she ever heard the name Angela Douglas Esquire again, it would be entirely too soon.

QUINN SAT EATING LUNCH IN HER OFFICE WITH JERRY GALLOWAY, Dean of the English department and her best friend.

"Guess who called me last night."

"I don't know, Jerry. Who?" Quinn asked, spreading mayonnaise on her sandwich.

"Angela Douglas." Jerry was grinning from ear to ear.

"Really," Quinn replied dryly.

"Yes, really and she said that she enjoyed going out with you last night. She also said that you were so easy to talk to and an absolute joy to be around. She's talking second date."

"Spare me."

"You didn't like her?" Jerry asked surprised.

"No. Not even a little bit. She grated my last nerve. You hear me, Jerry. I have not a single nerve left. Look at this." Quinn took a plastic knife and poked the back of her hand. "See this? I don't feel it. She was a chatterbox. And all she wanted to talk about was herself. I managed to get four words in during the entire dinner. You know what I said? 'What are you having?' That's it. After that, she monopolized the whole evening! I do not know where you found this one but—"

"She's one of April's sorority sisters," Jerry interrupted. "She wasn't certain about your chemistry, but decided to take the chance and set you two up."

"Jerry," Quinn whined.

"Okay, she was not a perfect match, but in our defense, it hasn't been easy finding women for you. That one date rule of yours doesn't help. We're running out of women to introduce you to. I must confess, we've been scraping the bottom of the barrel. Angela was possibly the last decent person we could find."

"Good."

"Quinn, all of these "first dates" have got to stop. Now it's time you were in a serious full-service relationship."

"You mean settle down. Why? I was in a serious relationship and it ended."

"Ingrid dumped you for her career." Jerry stuffed the last of the pastrami sandwich into his mouth, chewing purposefully.

"No, Ingrid did not dump me. We dumped each other. We knew at the start of our relationship that neither of us was head over heels in love. I mean, there was definitely love, but it was more about companionship. We made a great team. Our decision to split came way before the job offer in Germany. We were slowly drifting apart. People change. It happens. It was an amicable parting of ways. The offer to teach at the Freie Universitat in Berlin was a fantastic opportunity for Ingrid. She always wanted to live in Berlin and she's doing wonderfully."

"Great, I'm happy for her, but where does that leave you? Quinn, it's been five years since the two of you broke up. Don't you want someone to come home to at night, to share your thoughts and dreams with? You're a beautiful woman with a generous heart. Don't you think it's time to take a chance on real love—not companionship, but *real* love?"

Quinn gazed at Jerry. He called things as he saw them. But he was a cuddly bear of a guy who she could always confide in and whom she'd come to depend on. She sighed heavily, carefully considering her answer before saying, "Jerry, I hear what you're saying and I haven't given up on love, but right now, it's just not in the cards for me. I like who I am and enjoy not being responsible to anyone but me. So if it's all the same to you and your wonderful wife April, I'll stick with doing things my way."

"So the 'one date rule' continues," Jerry stated, wiping the sheen from his balding head.

"It does." Quinn smiled freely. "Oh, and one more thing, Jerry."

"What?"

"No more blind dates. They're killing me."

"Alright, Dr. Kendall, but you mark my words, someday soon love is going to sneak up on you and knock you on your keester."

"Yeah, I know," Quinn said, rolling her eyes.

"You have got to be kidding," Draylen Corliss huffed as she looked at her class schedule, shaking her head. She wondered how she could have confused things so. Looking at the clock on the wall, she realized that she was not going to make it on time. "This is not a good way to start," she voice aloud to no one.

"Hi. I'm Margaret. You look like you need some help."

A startled Draylen turned to see a peppy young girl with curly red hair, about twenty years-old. She was wearing a name tag with Student Assistant underneath her name.

"Hi, Margaret. I'm just a little turned around. I thought I was supposed to be going to my Anthropology class, but now I'm going to be late for a creative writing class."

"I can help you with that," Margaret said. "Let me see your class schedule." Draylen handed over her schedule.

"Oh, you've got Dr. Kendall. It's hard to get into her class. There's always a waitlist." Margaret added, "And I see you're on it. I can show you a shortcut to her classroom. Turn around and follow that blue line on the floor. When it turns to green, make a left and that will take you right to the English department. Her class is the second door on the left. You should make it just before she closes the door."

"Thank you Margaret."

"You're welcome and good luck getting into her class."

Draylen wished she were in better shape as she power walked down the crowded halls darting in and out between students and faculty. She could not believe she was doing this for a second time, of course the last time was over twenty years ago. She received her undergraduate degree, and vowed never to darken the doors of higher learning again. She was schooled out. Her mother, a retired educator and her father, a retired city worker were disappointed that she never went on to get her master's degree. Draylen hated letting them down but she was over school.

In elementary school she was in the accelerated program. On the weekends, there were pre-enrichment courses to prepare for high school. In high school, there were college-prep classes. Summers were not spent hanging out or working like most of her friends. Instead she was taking college courses at the university. When she finally walked across the stage to receive her Communications degree, she felt free. She had fulfilled her obligation to her parents. Now she was free to do whatever she wanted.

Draylen ran the last corridor and managed to reach the classroom just before the door closed. She wedged her foot in the door. "Wait, please." As the door opened wider to allow her access, she breathed a sigh of relief.

"Thank you," Draylen said, adjusting herself and removing the backpack from her shoulder.

"You almost missed your first day of class. Gotta do better."

"Thanks again," Draylen said humbly letting her brown eyes fall upon the instructor for the first time. Her breath halted briefly as their gazes locked for a scant moment in time.

"You're...welcome. Please take a seat, Ms.—"

"Uh...Corliss. Draylen Corliss. I'm on the waitlist."

"Okay, have a seat Ms. Corliss." Quinn continued to peer intently at Draylen, unable to shake the disturbing vibe that overwhelmed her senses.

Draylen wanted to be seated, however Dr. Kendall had not released her from her intense stare, and she felt as if her feet were riveted to the floor.

Quinn, realizing what she had been doing, quickly closed the door and walked to her desk, freeing Draylen to go in search of an available seat.

"Hello, class. My name is Dr. Kendall and I'll be teaching this Creative Writing class. I know for many of you this is an elective course, for English majors, it is a requirement. This is not an easy class, as some of you may have been led to believe. It involves a lot of writing. Expect to have two to three papers of no less than five pages due each week. I would encourage you not to miss any assignments, because they will weigh heavily on your grade. The final will be ten pages and worth forty percent of your grade, but we'll get more in depth with that as the class progresses. Now if this is an elective class for you, or if you feel you are not prepared to take this class, then you may want to drop before the withdrawal period ends."

Quinn looked around the room. She could already tell which students would not be there on the next class meeting. She always loved the first day of each semester. The students were often a source of amusement. Somehow they believed creative writing would be simple, requiring little to no effort. For those that decided to stay, they would find themselves struggling by the fourth or fifth day of class. Then there were the true writers, the ones who really excelled. It was always a joy for her to witness the birth of new talent. She only hoped to have that pleasure this semester.

When class ended, students quickly emptied the room. Draylen waited behind to speak with Dr. Kendall. After listening to the stirring lecture on the power of the written word, she was convinced she had selected the right course. It would be challenging, but she was used to hard work if her earlier academic background were any indication. If only she could be admitted, then she'd prove to Dr. Kendall and most importantly to herself that she belonged in this class. When Dr. Kendall ended her conversation with the student before her, Draylen approached the desk.

"Dr. Kendall?"

"Ms. Corliss, what can I do for you?"

"I was wondering how long it would be until I know whether I'm accepted into your class."

"So, you still want a spot in this course, huh?"

"Yes, I do," Draylen said confidently.

"I didn't discourage you with all the work requirements?"

"No. If anything, you made me want to be here more than ever." She smiled as she looked at Dr. Kendall. She couldn't explain it, but there was something happening within. It was almost like she couldn't get enough air in her lungs.

Dr. Kendall studied Draylen's full pouty mouth as she formed every word. She was an understated beauty. From the wild fiery honey-blonde mass of coils atop her head, to her African print top she wore that hugged her full bosom. She shook her head to erase the image from her mind. Draylen was a student, she reminded herself and therefore off limits. Student and faculty relations were a no-no according to university guidelines. She prided herself in adhering to all rules and regulations.

"I should know by the end of the day. I can let you know then. What is your student e-mail address?" Draylen scribbled the information on a piece of paper and ripped it from her pad, handing it to Dr. Kendall.

"As soon as I know, you'll know. Although I'm pretty sure you'll be admitted. I have a sixth-sense about things like this," Dr. Kendall revealed, as she tapped at her temple.

"Okay...well I'll see you next session."

"Alright. Oh and Ms. Corliss?"

"Yes?"

"You got lucky today, but moving forward, my class starts on time. Once I close that door..." She let her voice trail off.

"Don't worry. I'll be here on time from here on out." Draylen gave a big smile and a wave before exiting the room.

Quinn sighed aloud as she let her eyes follow the curves of Draylen's backside.

2

"Excuse me, please," Draylen yelled over her shoulder to a group of students, she nearly tackled as she ran at breakneck speed down the hallway. Only three weeks into the semester and already she was doing the very thing that she promised not to do—be late for school. She knew that she shouldn't have taken that last minute proofing assignment, but Brad practically begged her, saying that he was on a tight deadline. She couldn't turn him down. He valued her as a top proofreader and made sure she got plenty of work, even when other contracted workers were getting the minimum. However his request couldn't have come at a worse time. She was taking a full course load and this week there was homework due in every class. She didn't get off the computer until almost three in the morning. Somehow, she thought that she could still get to school on time—that is until she mistakenly pressed the off button instead of snooze on her alarm and overslept.

Dr. Kendall did a quick survey of the class before looking at the clock on the wall. It was officially nine-fifty a.m. And Draylen Corliss was absent today. She thought it odd for her not to attend class. Up until now, she had not missed a single session. She hunched her shoulders and sighed. Her attendance rules were finite and applied to all of her students, even Ms. Corliss. She grabbed hold of the door knob just as a hand landed atop hers. She looked up to find a smiling Draylen out of breath. "Whew," she panted as she gawked pleadingly at Quinn, who gave her a look of warning before smiling.

"Get in here and take a seat before you pass out." Quinn was glad that Draylen had not let her down. It was the third week and already several students had withdrawn. She didn't know why, but she had hoped Draylen had what it took to continue.

Just before class ended, Quinn began passing out papers to the students. "I am handing back your graded assignments. I must say that I was impressed by the amount of effort some of you put into your stories. If this is any indication of what I can expect from you, then I look forward to reading your offerings." Quinn went around the classroom returning graded papers to the students. "When you've received your papers, you're free to leave."

"Yes!" Draylen said in a hushed whisper, slightly raising her fist in victory. Another 'A' to add to all of her other assignments. So far things were going great in all of her classes. She had no complaints, though in the beginning, there were doubts about returning to school after a twenty year absence. So much had changed since she ran the halls of higher learning. She only hoped that she could keep the momentum going.

"Ms. Corliss, may I speak with you for a minute?"

"Sure," Draylen said as a sense of dread washed over her, taking her back to high school when she had been asked by her English teacher to wait after class. Then she was accused of not turning in a homework assignment. However she had completed the assignment early and handed it in. Frustrated, she cursed the teacher and stormed out of the class. She remembered how she felt having to break the news to her parents that she'd been suspended until they had a conference with the instructor. It would have been ugly had her mother not been present the evening she did the homework assignment. Draylen composed herself. She was certain that whatever Dr. Kendall wanted to discuss was not as drastic as that. Nevertheless, she wondered what it could be.

"You look like a deer caught in headlights. Are you okay?" Quinn watched as Draylen's expression went from confused to terrified in the span of a minute.

"I'm fine. I'm just a little concerned as to why you need to talk to me."

Quinn let out a hearty chuckle. "I didn't mean to alarm you. It's nothing bad, I assure you."

Draylen let out a sigh of relief. "Oh, okay then. What is it?"

"I've been really impressed with your writing and wanted to invite you to our Writer's Club."

"Oh. Is it something I have to do for extra credit?"

"No, no, no. It's a club founded by a few of the professors in the English Department. We meet once a week, on Thursday evenings. We read our short stories, poems and essays and then critique each other's work."

"I don't know about that." Draylen back-peddled. She didn't mind Dr. Kendall criticizing what she'd written, but didn't feel too comfortable with others doing it. It was only recently that she'd come to terms with her love for writing and vowed to learn more, with hopes of one day pursuing it as a career. Any bad critique could send her running and cause her to once again put aside her dream of being a writer.

"It's not as bad as all that. It's constructive. Trust me, no one will give your works the stink-eye. Many of the members gain lots of knowledge and become even better writers. In fact, several of them have gone on to be published. On top of that, it's a lot of fun. Free food and drink, plus you get to see some of your professors let their hair down and even be a little vulnerable...when it comes to their work, that is." Quinn began shuffling papers and storing them in her folder. Draylen was making *her* feel a bit vulnerable, she had to admit, although she wasn't sure as to why.

"Well...it does sound interesting, Dr. Kendall. Can I think about it?"

"Sure. The next meeting is this Thursday. I'll send the information to your e-mail, just in case you decided to come."

"Alright. I'll give it some thought. Thanks for thinking of me," Draylen said as she gathered her backpack, placing it on her shoulder.

"No problem. I hope I didn't make you late for your next class."

"Uh-no. I've got a forty-five minute break. I usually read and finish any last minute homework. I'm good."

"Well, enjoy the rest of your day," Quinn said.

"Thanks, I will," Draylen said before leaving the classroom.

And the best actress award goes to Draylen Corliss for her portrayal of the calm cool collected student, Draylen thought as she headed to the library. She was anything but calm. Why did Dr. Kendall make her feel so...awkward and unsure of herself? It certainly didn't help that she was so attractive—sexy. She could have been a run way model, though she may have lacked the three inches needed to meet the six foot required for most fashion runways of Milan.

At times during her lectures, it seems as if Dr. Kendall was talking only to her. It was a ridiculous thought, considering that there were at least a good twenty-four students in the class. Nevertheless, she couldn't help but entertain it whenever it crossed her mind—which was often. Teachers didn't look like Dr. Kendall when she was an undergrad twenty years ago. They were stiff, stodgy and dressed in flannels and various man-made fabrics. There was always an understood boundary that separated them from the students—a line which neither student nor professor ever crossed.

Dr. Kendall was a free spirit who was not afraid to interact with her students. When she spoke it was as if her voice bathed the class in sultry jazz melodies. She definitely knew how to captivate an audience. She was an excellent instructor, Draylen thought. It's no wonder her classes were the hardest to get into. Draylen smirked. Did she have a crush on Dr. Kendall? Stranger things have happened. Besides, it was harmless. She had no intentions of making a fool of herself and revealing these school girl feelings to her, so what was the harm? Anyway, there were rules in place that banned student/teacher relationships, weren't there?

Even if there weren't rules at the university, she had her own rule. She called it the steer-clear-of-any-and-all-things-pertaining-to-love rule—sure to keep her heart from being destroyed and leaving her life in shambles. She enacted it three years ago after her seven year relationship with her partner Dava ended badly. She was not done loving her and did not see the end until it was too late. Left for another woman. It was a textbook breakup. However there was one subtle difference—she had fallen in love with her best friend. It was just one of those things that happened. It surprised them both having been best friends since grade school.

They shared everything, the most intimate deepest darkest secrets. Then one day love stepped in changing the dynamics of their closeness. People always say that they want to fall in love with their best friends. That is perfectly fine when things are going well. But when they turn sour and it's over, it hurts twice as much because not only have you lost your partner, but also your best friend. Draylen recalled the dark times of not having her lover nor her best friend to lean on when the emptiness covered her like a shroud.

In the beginning, she didn't know which she hated losing the most, her partner or her best friend. As time went by, she realized she missed her bestie most of all. When Dava re-surfaced recently wanting them to work at restoring their friendship, Draylen jumped at the chance and vowed to let nothing ever come between them again.

"BRAD, IF YOU'RE CALLING ME TO DO ANOTHER LAST MINUTE JOB, I'm going to have to say, no."

"Relax, Draylen. I'm not calling to give you last minute work. In fact, I'm calling to say that the client was pleased with the quick turn around and as a result of your excellent work, you can expect a little something extra on your next paycheck."

"Great. Now that's what I like to hear, Brad," Draylen cheered. She'd been working for Bradley Mitchell's company as an independent contractor for six years and in that time they had become the dynamic duo. At first Draylen worked with a half dozen other clients in order to make ends meet and keep herself financially stable. However, when she took on Bradley's company one year ago, he was so impressed with her skills that he ended up giving her more work than she could ever imagine, forcing her to turn away some of her other clients.

"So, how is school? Is it kicking your butt? If it is, your work has not suffered because of it. Thank you very much."

"You're welcome Brad. And no, school is not kicking my butt, as you put it. I was hesitant in the beginning, but now that I'm in the groove of things, I quite like it. I even look forward to attending. In fact I was invited by one of my professors to join a club. I'm thinking about going to their meeting tonight—then again, I don't know. A lot of the faculty will be there. You know me, I don't like being put on the spot. That's why I do so well working from home—no pressure."

"You should go," Bradley encouraged. "You need to get out more. I don't know how you 'work at home' people do it. Honestly, I'd be climbing the walls if I didn't have interaction with people all day, five days a week."

"Oh. It's not as bad as you think. Besides, I do get out—maybe not as much as the average person and definitely not as much as you, Bradley, but I do have a social life."

"Not much of one," Bradley countered. "I know how many hours you clock with the company plus I am aware that you'll do the occasional job with my competitors."

"Brad—"

"Don't even lie," Brad interrupted. "I overlook it because you do most of your business with me and I appreciate that. Anyway, as I was saying, you clock many hours—far more than any of the other Independent Contractors and a few of them outsource to their employees. You've never missed an assignment. I say to you, go to that meeting and shake things up. It might just change your life. Put the work down and leave the house. That is an order."

"I am a little curious," Draylen reasoned. "Alright, I'll go. Thanks, Brad. You're the best."

"No problem. I forgot I may have another last minute proofing job that I need—"

"Bye, Brad," Draylen snickered into the phone before touching the 'end call' option on her phone.

3

Draylen paced nervously outside the media room door, wondering whether she should retreat. Brad was right, in the last few years, her life had taken a drastic turn, leaving her with a lot of time on her hands. She chose to fill most of that time keeping busy with work—however even with that, there were still too many unclaimed hours at the end of her days. Work had become pretty mechanical. With some jobs, Draylen believed that she could literally do them in her sleep. The idea of school happened quite by chance one day while she was thoroughly engrossed in a manuscript she was proofing. The author talked about dreams deferred and how important it was to pursue them before it was too late. Life was short. Draylen knew this in theory, however it wasn't until reading those pages that the message finally resonated with her. It was as though the words leaped from the page and were embedded into her brain.

"Hello. Welcome to the Writers' Club. Come in." The woman, who was dressed simply in a flowing multi-colored frock and sensible shoes, looked like a hippie from Woodstock. She smiled as she opened the door wide to let Draylen into the festive space. "I'm professor Daltry and whom might you be?"

Draylen attempted to speak but found her voice had failed. She cleared her throat before saying, "My name is Draylen Corliss and I'm—"

"Oh, you're Quinn's student."

"Who?" Draylen asked with a furrowed brow.

"Quinn. I'm sorry you may know her as Dr. Kendall."

"Yes." Draylen nodded.

"She told us all about you. I can't wait to read your work."

Draylen's eyes grew large. She was uneasy about others reading her stories. Right then she decided that she was not ready to be a part of a club like this. She would stay for ten minutes and no more, then make her exit before anyone noticed.

"Don't worry. We're all sensitive when it comes to our personal creative works, so you have nothing to worry about—I assure you." Dr. Daltry placed a reassuring hand on Draylen's shoulder before saying, "Feel free to mingle. I'm sure you recognize a few of the faculty here. There's plenty of refreshments. Help yourself and I'll let Quinn know you're here."

"Okay. Thank you," Draylen said nervously, her voice reaching slightly above the up tempo music that served as the backdrop for the cheerful gathering. There had to be at least twenty people circling about, laughing and interacting. Draylen saw two of her instructors, one of which was her usually stiff and very dry Russian Novels professor—the other being her oh-my-God-she's-so-boring Chaucer Professor. The fact that either of them were capable of showing any kind of emotions, proved that miracles did exist, Draylen thought.

"You know you have a habit of showing all your emotions on your face."

Draylen was surprised to find Dr. Kendall standing beside her. She shivered feeling overcome by her nearness. "What do you mean?"

"The way you're looking at Dr. Gall and Dr. Vance."

"I'm not...I mean, I was looking at them, but I wasn't...I—"

Dr. Kendall interrupted by saying, "You were thinking, I can't believe it, they smile, laugh and have a good time? I didn't know they could do that. They're the dullest teachers on the planet." Dr. Kendall looked to Draylen with a raised brow.

Draylen, shocked that Dr. Kendall had hit the nail firmly on the head, opened her mouth to refute her summation, but soon accepted defeat and closed it.

Dr. Kendall burst into uncontrollable laughter which only got louder when she looked into Draylen's eyes that were wide and filled with a mix of horror and embarrassment. Draylen reached up involuntarily and covered Dr. Kendall's mouth in effort to stifle her. "Shh! Professor Kendall, you have got to stop. You're causing a scene," Draylen whispered admonishingly, as she noticed some of the people turning towards them, curiosity piqued. "You're gonna get me in trouble if Dr. Gall and Dr. Vance catch on to what you're laughing about. I do not want to fail their classes because you've got a case of the giggles."

Dr. Kendall composed herself with great effort. She would have never guessed that Draylen was so high-strung. She could definitely have some fun with her, she thought. She would love more than anything to help tear those walls of rigidity down and loosen her up. She quickly came to her senses as she wondered where that last thought came from.

"Whew! Thank you, Dr. Kendall," Draylen sighed as she removed her hand from Dr. Kendall's mouth.

"I'm sorry Draylen. It's just...I mean, the look on your face was priceless...Anyway, don't worry about Dr. Gall and Dr. Vance. They know what the students say and they're perfectly fine with that. You'll find that they are lovely people with great senses of humor."

"I hope so," Draylen said trying to relax.

"I'm glad you decided to come and see what we're all about. We'll be getting down to business in another fifteen minutes or so. We tend to meet and greet, then we start the readings and critiques, and then more eating and greeting at the end."

"I appreciate your inviting me, but I wasn't planning to stay."

"Why not," Dr. Kendall questioned, trying to stave off her rising disappointment. Having Draylen there, and standing so close to her was the high point of her day. Lately her life had become rather mundane and predictable.

When Draylen joined her class, she knew there was something special about her and knew that she would do anything possible to clear her from the waitlist. Luckily, space opened up allowing for Draylen to stay in her class, without her having to compromise her ethics. Draylen was a rare find and there was no way that she would allow her to run away from the very things that could benefit her.

"Dr. Kendall, this is really not my scene. I feel awkward. Just about everyone here is a professor or administrator. Is that the Dean of the department?" she asked. "Oh, now I know I've got to go. Like I said, I don't belong here. I'm gonna' go." Draylen turned to leave, but was stayed by the gentle hand resting upon her shoulder.

"I'm not letting you go."

"What?" Draylen gasped.

"I don't accept your excuse," Dr. Kendall declared.

"Dr. Kendall—"

"Quinn," Dr. Kendall corrected. "I insist that all the people I kidnap call me by my first name. It's only fair."

"I could make a scene up in here then you'd have no choice but to let me leave," Draylen said, smiling smugly.

"Ah, but you won't do it."

"What makes you think that?"

"Just something I've observed about you."

"And just what have you observed about me? I'm dying to know," Draylen said.

"You're a private person who abhors confrontation and anything that places the attention on you. I wouldn't say that you're shy but you do keep to yourself." Quinn cocked her head to the side smiling with confidence.

Draylen stared expressionless at Quinn. For the second time this evening, she managed to read her precisely. She was uncomfortable with it because Quinn was able to do it so effortlessly. Many times in the past she'd been told that she was a complicated woman capable of driving the sanest person crazy. While the average person would have taken those words as an insult, not her, she embraced them. Why would she want to be simple or easily solved? Simplicity is boring and that's one thing that she never wanted to be.

"So is this what you do, spend your time reading people to their detriment?"

"Not really. I'm just overly aware. Like your displeasure about being surrounded by professors and the Dean."

"I told you that."

"I know. I just thought I'd say it again. But I have a solution to this problem," Quinn asserted.

"And what is that?" Draylen asked.

"This...Hey Jerry, get over here! I have someone here who wants to meet you," Quinn yelled, waving her hands profusely.

"You did not just call the Dean over here," Draylen shrieked as she watched the robust man make his way through the crowd of people. "Quinn what are you doing to me?"

"I'm trying to help ease your mind. Trust me."

When Draylen would have run for cover, Quinn thinking a few steps ahead, quickly took her damp hand and held on to it.

"Lady, you are two kinds of crazy. Release my hand so I can get the hell—"

"Hey, Jerry," Quinn interjected. "I wanted to introduce you to the student I told you about. This is Draylen Corliss. Not only is she new to our club, but she is also new to the University."

"Well, hello Draylen. Quinn has told me so much about you," he said extending his hand. Draylen attempted and finally succeeded in freeing herself from Quinn's grasp, in order to shake Jerry's out-stretched palm.

"Pleased to meet you, Dean Galloway," she said timidly.

"I'm not Dean Galloway. He's an old fart that can't even stay up past nine. I'm Jerry, the Dean's alter-ego. I love to have fun and have been known to come in by one a.m. on a weekday. But don't tell the Dean. He still can't figure out why he's always so tired in the mornings. But that's our secret." Jerry gave a playful wink and a nod that made a chuckle escape from Draylen's tightly pursed lips.

"It's nice to meet you Dean...I mean, Jerry."

"The pleasure is all mine." Jerry looked around at the other members before refocusing his attention back to Quinn and Draylen. "What say we get this show on the road? I'm ready to hear some new work. Draylen, do you feel brave? If so we can call on you first, kind of like death by fire." Jerry gave her the crazy eyes with a devilish grin.

"I didn't realize that I had to bring anything on the first day. I'm sorry." Relieved was more like it, Draylen thought, while giving a silent shout of thanks to God for saving her from public scrutiny.

"That's okay. There's always next meeting," Jerry said.

"Gee and I really would have loved to share my writing with you all," she lied. She couldn't believe herself, but since she had already decided that this would be her only time in attendance, she figured no harm no foul.

"Actually, Draylen," Quinn said intervening. "I happen to have graded your last homework assignment only this afternoon, and I brought it with me to the meeting," Quinn said with a sly smile covering her face.

"What!" Draylen shouted.

"Yeah," Quinn continued. "I took a chance on you coming tonight and I know how you students are always so anxious to see the grades you've received, so I thought I'd let you have yours early. I—"

"You really didn't have to do that. I mean really...you didn't," Draylen hedged.

"Oh, come now. It was no problem and I don't mean to let the cat out of the bag, but it's an 'A' just like all the rest."

"An 'A' Wow! Then surely you won't mind letting us hear a paper that comes with such a high mark," Jerry quipped.

"Yes. Surely I wouldn't," Draylen mumbled as she turned slightly towards Quinn with a look of pleading terror in her eyes.

Quinn picked up on Draylen's angst thinking that possibly her plan to put her at ease may have backfired. She had to think quickly or Draylen would surely self-destruct. "You know, Draylen, I was wondering if I could have the honor of reading your story. That also gives you time to sit and observe how we do things, since it's your first time here. Is that okay?"

"Yes," Draylen managed before her eyes rolled back in her head. "I think that is a great idea."

"Then it's settled. Come on Draylen," Jerry said guiding her over to the circle of chairs. "You can sit next to me."

"AND THE PRIZE OF THE EVENING GOES TO MS. CORLISS," JERRY cheerfully announced.

"Thank you, but I wouldn't go that far. There were a lot of wonderful creative works read here tonight," Draylen said, taking a sip from her glass of punch. She had planned to leave as soon as the last story was read, however she had no idea that she'd be the focus of all the attention during social hour. Whether it was one by one or two by two, club members all came to her with congratulations on her story. During Quinn's reading of her paper, she sat on pins and needles nervously watching many of the expressions around the room. When Quinn got to, "And as the sun said its final farewell signaling the end of the day, two lovers drifted apart knowing that forever was not in the cards for them. Their love had died," everyone in the room was moved by her words. Dr. Vance even dabbed at the corners of her eyes with a napkin at the story's end.

When the floor opened for critiques, no one said anything; the room was silent. Then one of the members stood up and clapped her hands. Before she knew anything, the entire room was standing and shouting, 'bravo'. Never before had she experienced anything so exhilarating, rendering her speechless. All she wanted to do was go home to the safety of her apartment, climb under the covers and relive that moment in her mind over and over again.

"You did great, Draylen. You even managed to move a few of us to tears, especially Dr. Vance. I think the last time she shed a tear it was at the birth announcement of William Shakespeare— she was there, you know. I can't wait to hear your next offering. If you'll excuse me, I have to work the room or else some of the faculty will feel neglected. I'll see you around these hallowed halls." Jerry gave a quick wave of his hand before disappearing into the crowd.

Before leaving, Draylen took one last look at the throng of people milling about the room in heightened discussions and merriment. She smiled trying desperately to commit this moment to memory. Draylen walked the corridor leading up to the security desk. She was surprised to find Quinn standing expressionless, save for an intense gaze that reached out to her.

"I figured you'd be heading this way soon," Quinn said.

"Yeah, you know what happened when Cinderella stayed too late at the ball." Draylen gave a heartless chuckle.

"She marries the prince and the two of them lived happily ever after," Quinn added.

"I mean before that."

"I know." Quinn gave a faint smile before adding, "I'm on my way home, as well. May I walk you out to your carriage? I believe you'll have just enough time before it turns back into a pumpkin."

Draylen scribbled her name on the sign-out sheet before returning her attention to Quinn. "There's no chance of that happening, I took public transportation," she said as she walked out of the glass door with Quinn close behind.

"I can give you a ride."

"That's okay. I'm fine."

"Draylen, it's late. I'm taking you home." Quinn walked ahead to the well-lit parking lot across the way, leaving Draylen to stand in the same spot, trying to decide what to do. Finally she let out a cry of exasperation before catching up to Quinn.

4

"Here you are, safe and sound," Quinn said shifting the car into park. Those were the first words either of them had said since leaving the parking lot. There were things that could have been said but it was all pointless. Tonight she did get to witness the birth of a new writer and it was thrilling. She knew that even though Draylen sat motionless right beside her, she was affected by tonight as well.

"Thank you Dr. Kendall, I appreciate this," Draylen said as she gathered her belongings. She depressed the button on the seat belt. However her efforts to free herself proved unsuccessful. She tried again to fully disengage the lock, but it would not budge.

"It seems that your seatbelt does not want to let me go," She said. Seeing her strenuous efforts to unlock the belt, Dr. Kendall came to her rescue.

"I'm sorry about this. It just started doing that. Let me help you. There's a certain way that you have to push down for it to release. Quinn unfastened her belt and reached over the storage compartment that separated them, taking hold of the base.

Draylen could see that she was having some difficulty. "Let

me hold that for you," she said and reached down covering Quinn's hand to steady the base and allow her to concentrate on the locking mechanism. Neither of them could predict that such a simple holding of hands would set off a sexual chemistry capable of reducing them to their purest needs. The attraction overtook them and their faces were mere inches apart. Operating on raw magnetism, they moved in closer—each struggling to temper her passion.

It became obvious what was about to happen even as their eyes closed and the heat from their breath intermingled. They held firm to the base for leverage anchoring them in what was rapidly becoming unchartered territory. Quinn's heart pounded as she opened her mouth to cover Draylen's slightly parted lips. Her fingers tensed on the button as a soft moan escaped from the back of her throat. Just as their lips were about to make contact, a click. The belt gave way, freeing Draylen as it recoiled back to its resting position, leaving their pent up emotions, dangling in mid-air. The moment died.

Quinn looked down at their hands, still joined at the base of the lock. Gradually Draylen let her hand fall from around Quinn's, her fingers grazing ever so lightly over tensed knuckles as it returned to her lap. Quinn let out a labored sigh trying to clear her mind of what almost happened. "It looks like you're free to go. I'm sorry about the seat belt. I'll make sure to get that fixed."

"Thank you for the ride. See you in the morning," she mumbled as she opened the door. Before she closed it, Quinn called her name.

"Yes, Dr. Kendall?"

"About class tomorrow—"

"I know. I'll be on time." Draylen closed the door and walked through the security gate leading to her apartment.

QUINN WAS PLEASED WITH HERSELF WHEN SHE ENTERED THE school's library. She worked diligently all day and managed to complete everything on her to-do list. Never one to let things fester, she stayed late into the evening grading papers, completing administrative tasks required by the university and drafting her lesson plan for the next two weeks. Many of her colleagues used the same lesson plans from one semester to the next. To Quinn, routine could get dull fast which often made for an unexciting experience for her and the students, so she was always changing things up.

All of her tasks were complete except for the final thing on her list, returning a reference book that she had borrowed earlier in the day. She waited patiently as the librarian came to the counter, scanned the barcode on the inside cover of the book and printed out a receipt, handing it to her. She smiled as she turned from the counter—a sense of fulfillment washed over her. It was now official, she had done everything on her list. The only thing left to do was to go up to her office, spruce up her desk, get her things and head home for the evening.

She had no plans for the evening. Since Jerry's last set up went so terribly wrong, she resolved to slow her dating activities down and put more space between each social encounter. She decided that she was in no hurry to be disappointed, so she would pace herself. Heading for the exit, she couldn't believe her good fortune. Draylen Corliss was off in the corner of the library fast asleep. Quinn's first inclination was not to disturb her but, somehow that didn't go over well with her impulses. She walked to the back of the room, her pulse racing faster with each step. Finally she was standing over her, watching as she slumbered. She smiled when a soft snore came from her cute nose. Her eyes took in Draylen's beautifully coiled hair, the color reminded her of a sunset that she'd seen in her travels to Mexico one year. It was wild and woolly. She longed to lose her fingers in each strand. She stooped down until she was level with her face. She swallowed as her gaze fell upon her mouth with those lips she had come so close to kissing weeks before. Gently she shook her awake. "I hope that it's not my homework assignments keeping you here all night."

"Hi, Dr. Kendall.," Draylen jolted, quickly straightening her disheveled appearance and groggily wiping the sleep from her eyes. Knowing that Dr. Kendall had been watching her as she slumbered knocked her off guard and she scrambled to find words. "I was just reading my Chaucer for Dr. Vance's class. She's giving us an open book quiz at our next class session. Experience has taught me to be prepared. Just because it's open book, a lot of time is eaten up searching through the pages for the answers. It's always good to have the material read and studied beforehand."

"That's the mark of a bright student. So tell me, when you were snoring just now, was that all a part of your study technique for the upcoming quiz?"

"I was snoring?" Embarrassed, Draylen looked around the room.

"You were, but it was light snoring. I didn't pick up on it until I was standing right over you." She came to her feet as their eyes locked.

Draylen snickered. "I thought I was reading the last of The Canterbury Tales. I convinced myself that staying after class and studying here in the library would be a more efficient use of my time. But I guess that only works if I'm not sleeping when I should be studying."

"Sometimes studying in a library where everything is overly

quiet can work against you. You probably would have gotten more accomplished in the comforts of your home."

"Well no chance of that. When I get home I have to go to work." Draylen turned her attentions to the book, taking note of where she had left off.

"I'll let you finish then. I only came in to return a book when I saw you over here. Happy studying. I know that you'll do well on the quiz."

"Thank you Dr. Kendall." Draylen stared at her before skimming her notes. Quinn took that as her cue to leave. As she exited the library, she could only wonder what Draylen was thinking when she looked with her head cocked to the side and her brow furrowed.

IT WAS A WHOLE HOUR LATER WHEN QUINN FINALLY TURNED OFF her desk lamp, grabbed her satchel and locked up her office. As she left the stairwell heading for the front exit, she saw Draylen by the coffee vending machine waiting for her brew to completely fill the dispensed cup.

"So we meet again Ms. Corliss. Did you finish your studies for the evening?" Quinn asked.

"Yes I did. I thought that I'd get myself a little pick-me-up to drink on the way home so I can be bright-eyed and bushy-tailed when I start my job tonight." The coffee stopped and the cup was released. Draylen lifted it from the holding receptacle but before she could take a sip, Quinn carefully removed the cup from her grasp.

"Uh...What are you doing?" She asked completely stunned.

"Trust me. I'm doing you a favor." Quinn dropped the cup into the nearby garbage can then grabbed Draylen by her forearm.

"Why did you do that?" Draylen asked with a tinge of displeasure. But before her temper started to flare, she was spirited off to the stairwell. When they reached the English Department, she was taken down a short hall and waited while Quinn unlocked a door marked 'Faculty Lounge.' Once inside, she turned on the lights.

"Ms. Corliss, please have a seat, I'll be right back."

Draylen was hesitant but took a seat and let her eyes drink in the surroundings. Gently worn leather lounging chairs aligned two of the walls with rich dark wood moldings outlining each wall and door jamb. A fully stocked kitchenette complete with modern appliances was in plain view. Five bistro tables with matching chairs were sprinkled about the spacious area. A tall bookshelf filled with books and magazines rested along another wall. In the far back of the room were two sets of comfortable looking recliner chairs.

"I hope that I wasn't gone too long."

"No, I hardly noticed. But why are we here Dr. Kendall?"

"We're not in class. You can call me Quinn, it's perfectly fine."

"Okay Quinn, why are we here?"

"Ah! Let me show you." She walked over to the counter and removed a plastic covering from a concealed device, placing it aside. She then moved to the other side of the counter. "Tah dah!" Quinn smiled and held out her hands like a presenter on The Price is Right.

"An espresso machine?" Draylen asked.

"Yes!"

"Is this my university tuition at work?"

"No, it's not," Quinn said, chuckling as she went about operating the machine like a skilled barista. "This was a gift or shall I say a re-gift from Dean Galloway and his lovely wife. You see, Jerry has a bad habit of watching the shopping channels on television, making many hasty purchases, much to his wife, April's chagrin. Anyway, he bought this and when it arrived he became intimidated by the phonebook sized instruction manual. The next day he brought it in here and this is where it's been ever since."

"I see," Draylen said.

"There are only three of us who actually use it. The other faculty can't be bothered. I've even shown them how to work it, but some people don't care to learn new things, which is surprising since we're in the business of educating. Go figure. Anyway, how many hours do you have to work tonight?"

"Maybe four intense hours of deep concentration. I doubt that I could do more than that—not the way I'm feeling." Draylen yawned further illustrating her point.

"Great. I'm just trying to determine how strong I should make your drink. This is my personal stash, top of the line imported from Brazil. It's very robust, but I can make it stronger."

"Whatever you feel is best," Draylen said astonished by the ease with which Quinn handled the complex machinery.

"What kind of work do you do, if I'm not being too nosey?" Quinn asked.

"I'm a freelance proofreader, which requires me to be alert."

"Definitely. How long have you been doing that?"

"Almost ten years."

"Do you like it?"

"It's a job. It's not exciting, but I do provide a valuable service and at the end of the day, it can be rewarding. The bottom line is that it pays me well. I'm able to meet my expenses and do some of the things that I want, like going back to school. I don't know that I could ask for more. And the cherry on top is that I get to work from home. It's funny. At times I have to do a business call with a client and they have no idea that I'm in my pajamas.

They're completely clueless. For all they know, I could be talking to them in the nude."

"I'd pay good money to see that," Quinn mumbled under her breath.

"Did you say something?"

"Uh-no. I was just wondering how you manage to work such a demanding job while going to school full time."

"The first week was an adjustment trying to juggle the two, but that was because I was in the middle of a project for a very important client. But now I am able to schedule my time properly, so it all works out."

"Yeah, but it couldn't leave much time for a social life or time for yourself, you know, to relax." Quinn looked over her shoulder to study Draylen's expression. She couldn't help herself. She had to satisfy her need to learn more about what made her tick.

"You'd be surprised how much I'm able to get out. In fact, lately I've been making time for fun and relaxation—in moderation of course."

"Of course." Quinn placed lids on top of the two prepared coffee drinks before cleaning and covering the espresso machine, and wiping down the counter. "I'm glad you're able to take time out. I think it is essential to enjoying life." She walked over to Draylen, allowing her gaze to cover her from head to toe before falling back to her expressive eyes. "Here. I added some sweetener for you. You seem like someone who enjoys something a little sweet. Was I wrong?" She stared, drinking in every molecule of Draylen, losing herself in her presence.

"You got it right," Draylen said as she found herself drawn into Quinn's sensual playfulness and its limitless possibilities. "I'm addicted to sweet and savory things." She quirked her brow and a slow smile teased at the very corner of her mouth.

Quinn was enjoying their wordplay and could have kept the

game going for hours on end but knew that eventually it would lead to something that neither of them was ready for. "Go on. I can't wait for you to try your espresso and tell me what you think."

Draylen was a little disappointed when Quinn ended their rousing banter but decided that it was the right call. They had to keep their wits about them—they each stood to lose a great deal if they didn't. Quinn could lose her university job while she, on the other hand, ran the risk of getting her heart broken once again. Bringing the cup to her face, she inhaled the rich hearty aroma before taking a cautious sip. "Whoa! This is serious business right here," she said wasting no time getting to her next taste of the delicious concoction. "Mmm, this is pure heaven. It's —it's like recess in a cup."

"I've never heard it described quite like that." Quinn laughed as she watched Draylen down the drink as fast as the scalding liquid would allow.

"I think it's tickling my insides," she said laughing aloud.

"I think you're experiencing a caffeine high. I've just never seen it happen so fast with anyone."

"I'm really not much of a coffee drinker," Draylen said. "My only indulgence is Caramel Macchiato and I have them just a few times a month."

"Maybe you should just drink half of that. Who knows what condition you'll be in when it wears off, and it will wear off. In fact eat these..." She handed Draylen two pre-packaged biscotti's. "They're delicious with espresso and it will help to coat your stomach. You probably haven't had anything to eat since lunch."

"No, I haven't. I'll get a sandwich later when I get home."

"Do you need a ride?"

"No, it's not necessary. I've got my transit card."

Quinn opened the door and held it open for her before

turning out the lights in the lounge. "You're riding with me." When Draylen motioned to protest, she gave her a look that said, 'don't argue with me.' Draylen acquiesced and together they left the building and headed for the parking lot.

5

B y the next morning, Draylen had finally come down from the espresso high and felt that a refueling was in order, which led her to her favorite haunt.

"One Caramel Macchiato up!" shouted the barista from behind the counter. Draylen wove her way through the people standing at the front of the line to reach her ordered beverage. She took a couple steps over to the prep area for a cardboard cone and then added packets of sweetener to the brew before returning to the small bistro table tucked away in the corner of the café.

Today was too beautiful to stay cooped up in the house. The sun called to her. She was in a good mood. Having completed all of her course work for the week, she decided to treat herself to a Saturday of coffee drinks, light reading and people watching—a guilty pleasure of hers. She stirred the frothy concoction before taking a cautious sip and replacing the lid. She opened her book to the page being held by the marker and resumed reading.

"Is it good?"

Draylen recognized the voice right off, but did not look up immediately, opting to brace herself by first marking her page in the book and closing it, before meeting Quinn's hypnotic gaze. "It's interesting—a little dry in the beginning, but it's starting to pick up. Dean Galloway suggested it as a good reference tool for writers."

"Quinn read the title upside down from her standing position. "Yes, that is a great book. We all find ourselves using it at one time or another. I have an extra copy. I'd be happy to let you have it and save yourself sixty bucks."

"Are you sure? I mean, that would be great."

"Sure, I'm sure. What do I need with two copies of the same book?" Quinn chortled.

"Why do you have two?"

"I thought I'd lost the first one, so I bought it again, only to discover that I had packed it away with some other books. I found it one day while cleaning out my office."

"I see," Draylen nodded. She pursed her lips together and let her hand rest atop the book tapping out an S.O.S message with her fingers—a desperate attempt to drown out the awkward silence between them. She looked to Quinn who was standing above her, surveying the bustling café bookstore, and realized she hadn't invited her to sit down. "I do have manners, but I seemed to have left them at home today. Would you like to sit down?" She pushed the chair from under the table using her foot.

"I'd love to," Quinn said, placing her coffee cup onto the table and then sitting in the offered seat. "You must have gotten here early to get this table. This is choice seating. You can see everything and still keep your privacy."

"Spoken like a regular. Do you come here often?" Draylen asked.

"I do, when I have the time. What about you?"

"I'm here a lot. I guess you could say that this is my second home. Sometimes I read but mostly I watch people, and write stuff." Draylen shifted in her seat. Quinn had a way of looking at her with such intensity that she was subconsciously drawn into her world.

"How is school going for you?" Quinn asked.

"Everything's great. I guess the only thing that I've had to come to terms with is being in school with kids half my age. I'm older than some of their parents, so, it's definitely an adjustment —but everything is clicking. Going to school now is so different from when I went twenty years ago. I don't have the added pressures of trying to find my place in the world and everything that comes with that—I'm already established. Also I'm a lot more receptive to learning. Everything is fascinating to me. I actually look forward to homework. The 'me' of twenty years ago would be trying to figure a way to get all the partying in first and then the homework."

"Wow! Talk about living dangerously."

"Not really. School always came easy for me. My mom was an educator before she retired, so I spent a lot of time in school and more school. By the time I got to college I was over it. I discovered that school was mostly memorization. You know, honestly, I can't say that I learned much academically. The real growth came with trying to be independent—everything else was pretty dull. I went through the motions." Draylen gulped down the rest of her drink. She noticed Quinn looking at her watch for a second time. "Are you late for an appointment?"

"No. Actually I'm going to see the Meryl Streep comedy. I've heard good things about it, so I thought I'd check it out. I want to get there for the first showing."

"From the trailers I've seen it looks like it will be hilarious."

"You want to..." Quinn cleared her throat..."Come with me? Comedies are more fun when you can share in the laughter." Quinn couldn't believe she was technically asking her on a date. She could tell that Draylen was carefully considering of her invitation. She wanted to go. Her body language all but told her true feelings. She just needed one final push in the right direction. "Come on. It's my treat. Besides, I owe you for what I did to you at the Writers' Club meeting."

"No, I owe you," Draylen corrected. She had never thanked Quinn for reading her story at the meeting. She should have and wanted very much to do so but had not been able to form the words. "Alright, I'm in. Let's go."

"I DID NOT SEE THAT ENDING COMING, DID YOU?" QUINN INQUIRED as the crowd of movie goers spilled out into the lobby area.

"No. I never heard of a comedy with a surprise ending. I smell a sequel," Draylen surmised.

"Definitely. A sequel is inevitable." Quinn stared at Draylen, waiting to see what the next move would be. Had she even realized that they were actually on a date? How did she feel about that, she wondered. Then instantly she knew the moment it crossed Draylen's mind. Her expression changed from jovial to detached and gloomy. She stood rigid enough that the slightest touch would cause her to break into tiny little pieces. Removing her phone from the pocket of her denim jeans, she pressed the pad to check the time. "Well, I've gotta go. I have to be somewhere soon. But thanks for...this. It was fun...See you in class on Monday." She barely waited for a response from Quinn before she scurried from the theatre, leaving Quinn still standing in the same spot watching her fleeting frame.

6

The Writers' Club let out early, much to Draylen's relief. The meetings had been rescheduled to Fridays for the next few weeks on account of upcoming faculty meetings. Draylen had another successful reading. Since becoming a member, her writing had received high praises from the other members which served as a boon to her confidence. Tonight she read an experimental piece about urban decay as reflected in the eyes of two African-American families. She was uncertain how it would be received by the culturally diverse audience. She was always surprised by the positive responses she got. Had she only pursued writing during her undergraduate years, she thought, maybe she'd be a writer by now and not just dreaming about it.

She signed out at the front desk and headed through the doors leading to the parking lot. She stopped short at the sight of Quinn who stood just beyond the exit. Draylen knew that she had been waiting for her. At the meeting she sat away from Quinn, not wanting to be affected by her closeness. During the social time, she mingled in circles separate from Quinn. If Quinn made eye contact with her, she'd quickly look away, even though she could still fill the heat from her stare. And now here she was, caught up in her gaze—again.

"Hi." Quinn smiled.

"Hey."

"That was a great story that you read tonight. I was really impressed by it."

"Thank you," Draylen said, chewing her bottom lip. "I wasn't sure about it, but I decided to take a chance. Most people tend to turn a deaf ear whenever you talk about the injustices that go on in the African-American community. I didn't want it to come off as a rant, with me standing on my soapbox spouting rhetoric."

"I'm glad you did. It paid off, wouldn't you say?"

"Yeah, it did. I enjoyed your piece as well. The way you compared the worn shoes to life, it was a cool metaphor. I also see what you mean in class when you talk about the importance of imagery."

"I'm happy that you were able to get that from those few pages of the story," Quinn said.

"You made it easy." Draylen quirked her brow and smiled sheepishly.

"Thank you."

"You're welcome."

"Do you need a ride home tonight," Quinn asked, not wanting their conversation to end.

"Nope." Draylen reached into her light denim jacket and extracted a set of keys, dangling them in the air. "I'm under my own steed tonight. It's my friend's car. She lets me borrow it from time to time."

"Oh, good." Quinn pasted on a smile though she was clearly disappointed. She had hoped to take Draylen home, that way she'd have more time to spend with her. But now that was not to be. She had to do something to prolong their time together, she thought, but what?

"Well, I'd better g—"

"Do you want to get some dinner?" Quinn blurted then waited patiently while Draylen deliberated in her mind. She could tell that her offer was about to be shot down and therefore she had to do some quick thinking to turn the odds in her favor. "Come on, say yes. I know a great out of the way place with delicious food and a wonderful atmosphere." When Draylen still hadn't responded, she added, "It's Friday. The night is still young. You don't want to be home on a Friday night any more than I do. Say you'll come...you took one chance tonight, take another one," (on me, she found herself wanting to say, take a chance on me).

"Um...I guess I could get something to eat. I was only planning to warm some leftovers."

"Great, then you can follow me." Quinn beamed, showing her perfect set of teeth.

"Sounds good," Draylen said as they walked to the parking lot.

"How long have you been a professor?" Draylen managed between bites of key lime pie.

"Going on nine years," Quinn said as she stirred her glass of soda with her straw.

"Do you like it?"

"I do. It was stressful in the beginning because I thought that I needed to conform to everyone's idea of what a professor should be and how they should act. So I would try to be this regal instructor that called all of her students by their last names and stood at my desk looking down on them as I lectured. It just wasn't me. Finally I decided to be myself, and that's when I started to really enjoy what I was doing. Of course when I became tenured, I was able to relax even more. I love teaching because I take pleasure in watching my students learn new concepts and ideas. It's a huge responsibility to help mold minds. I try and give my students the framework and allow them to fill in the blanks with their own thoughts. I never want to stifle a person's creativity." Quinn took a sip from her soda. "I'm sorry for the long answer. I tend to get really excited when I talk about teaching."

"No, you're good. I have to say that I do enjoy being in your class. I'm glad that I was able to get in."

"So am I." Quinn covered Draylen's hand and was pleased when she didn't recoil.

7

Quinn sat at the desk with her hands folded. She had given an in-class writing assignment. As she waited for the period to end, she found herself staring at Draylen who sat with a bowed head as she worked. Things were happening that, try as she might, she could not stop. Her feelings for Draylen were growing far beyond what was considered appropriate for a teacher/student relationship. Were there any doubts, she only needed to look at what happened at dinner on Friday. The evening was going great and after a while, Draylen began to relax and open up. She was amazing, funny and beautiful. Quinn could not have asked for a better evening. They left the restaurant, still reeling from such a magical night. As they were set to part and go their separate ways, she hugged Draylen. It had not been planned. She acted on pure emotion. When she pulled back, overcome by passion, she longed to kiss her deeply, and would have were it not for the look of caution Draylen gave her. Slowly she braced herself, letting her hands fall to her side before stepping away.

She sat there at her desk, wanting very much to reach out and caress her smooth caramel skin and taste those succulent lips surging deep within to feast upon her tongue. Even though she wanted to do all of these things, she knew that she had to push those desires behind her if she was to make it through the semester with her heart and her job intact. She was caught off guard when Draylen raised her head and stared into her eyes for what seemed like an eternity. Most of the time she was able to read her biorhythms like an open book. Unfortunately this was not one of those times. She was the first to look away unable to handle Draylen's scrutiny. When class came to close Draylen looked straight ahead as she exited the classroom.

"ARE YOU ALRIGHT," JERRY ASKED AS HE SAT ON THE CORNER OF Quinn's desk.

"Yes. Why do you ask?"

"I just spoke to you in the hall and you walked right past me."

"Oh, I'm sorry. I must have had something on my mind." Quinn sat at her desk with her head resting against the palm of her hand, staring off into space.

"Quinn, is there anything you want to talk about?"

"Well...Uh, no. Everything is fine." She began mindlessly shuffling papers, moving them from one side of her desk to the other.

"Alright. Remember that we're good friends. You can talk to me about anything. My door is always open." Jerry got up and walked to the door.

"Okay," Quinn said before he left the office.

Quinn shook her head trying to clear her mind. She needed to purge these feelings for Draylen once and for all, she decided.

AFTER QUINN'S CLASS, DRAYLEN FOUND IT QUITE DIFFICULT TO concentrate in her other sessions—she was simply going through the motions. She hadn't been able to get Friday night off her mind. How could she? Quinn was becoming so much a part of her world that she felt powerless to do anything about it —but she knew that she had to do something. The last thing she needed was to get involved with her professor or anyone for that matter. She had no choice. She'd have to put some distance between them or suffer the consequences.

8

It was ten a.m. and everyone was present and accounted for —everyone except Draylen. She was a no-show. Quinn had even relaxed her rule, leaving the door slightly ajar, just in case Draylen did her last-minute entrance, but she didn't. Suddenly she could think of nothing else and as the class went on she found herself from time to time, glancing over to the empty seat and wondering what could have happened that would cause Draylen to miss her class. It was not like her to miss a class, she reasoned. She found herself thinking of all sorts of things that could have gone wrong with her. She then reminded herself that she was just another of her students and therefore she could not afford to put so much thought into her absence. How could she put an end to her feelings for Draylen if she was constantly letting her consume every corner of her mind? Draylen was an adult. If she missed class then it must have been her choosing— case closed. This was her reasoning even as she parked her car in front of Draylen's apartment building.

"Who is it?" Draylen said, answering the ringing bell.

"It's Dr.—it's Quinn."

Draylen pressed the buzzer then unlocked and opened the door. Of all people she did not expect to hear from Quinn. In fact she was the last person she needed to see. Quinn walked through the door in a fit of frenzy, as she closed the door behind her.

"Are you okay?" Quinn asked.

"Of course, I'm fine," Draylen assured her as she furrowed her brow.

"Why didn't you come to class?"

"I was behind on an assignment for my job," Draylen said as she walked further into the living room rather than look into Quinn eyes.

"Oh, really?" Everything about her body language said that she was lying and Quinn was determined to find the truth.

"I've been calling your phone. Why haven't you answered?" Quinn followed Draylen into the room and stood facing her.

"How did you get my number," Draylen asked somewhat confused.

"I looked it up on your class record. It wasn't hard," Quinn said. 'Now why haven't you answered my calls?" she repeated impatiently.

"I usually turn it off when I'm working."

Quinn knew she was not being upfront with her, judging by the way she paced the wood-varnished floor.

"What if there is an emergency, then how does someone reach you," Quinn challenged.

Draylen walked over to the desk and retrieved the landline phone holding it up to Quinn. "People know to call the house phone if it's an emergency." She returned the phone back to the desk, before asking, "Why are you here, Dr. Kendall?"

"I thought something might have happened to you, that's all." Now Quinn was the one pacing the floor.

"Daniel Jacobson was absent the other day. Did you show up at his home asking him why he wasn't in class?"

"No, but Daniel has a pattern of missing my class, you don't."

Sensing her advantage, Draylen pressed further. "Okay and is that the only reason?"

"What is that supposed to mean?" Quinn hedged.

"I think you know what I mean." Draylen was now mere inches from Quinn staring her down.

"What?"

"Nothing. Just forget it," Draylen replied, backing down. "I was busy when you got here, so I have to get back to it," Draylen said as she walked Quinn to the door. Before she could open it, Quinn leaned against the door, obstructing her.

"What are you doing?" Draylen asked astonished by Quinn's actions.

"I get the feeling that you're trying to avoid me. Is this true?"

"Why is it your concern about anything I do?" Draylen asked.

"I don't know. Maybe it's because I'm a human being. Draylen, my care and concern for my students doesn't stop just because the school bell rings."

"That's why you're here—out of concern for your student?" Draylen closed the space between them, preventing any possible escape.

"Yes, what else would it be?" Quinn said, feeling her face flush. The heat of Draylen's nearness was becoming unbearable. Draylen reached above Quinn's shoulders placing her hands on the door, trapping her. Quinn closed her eyes and tried to steady the rapid beating in her chest. Draylen stared at her, not moving. She had more than made her intentions known. When Quinn opened her eyes Draylen was rewarded with unabashed surrender like none she had ever encountered. That's when she kissed her. Her kiss belied the power of emotion that had been welling up inside of her for weeks. It was thorough and demanding.

Quinn could not prepare herself for the surge of heat that consumed her at the slightest touch of Draylen's soothing lips. It was as if she was transmitting coded messages to her through her sun-drenched kiss. She wanted to live inside of it forever, but it was not to be. The kiss ended leaving her mouth singed and the two of them breathless. As if on automatic pilot, Draylen's hands came down to her sides, freeing Quinn from wanton captivity.

Having fought feverishly for an ounce of resolve, Draylen was the first to speak. "Professor, I thank you for your..." She cleared her throat... "Concern." Her hand came up to slowly caress Quinn's olive cheek before moving down to her neck, then retracing her steps.

"I wouldn't advise you to show this much compassion for any more of your students. I don't think that would be a good idea, do you?" Her voice was low and seductive as she spoke.

Quinn could feel herself slipping into a sensual invasion that she had no desire to escape. She allowed her cheek to lean into each caress, slowly learning Draylen's touch, burning it into memory. She had become so in tuned to her tender hand and its pleasant assault that a few minutes had gone by before she realized that the caressing had ceased and Draylen was gazing intently, reveling in the moment. Quinn would have been embarrassed being caught so enraptured and vulnerable, were it not for the playful, satisfied smile at the corners of Draylen's mouth.

"I'd better go and let you get back to what you were doing," Quinn stammered, prying herself from the door. She reached for the knob at the same time as Draylen. That simple contact was enough to stoke the embers burning beneath the surface.

They each recoiled, not willing to play with fire any more than they already had. When enough time had passed and ardors were under control, Quinn grasped the handle and with a quick turn, opened the door, further cooling the temperature of the space. With a heavy sigh, she made her exit.

9

Quinn sat staring at the empty seat as she listened to a student read from his paper. Draylen was absent for the second time and she didn't understand why. What was going on with her? Since the night they had shared the mind-blowing kiss, things had returned to normal. Draylen was present for every class, but now her seat was empty and had been for the last few sessions. If she continued on this way, then she would have no other choice than to fail her—she knew that she could never bring herself to do this no matter what. Draylen was her best student, filled with so much promise.

She grew somber with each passing minute and decided it best to dismiss class early so that she could get herself together and make it through the rest of the day. She vowed not to call Draylen no matter how much she ached to do so. She would wait to speak with her at the next Writer's Club meeting.

"So...where is she?" Jerry asked.

"Who?" Quinn asked although she knew exactly who he was referring to.

"Draylen Corliss, our star writer. I thought I'd be captivated by one of her short stories tonight. She's really good. Why don't you suggest to her that she submit some of her stories to 'The Write Off'? Getting published in our student publication would do wonders for her confidence. It's a good place for her to start." Jerry would have continued talking but noticed that Quinn was not listening to him. "Quinn, is everything okay? You're doing that staring off in the distance thing again."

"Oh...No, I'm fine. Draylen has been working a lot of overtime. I guess she's still playing catch up, that's all." Quinn was upset that Draylen did not bother to come to the meeting tonight. Like class the other day, she had blown the club off as well. She felt like screaming, but pasted on a smile as Dr. Vance and Dr. Gall approached them.

"What happened to Draylen? We were hoping that she came tonight. We love her stories," Dr. Gall said.

"Yes, I was just discussing with Jerry that she's been working a lot," Quinn said.

"Maybe that's why she said that she was leaving school," Dr. Vance added.

"What?" Quinn said, clearly shocked by the news. "Are you certain of this?"

"Yes, dear. I was in the admissions office this afternoon and I saw her there. She told me that she loved being in my class but was sorry to inform me that she would no longer be attending. She was dropping out of school. She said it was due to circumstances beyond her control."

"Maybe that's why she didn't show up tonight. She probably felt like she wouldn't be welcomed. What a shame," Jerry sighed.

Quinn had taken all that she would take from Draylen. To drop out without telling her—simply disregarding her feelings?

Well that was it. She resolved to have it out with Draylen Corliss and let her know that she would not stand for it.

"Quinn, are you feeling okay," Dr. Vance asked.

"Yes, why do you ask?"

"You're starting to look a little flush."

"I...have a headache... I need to get home. If you'll excuse me, please."

"Of course," Jerry said with a look of concern. "See that you take care of what's bothering you." He quirked his brow when Quinn gave him a questioning look.

"Call me." Jerry continued. "If you're not feeling better, I can take over your classes for you tomorrow."

"Thank you. Goodnight everyone."

QUINN DID NOT WASTE ANY TIME GETTING TO HER CAR. SHE WAS SO hurt and angry. Draylen could have told her that she was leaving school, but to quit without the slightest mention to her. Doesn't she care about my feelings, she wondered.

When she got to Draylen's apartment, she looked up and saw the lights were off. She decided to ring the doorbell anyway, but came away disappointed, She was not home. All of her attempts to reach her by phone fell short as well—all of her calls went to voicemail. She was beside herself with untapped rage. She had to see Draylen. There was only one other place she could be, she hoped.

Quinn entered the bookstore after speeding like a mad woman. She was pleased that traffic was light and that there were no police around as she drove forty-five miles an hour on residential streets. She was glad that she arrived minutes before the store was set to close. She let her eyes dart around, checking first the table in the far back of the cafe, Draylen's favorite spot.

Next, she looked about the book area, but with the exception of a few people heading for the checkout, Draylen was nowhere to be found. Quinn decided to cut her losses. Draylen was not there and she could think of no place else she may have gone. As she turned to leave, giving one last sweep of the place with her eyes, she came face to face with her, as she emerged from the restroom.

Draylen was startled and stopped in her tracks upon meeting Quinn's unyielding gaze. Instead of acknowledging her, she walked past her and out of the store, convinced that Quinn would follow. When they were both standing out on the pavement, Quinn was the first to speak.

"Hi, Draylen." Her voice was curt, as she did her best to suppress the full force of her anger.

"I already know what this is about," Draylen said as she rolled her eyes and braced herself for Quinn's verbal attack.

"Do you need a lift?"

Draylen was stymied by the question and stared at Quinn's blank expression trying to gage her mood. At a loss for words, she simply nodded then said, "Sure, I could use a lift."

"I'm parked just up the street," Quinn said pointing in the direction of the car. She hit the button on her key fob to unlock the doors. Draylen fell in step with her. Quinn waited until Draylen was seated and secure before going around to the other side and getting in.

Draylen cautiously looked over at Quinn who kept her eyes on the road, never once acknowledging that she was even in the car. She knew that Quinn was upset with her—she had to be, she thought, and yet Quinn said nothing. She didn't know what to make of that.

Quinn could feel Draylen's eyes on her, but she could not let herself look her way. She was too filled with emotion and she did not want to cause an accident.

She turned down Western Avenue and Draylen frowned. "This is not the way to my place."

Quinn continued on, making a right down Artesian before making a left onto a dead end street. She pulled into the drive way of a contemporary brick bungalow in the middle of the block, and put the car in park. She disengaged the locks and opened her door. When Draylen made no motion to get out of the car, Quinn turned to her and said, "I asked if you needed a lift. I never said that I was taking you home." She exited the car closing the door behind her, leaving Draylen still seated on the passenger side.

Quinn walked the few steps of the driveway leading to her house, checked the mailbox, extracting a few bits of mail, then unlocked the door, leaving it slightly ajar. She tossed the keys on to the occasional table that separated the combination living room and dining room area from the kitchen. Once in the kitchen she leaned against the large island that stood in the middle of the travertine floor, then waited. At the sound of the door closing, Quinn walked over to the wine cabinet, taking down two wine goblets and placing them on a serving tray. She opened the wine cooler and selected a bottle. Sitting it on the tray, she brought it to the living room to rest on the cocktail table.

Draylen watched from the entryway as Quinn took a seat on the sofa. She looked around at the stylish house comprised of varnished concrete and metals. The rich fall-colored fabrics of the sofa, loveseat and two full-bottom chairs did much to give warmth to what would have otherwise been a very cold existence. Expensive art hung on the walls. Quinn definitely had an eye for beautiful things, she thought.

"Would you like some wine?" Quinn asked, already pouring one glass and then the other. She held out one of the glasses, clearly out of reach from Draylen who remained standing in the entryway. Finally she walked in measured steps until she was able to take the goblet from her hand.

"Please have a seat," Quinn offered.

Draylen sat at the opposite end of the sofa, closest to the door and watched Quinn with leery eyes. Quinn took a sip of the wine, letting the flavors play upon her tongue before allowing the cool liquid to flow down her throat. She rolled her eyes, tossing her head to the back of the sofa, as she reveled in the sweet nectar. Taking another sip, she relaxed easing comfortably into the cushiony sofa, running her fingers casually through her shoulder length silken curls. Draylen watched her, feeling more like a voyeur than an invited guest.

"Did you try the wine?" Quinn asked as she slowly opened her eyes and looked at Draylen.

"No, not yet," She said refocusing her attention on the glass resting in her hand.

"Take a sip and breathe in through your mouth, like this"— she demonstrated for Draylen—"then swallow. That's how you get the true flavor. It's a Riesling, one of my favorites."

Draylen followed Quinn's directives and smiled the moment she captured the full-bodied essence of the liquid. "It's nice."

They had reached the last of the bottle and still had not discussed the issues gnawing at them. They were relaxed and sat in silence, at times looking at each other and then off into the distance. Quinn removed her shoes and tucked her feet beneath her. Draylen took a labored breath as she watched her under heavy-hooded eyes. She could not believe how graceful she was, even when doing nothing but sitting on the sofa.

Quinn could feel certain points of her body being caressed though there was no physical touch to speak of, only Draylen's beguiling gaze. She told herself that she didn't want to have these feelings—not now when she was still so angry with her.

She had to focus on the anger or else find herself in deep trouble.

"Why did you drop out of school today?" Quinn stared at the floor to avoid making contact with Draylen's coaxing brown eyes.

10

"It was getting to be too much for me."

"You didn't have to leave school. There are all sorts of tools that the university has in place to help our students. There are tutors...you could speak to a peer counselor. I could have helped you." Quinn could feel the lump forming in her throat as she tried to keep her emotions under control. "I would have helped you. Why didn't you come to me?" She took a chance and looked at Draylen. "If only you had asked me."

"Quinn, I couldn't ask you for help, not when you're the problem." Draylen turned into Quinn's questioning stare until it became more than she could handle and she had to turn away.

Quinn's jaw dropped in outrage. "I'm the problem?" She yelled, placing her feet on the ultra-plush hand-woven ivory rug. "What does that mean?" She stood and began to pacing the room.

"Do you know how hard it is to sit in that classroom with you for fifty minutes and pretend that I don't feel things—that I don't want you?" Draylen rested her head in the palms of her hands. "I just couldn't take it anymore!"

"But quitting school, Draylen? You were doing so well in all of your classes...Dammit! Why didn't you just come to me? I could have—"

"You could have what?" Draylen raised her brow.

"Something could have been done, but you didn't come to me. Instead I had to find out about it at the Writers' Club meeting. You do remember the meeting. You missed it and everyone was asking me where the hell you were. I felt like a damn fool making excuses for you when all the time you had dropped out. I can't believe you. Oh, and by the way, everyone told me to tell you that they expect to see you next week."

Draylen could feel the heat radiating off Quinn's body and knew that she was beyond miffed with her. Things were a lot worse than she thought possible. "I'm going to go now before either of us say things we don't mean." She stood up slowly, feeling the effects of the wine. She made it to the entryway, but before she could open the door, Quinn had barricaded it with her body.

"No, I won't let you go. It's too late for you to be out alone, besides you've been drinking. If you don't want to talk anymore, then fine, but you're not leaving here tonight." Quinn glared at her intently as her pulse quickened and a sheen of moisture covered her forehead.

"Is this more of your...concern for your student?" Draylen asked, making air quotes with her fingers.

"No. This is..." Quinn grabbed Draylen bringing her body flush with hers and plowed into her with a hungry and thunderous kiss that lacked all the constraint of their last encounter. Quinn did not seek permission before thrusting her tongue past Draylen's lips. There was no chasteness, only powerful lust that shook them both to the core of their souls. They took turns feasting on one another, letting their tongues dance as they tried desperately to get their fill, only to discover their passions were bottomless, and their thirsts unquenchable. This time there would be no cooler heads prevailing. They had already gone way past the point of no return—which would have been somewhere around the first sip of Riesling. Quinn managed to free her mouth from the hot ministrations of Draylen's lips. Her first attempt to speak faltered when Draylen began sucking and nibbling a path from just behind her ear down to the swells of her exposed cleavage, and she stayed there, tempering her desire to go further. She looked up into Quinn's sensuous gaze pleading even as her hand cupped her breast, manipulating it through her outer coverings.

"Oooo! Draylen, please," Quinn crooned as Draylen reached beneath her starched white cotton shirt and lifted a breast from the confines of the silky bra. Quinn cried out as Draylen's soft hand made contact with the taut nipple, teasing it with her thumb and forefinger.

"Quinn, I need more. I want you, now."

Quinn was barely able to make out the words through the dizzying fog that enveloped her. Quickly she reacted, taking hold of Draylen's hand. "Come with me," she said between gasps of air. No more games tonight, Quinn thought, as they entered her bedroom.

Quinn pulled the chain of the antique lamp bathing the impeccably neat room with a soft white glow. As she turned to face Draylen, she became filled with trepidation. How long had she dreamed of this night, making love to Draylen? Then it was a fantasy, but now it was really happening. In all her teaching career, she had never become involved with any of her students —why now, she wondered. What was it about Draylen and why were these feelings so strong? It was as if she was compelled to submit to these passions lest she be consumed by them. A feeling of uncertainty washed over her. Even as her mind was casting doubt, she opened her arms to Draylen and was pleased when she walked into her soft embrace.

What began as a deliberate removal of clothing became a harried, shameless undressing where some articles were ripped or torn in the process—a small sacrifice for the pleasure set to come. Quinn let her gaze fall upon Draylen's nude frame. She took a deep gulp of air before releasing through partially opened lips. Draylen was far more perfect than she could have ever imagined. She was flawless, from her wildly coiled honey blonde hair, her bold brown eyes, and pouting mouth down to her full breast, and manicured mound that made up her femininity. From head to toe, Draylen was the perfect specimen. She was made to be loved and made love to.

"Draylen, you're beautiful," Quinn said in awe as she reached out and let her hands explore the smoothness of her neck and shoulder, her arms.

Draylen didn't know what to make of Quinn's careful perusal of her body, but she'd be damned if she'd stop her. "Quinn?"

"I've never seen someone so perfect," Quinn said while she ran her hands down Draylen's waist and over the expanse of her thighs.

"Quinn, I don't know how much more of your touching me I can take."

Quinn looked up to find Draylen trembling and in the throes of agony. Rising up to her full five-seven height, she reached for Draylen, clinging to her as she planted kiss after soul- searing kiss on her pliant mouth. Quinn released Draylen long enough to pull back the covers on her bed then quickly returned to her tender lips. As the kiss deepened, she walked Draylen slowly back to the bed, gently easing her down to the plush pillows, before climbing atop her quivering frame.

Quinn cupped Draylen's breast, causing her to explode on contact. "Quinn...please," Draylen begged when Quinn took her berry nipple into her mouth and laved it repeatedly with her tongue, letting it slide out over her playful lips, only to be captured once again. Draylen held her other breast consoling it, tenderly cooing until Quinn could move to it and give equal attention.

Draylen's head thrashed from side to side as Quinn parted her legs positioning herself firmly against the apex of her slippery walls. Slowly, methodically she began to move her hips in a rhythmic pattern that grew more frenzied at each pass.

Quinn could not stop the rapacious screams from escaping her lips as Draylen's fingers lightly skimmed down the surface of her spine.

"You feel so good," Draylen whispered as her appetite became more ravenous. Quickly she reversed their positions, pinning Quinn to the bed, and setting a new pace, one that would elevate their passions and enter the zenith just within reach. When Quinn made an attempt to challenge her and regain her position, Draylen held her hand firmly as she continued to move against her throbbing mound.

"Trust me, babe. I'm giving us what we need," she said spreading Quinn's thighs wider. "Ride with me," Draylen commanded, increasing her motion. Quinn followed suit undulating frantically, causing a fiery fusion of splendor. Neither of them could prepare for the wicked delight as their clitorises rollicked, intensifying the heat of their desires. And when the last vestiges of passion wrung from their glistening bodies and shudder upon shudder came in succession, they clung tight to each other until finally they transcended into true ecstasy, never to be the same again. They shivered as they gazed at each other with dizzying disbelief. Sated for a second then a third time, they lay listening to slowed breathing and normal heartbeats.

"Quinn?"

"Hmm?"

"I'm sorry. I should have told you of my plans to leave school.

I was angry because of my feelings for you. I wanted you to be angry too."

"Draylen?"

"Hmm?"

"Don't talk."

"You don't accept my apology?"

"I'm still very upset with you. However in light of everything we just shared, I'm willing to move forward—a clean slate. Does that work for you?"

"Yeah," Draylen smiled. "It works for me."

"Good, now go to sleep."

"Goodnight, Quinn."

"Goodnight, babe."

11

A week later at Draylen's apartment.

"Draylen?"

"Yes?"

"You told me to let you know when it's nine o'clock. Well, its nine o'clock," Quinn said glancing at her watch.

"Thank you," Draylen said yawning as she sat at her desk staring at her computer screen. She made a few more corrections to the manual she was proofing before closing out of the program. She removed her reading glasses and place them in the drawer before rubbing her tired eyes.

"Is that a tough assignment that you're working on," Quinn asked from the sofa where she sat grading papers.

"No, it's not tough, it's boring. I prefer to work on anything except instruction manuals. But more than anything, I prefer to work on you." Draylen walked over and snuggled up to Quinn planting little kisses on her cheek. The past week was wonderful with the two of them becoming almost inseparable alternating between each other's places.

"How much longer are you gonna be grading those—" Draylen was interrupted by the ringing cell phone, but she made no move to answer it. Instead, she returned her focus to Quinn.

"Aren't you going to answer that?"

"Nope. I'm busy." After the fourth ring the phone went silent. "Now again, how much longer—" The land line phone began ringing.

"Are you going to answer that?"

Draylen look at the ringing phone then back to Quinn. "No."

Quinn scrunched her face. "But it could be an emergency."

Draylen saw the pleading in Quinn's eyes. "Fine," she sighed as she went to the phone lifting the receiver from its base.

"Hello...yeah...No, I can't, I'm busy...Not now...yeah...I'll let you know. Bye." Draylen returned the phone to the base, and reclaimed her seat on the sofa.

"Who was it? It didn't sound like an emergency," Quinn asked.

"Just people not respecting the fact that I want to be alone with you...So how much longer are you going to be with those papers?" Draylen quirked her brow repeatedly as she gave Quinn a cocky smile.

"I'm looking at an hour, at least."

Draylen pouted. "Aw, Booo!" she jeered. "I guess I'll take me a shower and watch some TV. She got up and stretched before heading to the bathroom.

"Oh, wait. Before you go, here..." Quinn held out some papers to Draylen.

"What's that?"

"These are the last two assignment you did in class. I've been meaning to give them to you, but I keep forgetting. I don't have to tell you that they're 'A' papers."

"Why don't you keep them? Consider it a parting gift from me to you." Draylen blew a kiss before leaving the living room.

Quinn looked at the pages as a devilish smile splayed on her lips.

~

MINUTES TURNED TO HOURS AS DRAYLEN WAITED FOR QUINN TO join her in the bedroom. She awoke and realized that she had fallen asleep to a crime drama marathon on TV. Not wanting to fully awaken, she reached out her hand, feeling about the bed for the remote control. When she did not feel Quinn beside her, she went in pursuit and found her in the living room seated on the floor by her desk.

"Quinn, what are you doing? It's almost one in the morning."

"I know. I walked over to the desk looking for a red pen and I came across these. Quinn held up a stack of papers. "Did you write all of these?"

"Yes. Now, let's go to bed." Draylen yawned.

"There's got to be at least thirty different stories here," Quinn said, fanning though the pages.

"Yes, I know and there are a lot more where those are concerned," Draylen remarked impatiently while rubbing the sleep from her eyes.

"Draylen, how long have you been writing?"

"I don't know, probably since I was a kid. I was always making up crazy stories. No big deal. Can we please go to bed?" She whined.

"No! I will not let you gloss over this. I've read quite a few of these and I have to tell you, they're really good. I mean when you came to my class I assumed that you'd only just begun writing as a hobby. I had no idea...I..." Quinn at a loss for words, shook her head.

"I told you that I like to write. Why is it so shocking to you?"

"Draylen, don't you understand? This is a whole book. You

should be published. Yours is the sort of works that should be on bookstore shelves."

"Yeah, I know, okay?"

"Why are you doing this?" Quinn asked.

"What am I doing? Trying to go to sleep at a reasonable hour. Oo! Call the police." Draylen flailed her hands about feigning hysteria.

"You know exactly what I'm talking about. You're doing what you always do whenever anyone praises your writings, you brush them aside just like you're doing to me right now. Face it, more than taking my creative writing class, more than being a part of the Writer's Club and certainly more than that damn proofing job, you want to be a writer. I think you should be."

"Oh, my gosh," Draylen exclaimed as she walked to the bookshelf and removed a large envelope, handing it to Quinn. "Open it." Quinn opened the envelope and began reading the correspondence before putting it back in the envelope.

"Are you happy now? Do you see why I don't get too excited about anything you or the people in that meeting have to say? It's pointless."

"Draylen, it's a rejection letter, so what?" Quinn said, hunching her shoulders. "Are there more?"

"No." she said shaking her head. "One is more than enough." Draylen walked over to the plush wingback chair and fell into it.

"Draylen, if you're a writer then rejection letters come with the territory. Everyone gets one at some point. Remind me to show you my box of rejects one day."

"Look, I don't care about your letters," Draylen interrupted. "When I decided that I was going to be a writer, I sent out my best story. I put a lot of work into it, only to get a 'thanks, but no thanks' letter from someone that probably wouldn't know the first thing about good writing, even if it kicked them in the rear.

The idea that someone could cancel me out with a form letter..." She waved her hand in the air dismissively.

"You can't let one meaningless letter put an end to a career that hasn't begun yet. That's stupid."

"So I'm stupid?" Draylen furrowed her brow.

"That's not what I'm saying and you know it. Look, if I stop talking, will you let me read some more of these?"

Draylen walked over to Quinn taking the stack of pages from her and returned them to the shelf. "Sure, you can read them anytime you want. But right now, it's past your bed time, Dr. Kendall." She put out her hand and helped Quinn up from the floor.

"I guess you're right. I'll be a little tired in the morning. That just means that instead of one cup of coffee, I'll have two."

"Oh, I think you'll need more than that." Draylen wrapped her arm around Quinn's waist while caressing her breast with her free hand. Quinn gasped. "You're gonna' need the whole pot," Draylen said kissing her neck.

"Oh, really?" Quinn said as they walked slowly to the bedroom.

"Really. And you'd better make it strong."

"Why don't I just forgo the hot water and just chew the coffee grounds?"

"Now you're talking," Draylen said before nuzzling Quinn's neck.

12

A week later, Draylen was frustrated. How had she managed to let things get so out of hand? She knew she should have ended things with Quinn long ago. As she took a gulp from the caramel macchiato, she told herself that things couldn't continue on this way. One of them could get hurt. She had to end it before it was too late. But how?

"I knew I'd find you here." Quinn smiled as she took a seat at the table.

"What are you doing here?" Draylen asked looking at her watch. "Shouldn't you be at school teaching a class or something?" A mix of surprise and confusion covered her face.

"I should, but I decided to take Jerry up on his offer to fill in for me if I ever needed it." She grabbed Draylen's hand and held onto it.

Draylen looked around cautiously before removing her hand. "Dr. Kendall, are you feeling sick or something—is that why you took time off work?" Draylen was aware that many students from the university frequented the bookstore and she did not want to bring any attention to them.

"No, I'm not sick," Quinn said. "I just needed a break. I

thought that maybe we could play hooky together. Between my job and the article that I'm writing for that magazine, not to mention your constant overtime, we haven't been together in a week."

"But we talk on the phone," Draylen consoled.

"Yeah, if you're not too busy. Do you even remember our last conversation Draylen? You called to tell me that you were too busy to talk. By the way, why are you always so busy lately? I thought you said you weren't going to take anymore quick turn-around jobs."

"I know what I said," Draylen snapped. She took a deep breath and released it slowly. "I'm sorry...I'm a little tired."

"That's okay," Quinn said as she reached for Draylen's hand. Draylen removed her hands from the table. Quinn looked away feeling slighted by the gesture.

"I took the jobs because the money was good." She glanced at her watch.

"Draylen, if it's money you need, then—I"

"I don't need any money," Draylen said cutting Quinn off. "I'm perfectly fine."

"Okay. But if you do—"

"No, I'm fine." Draylen looked at her watch again.

"Do you have to be somewhere? You keep checking your watch. Am I holding you up?"

"No. I'm waiting for someone," Draylen replied, letting her eyes dart around the café.

"Who?"

"Uh...A client," Draylen answered flustered.

"What client? I thought Bradley's company was in California. What client is this?" Quinn didn't like the evasive answers she was getting from Draylen. It was making her uncomfortable. What was she trying to hide, she wondered.

"Why are you grilling me? I do have other clients."

"I'm not grilling you, really I'm not. But you're acting strange. I just want to know what's going on."

"Look, I told you, I'm seeing a client. It's a new client based right here in the city and they're late. I don't like it when people are inconsiderate of my time, that's all."

"Says the person who came to my class late every other day." Quinn chuckled, but sobered at the sight of Draylen's scathing look.

"Why don't you go and I'll call you later." Draylen waved her hand dismissively.

Quinn stood to her feet. "I've got a better idea. I'll leave, only don't call me, at all." Quinn walked away leaving Draylen behind.

"Dammit!" Draylen swore.

QUINN WAS SURPRISED TO SEE DRAYLEN AT THAT NIGHT'S MEETING. She was good at getting lost whenever they'd had a disagreement. As it stood, she had not heard from Draylen since the incident at the café weeks ago. It was such a silly fight, more like a tiff, but she didn't think that it warranted their not speaking to one another. Before the meeting adjourned, Jerry announced the upcoming Writer's Conference being held in Seattle, Washington, during the weekend leading into fall break. When the meeting came to a close, Quinn watched as Draylen spoke briefly with a few of the members before walking past her and out of the door. She didn't even acknowledge her. Quinn had just about enough of Draylen's cold shoulder as she quickly followed behind her. She managed to catch up with her just before she left the building's exit.

"Draylen," Quinn called out, taking hold of Draylen's jacket sleeve. Draylen stopped and turned to face her, with a slightly perturbed expression.

"Hi."

"I didn't get the chance to speak to you before you left."

"Yeah. I'm kinda' in a hurry," Draylen said.

"Okay, I understand. I was just wondering if you planned on going to the conference."

"I don't know, probably not. I've got a couple things on my plate. I don't think that I can afford the time away."

"Well, you should really think about it. You can pick up some valuable information about the many aspects of writing. There are the seminars, workshops and you'll get to meet many important people in the literary field. I go every year, and I learn something new every time."

"It sounds great, but again, I don't know if I can get away." Draylen checked the time on her cell. "Quinn, I have to go now." Draylen walked out of the door with Quinn at her heels.

"Draylen, what's wrong? Why won't you speak to me? When did things get so bad between us that you won't even talk to me?"

"Quinn, please. Let's not do this." Draylen looked at the pavement beneath them, refusing to get caught up in Quinn's gaze.

"All I'm trying to do is get some understanding. Weeks ago we were making love. We exploded in each other's arms. And now you act as if it never happened. So, I'm sorry to delay you from whatever you've got to get to, but I need to know what's going on?"

Draylen gave a labored sigh before saying, "Our getting together was a mistake."

"What?" Quinn exclaimed, she gave a quick shake of the head in disbelief, trying to clear her mind.

"Quinn, we should never have become involved. We're two different people."

"Is this about the incident at the café?"

"No. It has nothing to do with that."

"Then what?"

"The truth is, I'm not looking to be in a relationship right now."

"You mean you don't want to be involved with me." Quinn felt her heart sink as she tried to steady her emotions.

"That's not what I mean."

"What do you mean?"

"I don't want to be in a relationship with anyone, okay?" Draylen turned away and began walking but could get only as far as two steps before Quinn was standing in front of her—blocking her path.

"I don't believe you."

"Well believe it. Look, I'm not angry with you or anything of the sort. I just want to...I need whatever it is between us to end. That's all that I am asking." Draylen chewed at her bottom lip to keep it from quivering.

"Fine, then I bid you good night." Quinn moved off to the side to give Draylen access to the sidewalk. She watched as Draylen pulled a set of car keys from her jacket before heading off to the parking lot. She waited to make sure that she was safely inside the flashy sports car and on her way out of the parking lot. She rolled her eyes. Draylen made her furious and still she was concerned for her safety.

13

Q uinn stepped off the elevator and ran right in to Jerry and his wife April amidst the throng of boisterous people moving about the hotel lobby.

"Hey Quinn." Jerry gave her a big hug.

"Hi, you guys," Quinn hugged April. "I was wondering what time you were going to get here."

"I let Jerry schedule the flight." April rolled her eyes. "Leave it to him to choose the one with a two hour layover."

"Jerry," Quinn whined.

"It was ten dollars cheaper."

"Really, Jer. You put April through hell all to save ten dollars?" Quinn chuckled, shaking her head. "What are we going to do with you?"

Jerry hunched his shoulder impishly. "Have you seen any other Beacham students or faculty?" He asked.

"Yes. I saw Sue Daltry, Amanda Pickford and six of our student members. Also Sue said that Anne Brooks and her husband will be here tomorrow. They couldn't get a flight out until morning."

"Maybe we can all meet tomorrow for lunch and compare notes about the morning block of seminars."

"That's fine by me," Quinn said. "I can contact everyone and let them know."

"Great. Are you staying the whole week?" April asked.

"Yes, I think I will. They have some interesting speakers scheduled for the last day that I want to see. Are you staying as well?"

"No. We're leaving out Monday after April's seminar. We want to visit Kelly and the grandkids for a few days."

"Oh, that should be fun," Quinn remarked. Jerry and April's oldest daughter and her husband had three rambunctious little children who were the apples of their grandparents' eyes.

"Where were you headed before we bumped into you?" Jerry asked.

"To the front desk. The strip on my key card is not working properly, so I have to get a new one. Why don't you both go get situated. You must be tired. I'll talk to you later."

"Alright, we'll see you. I think Dean Galloway needs to take a quick nap. You know he's an old fart," Jerry said, speaking about his alter ego. Quinn and April gave each other knowing glances.

"Come on, Dean Galloway. Your chariot awaits."

"I'm not Dean Galloway. I'm Jerry! I like to have fun." April grabbed him by the arm as they headed for the available elevator car.

Quinn walked to the registration desk and waited in the shortest line. She could have kicked herself, she thought. All she had to do was call the front desk and have them bring her a new key card. She wasn't thinking about how busy the registration desk would be for the rest of the evening. Ten minutes later she made it to the guest services representative and explained her problem and was quickly given a replacement key. As she turned to leave, she was suddenly glued to the spot she was in, her pulse quickened. Draylen's name flowed from her lips as a soft whisper. Surely she must be dreaming she thought even as Draylen stood mere inches away, mirroring her surprised expression.

14

The ballroom was filled with people, some dancing to the live band, while others were seated at clusters of tables, in deep conversations. Everyone was having a wonderful time. As planned, several of the Beacham University students and faculty sat a table together laughing and talking, with Jerry holding court.

"I'm glad that you were able to make the conference, Ms. Corliss. You'll have fun and come away with a lot of information. You may even find a love connection."

"Jerry!" April exclaimed, elbowing him in the ribs.

"Well, I'm just saying that a lot of the people have met their significant others at this conference."

"Trust me, Jerry. I am only looking for information." Draylen briefly locked eyes with Quinn before she took a sip from her glass of punch.

"Speaking of mates. Quinn, we've got the perfect person for you. I mean, the two of you couldn't be more perfect. Let me tell you all about her—"

"Not now, Jerry. What did I tell you?" Quinn whispered.

"I know, Quinn. But I'm just so excited about this one. I can't wait for you to meet her. Tell her honey."

"Quinn, she is absolutely perfect for you. But we'll talk later."

Quinn chanced a look in Draylen's direction and saw that she had become quiet and withdrawn. Her eyes dull.

"Honestly, Quinn, after you meet her, your 'one date rule' will be a thing of the past," Jerry said.

"I'm gonna' get some more punch." Draylen excused herself and headed for the beverage station.

Quinn longed to follow after her but did not want to arouse the group's suspicions. She remained seated until most of the club members went off to dance and mingle, then she made her move.

"Why didn't you come back to the table?" Quinn asked.

"I decided to walk about, then I found myself back here at the punch bowl." Draylen took a sip from her glass.

"I see. It's good punch." Quinn looked around the ballroom, taking in the festive atmosphere.

"So, what is the 'one date rule'?" Draylen hated that her curiosity was getting the better of her, but she wanted to know.

"It's nothing."

"It must be something or else Jerry wouldn't be so adverse to it. Draylen watched as Jerry lit up the dance floor, drawing the attention of the crowd with his energetic version of the 1970's dance, the Hustle.

"It was something I created a while back after my last relationship ended. I had decided that I no longer wanted to be committed to anyone. I realized that I preferred my freedom. So to avoid any emotional commitment, I started a one date only rule. I figured that it would be hard to fall in love with anyone after having had only one date."

"Oh, I see."

"You do?"

"Yeah. It's actually quite ingenius."

"Yeah, it was." That is, until I met you, Quinn thought. Just then a man approached and asked Draylen to dance. "Boy was he barking up the wrong tree," Quinn mumbled under her breath.

"I'd love to," Draylen said beaming.

Quinn's head shot up in utter shock as she watched Draylen being escorted to the dance floor. She fumed as the man held her close during the slow tempo song. She boiled when his hand crept to the lowest part of Draylen's back. Only when the song had ended was she able to loosen the clench of her jaw muscles. She was thankful when Draylen had declined the man's offer for one more dance, and left him still pleading in her wake. Draylen made her way to the table for a fresh glass of punch.

"I felt kind of sorry for the poor man thinking that he had a chance with you. He didn't know like I do, that you don't want a relationship of any kind, and especially not with me."

"I would think that you'd be happy about that, with your 'one-date rule' and all. Goodnight." Draylen left the ballroom rather than let Quinn see the hurt she was unable to hide.

Quinn knew she'd blown it with Draylen, the moment she lost control of her emotions, letting jealousy rule her head. She could have handled that better, but she was enraged watching as Draylen let this perfect stranger dance seductively with her, touching her inappropriately, when she wasn't allowed within a stone's throw of Draylen. She would give Draylen time to cool off, while she did the same, but this wasn't over, Quinn vowed, not by a long shot.

15

The next day was a series of lectures and meet and greet seminars. By the end of the last workshop, Draylen was exhausted and overwhelmed by all the information. She was leaning toward dashing her writing dream. There was so much to know and she didn't feel like she was capable of sticking with it. Quinn caught up to her just as she entered the elevator.

"You look worn out."

"I am. It was more information than I could stomach." Draylen let the weight of her body rest against the back wall of the elevator car.

"I guess it's my fault. I should have told you to pace yourself. You can really learn everything you need to know by attending three workshops. The rest of them, you can do without. You'll find that many of the seminars overlap."

"Then why do they have so many of them?" Draylen inquired as the elevator reached the fourteenth floor and they got off.

"Well they have to do something to justify charging so much money to attend."

"I guess you have a point."

"If you want, we can go over any questions you may have."

"Maybe later, but right now all I want to do is take a nap and re-calibrate my mind."

They reached Draylen's room sooner than Quinn would have liked. This was the first time today that she was able to speak to her. In the seminars and workshops she had not been lucky to sit with her, instead she had to settle for gazing at her from a distance.

"Would you like to go out for dinner this evening?"

"Wouldn't that interfere with your 'one date rule'?" Draylen quipped.

"No. Last night was not a date. It was merely two people taking part in a shared group activity."

"And tonight, what would that be?"

"Again, not a date, just two people with a common goal in mind—warding off starvation."

Draylen chuckled before saying, "I don't know. Both of those well thought out descriptions sound like dates to me."

Quinn snickered before turning serious. "Well, they're not. So what do you say? I know of a delightful little place that has the best food. It's also out of the way, so we won't have to worry about running into the convention people. It will be just the two of us and Seattle's nightlife." Quinn waited as Draylen sought inner council. She was used to her lingering decision making process. Draylen never did anything without careful consideration, and she could not be rushed. Quinn took this time to fight a war of her own. She wanted to take Draylen into her arms and kiss her. She thought of nothing else since first laying eyes on her in the lobby yesterday. What would she do if I kissed her right now, she wondered. What would she do?

"Alright I'll go with you on this mission to get food," Draylen said.

"Mission, but not a date," Quinn stated for clarity. "I'll knock about eight o'clock. Is that okay?"

"I'll be ready."

"See you then." Before Quinn could stop herself she was drawn into her. The kiss was meant to be fleeting however neither of them expected the magnetic current of need that flowed through them, deepening the kiss. Draylen moaned her pleasure into Quinn's mouth as she opened to her, letting her feast as their tongues reunited in a familiar dance that each partner helped to choreograph. Draylen felt the dew beginning to flow between her thighs and gently pushed Quinn away. She braced her hands on Quinn's arms keeping them at a distance, while they each cooled their heels. Then clearing her throat she said,

"Maybe we shouldn't go out to—"

"I'll see you at eight," Quinn interrupted. There was no way she was letting Draylen finish that sentence. She couldn't let her squirm out of their date. She was making progress with her and did not want to go backwards. She walked briskly down the hall to her room, leaving Draylen to stare after her.

"A PENNY FOR YOUR THOUGHTS," QUINN SAID GAZING INTO Draylen's dreamy eyes.

"Pardon me?"

"You've been in deep thought about something for the past few minutes. I just want to know what you're thinking.

"I was just thinking how nice this restaurant is. It's not too big or small, its intimate, cozy."

"Wait until you taste the food. It's to die for."

"I can't wait, Draylen said. "How did you find this place?"

"One year at the writer's conference I met a woman who lives here in Seattle, she told me about this place and I've been coming here ever since."

"Oh. I guess you can learn all sorts of things at these conferences." Draylen sipped from her wine glass.

"I meant what I said earlier, Draylen. If you need any questions answered about anything that you heard at the seminars today, I can answer them for you."

"I really don't have a question. I'm just amazed at all of the different ways a writer can go about publishing their work and still nothing is guaranteed. It's a lot to take in, especially if you're new to the whole process."

"It can be, but if you truly have a love for writing then it's worth it."

"That's just it, I don't know if I feel that it's worth it to me."

"Would you write your stories even if no one paid you a dime?"

"Yes, I'm doing that now."

"Do you like when people read your stories and are touched by them?"

"Yes," Draylen smiled. It's like a shot of electricity."

"Then I'd say it's worth it. You're worth it." Quinn placed her hand on Draylen's arm, caressing the smooth skin with her thumb, as she captured her in an intense stare.

"Sometimes I think about putting more time in my schedule to write."

"Then you should. It can only improve your craft. Draylen, can I ask you something?"

"Sure, what is it?"

"Why do you work so hard?"

"Well, I'm trying to make some big purchases in the not too distant future. I'm looking to buy two properties on the South side of Chicago. My goal is to turn them into low income housing rentals."

"Wow. I had no idea you were into real estate."

"My parents have always owned property and they've managed to do well by it. My dad, before he retired, worked for the city doing carpentry, plumbing and electrical work. Then he started rehabbing buildings on the side. He's going to help me with all the hands on work, but I want to own the buildings outright without my parent's contribution. I believe I can do it."

"How much longer will it take you to save up the capital?"

"Hopefully by spring of next year. I know that it's a sacrifice right now, but I don't mind. I want to take charge of my life. I want to live comfortably, but I don't want to wait until I'm seventy to retire before I can enjoy the fruits of my labor. There are things that I would like to do. I want to travel and learn new things. I don't want to miss out on life just because I cannot financially afford the experiences."

"I'm glad you told me. It's another part of you that I get to see. Thank you for sharing."

"No problem. Now, can I ask you something?"

"I'm an open book. What would you like to know?" Quinn asked.

"What was it about your last relationship that made you come up with your 'one-date rule?' Did she break your heart?"

"Actually, no. We simply grew apart. She went off to live in Germany and I was left single, once again. I thought I would be distraught over the idea of being alone, but it was the complete opposite. I started to love my freedom, not being beholden to anyone but myself. But I found that most women our age are looking for forever, so I had to do something to ward off any ideas of permanence, hence the 'one date rule.'"

"How did I factor into your rule? By your definition, we went beyond what would be considered one date. In fact we went further than that, we obliterated it."

"What can I say, I never expected to be blindsided."

Draylen found herself imprisoned for a second time by Quinn's demanding gaze. She was relieved when the waiter arrived with their meal.

～

"I'M COMPLETELY STUFFED," DRAYLEN SAID AS THEY LEFT THE restaurant. "I should be ashamed of myself. I feel like a pig. That grilled lobster was insane. We may have to come back here before the conference is over."

"We can definitely do that." Quinn was excited that Draylen was already planning for them to spend more time together. Maybe her mind was changing.

"Are you ready to go back to the hotel?"

"Quinn, if you don't mind, I'd like to walk around a bit. I could use the exercise."

"Okay. The pier is this way. We can check out some of the stores over there." Quinn looped an arm through Draylen's as they headed for pier.

After an hour of walking and perusing the local tourist shops, they settled on a bench near the wharf to rest and soak up the crisp night air. There was a faint smell of brine wafting from the waterfront and a gorgeous view of the ink-blotted skyline.

"What do you think of Seattle's nightlife?" Quinn asked.

"The little that I've seen is quite impressive," Draylen said, fingering the ornate metal work of the bench's armrest. I wouldn't mind coming back for a visit, you know, to see some of their known attractions like the space needle and the Pike Place Market."

"Then maybe we can do that one day." Quinn knew that she was forcing her hand where Draylen was concerned but she wanted to be a part of her life, therefore she had to make great use of the time they shared together. She wanted to flood her senses with the idea of them being in each other's lives. Seattle held but a small window of opportunity for her to accomplish this. Once they arrived back in Chicago, it may be too late. Draylen would surely erect those impenetrable walls again, leaving her on the outside.

"Draylen?"

"Hmm?"

"Did someone hurt you? Is that why the thought of us being together frightens you?" Quinn asked.

"What would make you ask such a question?" Draylen's heart pounded in her ears.

"It's just that during dinner, you asked me if my heart had been broken. So I assumed that somewhere along the way, someone caused you a lot of pain. You can tell me Draylen. I'm a good listener."

"I've been hurt before, but that was a while ago. I've made my peace with it."

"Have you?" Quinn wasn't convinced.

"Yeah. Sometimes things have a way of happening and it's nobody's fault." Draylen's mind went to the day her life changed for the worse. Losing Dava was unexpected and left her a shell of her former self. But she was a witness that time could heal all wounds.

16

"I know that you said you don't want to be in a relationship with me or anyone else, but everything you've shown me, says that you do, and you want it with me. I'm trying to understand you, but I just don't feel like you're telling me everything. Can you help me with this?" Quinn's hand came up to methodically caress Draylen's cheek.

"Quinn I have my reasons, that's all I can say. I need you to accept them. Please don't push me. It just makes things harder for both of us. I would like us to remain friends, really I would. But if you feel that it's not enough..." Draylen let her words trail off. She didn't want to voice the possibility of them not being in each other's lives anymore. She had done her best the last few weeks to try and get Quinn out of her mind, but it was unsuccessful. She knew that the moment they laid eyes on each other in the lobby of the hotel.

"I think we should head back to the hotel," Quinn said as she helped Draylen to her feet and together they walked to the street flagging down a taxi.

The elevator doors opened on fourteen and the two of them made the slow walk to Draylen's door. The taxi ride back to the hotel was silent. Quinn was in a pensive mood, casting a somber light on an otherwise pleasant evening. Draylen hated that she was the cause of it. Hurting Quinn was the last thing she wanted to do, but she couldn't see another way of doing things. She had made a promise to Dava. How could she expect Dava to put everything into restoring their friendship if she was not willing to do the same?

She needed her best friend back in her life. She believed that in spite of the failed relationship, they could, with hard work, reach some sense of normalcy like they had in the past. But if she were being truly honest with herself, she would admit that Dava wasn't the only issue keeping her and Quinn apart—it was her fear.

Falling in love had its consequences. She was afraid to be with Quinn because loving her meant giving up her power, making her vulnerable to heartache and she did not want to relive those feelings again.

When they reached Draylen's room, they stood quietly, each searching for some way to put a positive spin on the evening, but neither of them could think of what to say. Draylen decided it best to leave things as they were—unfinished. She turned to insert her card into the lock, opening the door. She was halted when Quinn began to speak.

"Meet you tomorrow for breakfast before the seminars begin?" Quinn did not want the night to end on a sad note—that would only make tomorrow worse, not knowing where she stood with Draylen. Time was not on her side when it came to winning Draylen over. They'd be returning to Chicago in a few days and she was doubtful of her chances with Draylen once the plane touched ground. Draylen said she didn't want to become involved, but her words were one thing, her actions another.

"Is seven-thirty good for you?" Draylen asked.

"I'll be here bright and early." Quinn reached for Draylen

and was pleased when she walked into her arms for a brief mind-drugging kiss which ended much too soon for either of them, but Quinn had to step away and put a stop to her mounting need. "Goodnight, get some rest." Quinn watched as Draylen went inside her room and closed the door before trudging her way down the hall, each step heavier than the next.

17

Quinn woke in a surprisingly chipper mood. She was determined more than ever to win Draylen's heart. It was a new day and a new opportunity to convince her that they belonged together. She had her doubts in the beginning, but everything within her knew that what they had was special. It could be even better than before if Draylen allowed herself to open up and be free, and she knew that she could help her get there—show her how to let her guard down and feel. Quinn gave herself one last mental pep talk before knocking on the door.

"Who is it?"

"It's me."

"Quinn, why don't you go on down. I don't feel much like breakfast today," Draylen said through the closed door.

"Why not? Did you oversleep? If so, that's fine. Breakfast doesn't end until...Draylen, this is ridiculous. Can you open the door? I look stupid standing out here trying to hold a conversation with you."

"I'd rather not. Why don't you just go and I'll talk to you later."

"Draylen, what's going on? Open the door. I'm not leaving until you do." Quinn waited as the lock was slowly disengaged and the door opened by degrees. Quinn was impatient and pushed the door until she was able to enter. Closing the door, her eyes roamed the room in search of Draylen who had disappeared.

"Okay, Draylen, this is not funny anymore. Please come out."

The door to the bathroom opened and Draylen stepped out into the room. Quinn's face was stricken with shock. She could barely recognize Draylen with her swollen cheeks, slits for eyes and lips twice their normal size.

"Draylen! What happened to your face?"

Draylen looked to the floor, embarrassed by Quinn's reaction to her recent disfigurement.

"Get dressed. I'm taking you to the nearest emergency room. Quinn went to the dresser and began removing clothes haphazardly.

"Quinn, I'm fine. It's just an allergic reaction, that's all."

"Allergic? What are you allergic to?"

"Shellfish."

"Shellfish!"

"Yeah, this what I woke up to."

"Babe. Everything we had last night was shellfish or had shellfish in it. I would have never ordered any of that had I known that you were allergic. My God! People die from this kind of allergy. Why didn't you say something? I could have killed you." Quinn dropped to the bed under the weight of guilt.

"I didn't know that I would be affected by it. I just took a chance."

"You just decided to take a chance with your life? Just like that?" Quinn snapped her finger. "This has happened before?"

"Once when I was New Orleans and I had a lot of shellfish.

But that was so long ago, and I've eaten shrimp and lobster since then with no reaction so I thought that I'd be safe."

"You thought? You didn't think at all. What if your throat closed up? I know that is a symptom. What would you have done then? I could have lost you." Quinn inhaled holding for a ten count before exhaling. She could see that Draylen was upset and she didn't want to add to her misery. Not trusting herself to stand, she pulled Draylen gently to sit down beside her. "I think we should go to the emergency room. I won't rest until I know that you're all right...Please?"

"Quinn the worst is over besides, I do carry an Epi-pen just in case," Draylen said trying her best to reassure her.

"Babe, go get dressed."

"But you'll miss the seminars."

"I don't care. For the last time, will you please go get ready?"

Draylen reluctantly retreated into the bathroom.

QUINN BREATHED A SIGH OF RELIEF WHEN THE EMERGENCY ROOM doctor gave the all clear and they were able to return to the hotel. She helped Draylen remove her garments. Taking the tube from the prescription bag she carefully read the instructions.

"Do you need me to put the hydrocortisone on for you?"

"No," Draylen responded, slipping into her sleep shirt. "That stuff never works. Can you just get me some water so I can take the anti-histamine tablets? I'll be fine."

Quinn went to the bathroom and came back with the water. Draylen quickly downed the pills and got into bed.

"Are you in any pain?"

"A little, around the eyes, but mostly I'm itchy. I'll feel better once some of the swelling goes down." Draylen looked at the clock on the night stand. "Quinn, we made great time. You can make it to the other seminars and activities."

"I'm not going. I'm staying here with you."

"The doctor said that I'll be fine. There's really no point in you staying. I can't go downstairs. If you don't go, then how will I know what I missed?"

Quinn finally agreed against her better judgment. "I'll go, but I'm coming back to check on you as soon as we break for lunch."

"Then you had better take this." Draylen removed the key card from the table and handed it to Quinn. "In case I'm knocked out, which is a definite possibility. Allergy medication has that effect on me."

"Okay. I have my phone on me. Call if you need anything."

"I will and tell Jerry and the gang that I said 'hello' and I'm sorry that I can't make lunch." Draylen inched further beneath the covers, as Quinn left the room.

"DRAYLEN, BABE, WAKE UP." QUINN GENTLY SHOOK HER SHOULDER. "Draylen, wake up. Can you hear me?" Draylen nodded as she squirmed, opening her eyes gradually before they closed again. Quinn shook one last time until she came groggily awake.

"Hey sleepy head. I ordered room service. Get up. You've been asleep all day. You need to eat something." Quinn pulled back the covers and helped Draylen from the bed.

"How do you feel?"

"That all depends, Draylen croaked. "How do I look?"

"Well..." Quinn fought unsuccessfully not to scrunch up her face.

"I'll take from your expression that I won't be winning any beauty contests any time soon."

"Some of the swelling has gone down."

"Really, where?"

"Right here..." Quinn planted a delicate kiss on Draylen's puffy lips.

Draylen felt her mouth and noticed while it was still a bit enlarged, there was a drastic improvement. Quinn seated her at the table, handing her a napkin.

"I thought that we'd keep dinner simple. I got chicken broth and a turkey sandwich for you. I didn't want to take any chances."

Draylen pouted. "What did you get?"

Quinn lifted the lid off her plate. "I got the same thing. I decided to show some solidarity."

"That's kind of you."

An hour had gone by when Quinn noticed Draylen's body twitching. "You're miserable aren't you?"

"Yes, very. It's time to take some more tablets."

"I'll get them for you." Quinn retrieved the pills from the night stand, handing two of them to Draylen.

"Thank you," Draylen said as she swallowed them with the rest of her water.

"Now let's get you into bed."

"I have some time before the meds take effect. Do you want to watch some TV?" Draylen was having a good time being with Quinn and did not want the night to end. She missed their time together. Her desire to be with Quinn was depleting her resolve to stay away.

Quinn reached for the remote and surfed the channels until they settled on a Matt Damon action movie. She was pleased when Draylen snuggled close to her in the bed and as the heaviness of the day dissipated, she drifted off fast asleep.

Quinn awoke with a start, distracted by the sounds coming from the television, and was met with Draylen's reflecting gaze.

How long had she been watching her and what was she think-ing? She couldn't get a reading from her. She wanted to ask her what she was feeling but was too afraid of the answer she might give. Had she put her barriers back in place? Quinn was clueless and braced herself for the unexpected. However nothing could have prepared her for what happened next as Draylen curved her arm around Quinn's head pulling her into the most soul-searing kiss. Draylen held her hostage to the ministering of her hot mouth and probing tongue, setting their passions ablaze with unimaginable pleasure.

Soon Quinn took matters into her own hands, straddling Draylen's lithe body as she intensified the kiss, urging her mouth to open wider to her ardent exploration. A surge of heat enfolded them as they traveled closer to the enticing flames. It was all happening so fast, Quinn thought as she savored every moment. When Draylen whimpered, she was instantly aware of what they were doing and where they were headed if she didn't put an end to it. With painstaking effort, she pulled away from Draylen's swollen lips. Resting on her thighs, she struggled to restrain her desire. "Did I hurt you?" Quinn had been so ready to make love that she'd completely forgotten about Draylen's healing state.

"No, I'm fine," Draylen panted.

"I think I should go back to my room," Quinn said in a voice she did not recognize. "You need to get your rest." She carefully dismounted Draylen in an effort to leave, but was kept by a touch to her shoulder.

"Stay, Quinn."

Quinn sought refuge in Draylen's pleading eyes and wanted to stay forever, but the temptation to have her was too great and she was weak. "I can't. I'm afraid of what would happen if I did."

"Nothing that we didn't want to happen," Draylen replied.

"I don't know, Draylen. I was on my way to making love to

you, and you were responding to it. I've made no secrets about what I want, but you keep telling me that you want something different. I can't let myself go any further with you, especially when you're not sure of what you want yourself. Aside from that, you're not in any physical condition to have sex. We went farther than we should have gone." Quinn attempted to leave the bed but Draylen held fast to her arm keeping her there.

"I want you to stay. While you were asleep I did some thinking. I've been trying so hard to stay away from you, and I haven't had much luck with that. This whole thing has been so useless. I can't stand this. I know what I said about not wanting to be in a relationship, for which I have my reasons, but couldn't we just try to be together while we're here. I realize what I'm asking of you and I know it's not fair. Quinn, I have some...issues that I need to deal with."

"Tell me what they are. Maybe I can help you with them."

"It's not something you can help me with. I'm asking you for time. I can give you me, all of me, for now. Can you do this...be with me, here for the next few days?"

Quinn was silent, conferring with her inner counsel before coming to her decision. "I can't, Draylen. Three days is not enough time. I need more."

"What more?"

"Say that we'll fly back to Chicago together and that you'll give me the remaining days of my fall break, you and me together. If you can give me that time with you, then I'm willing to wait it out with you while you decide whether or not I'm what you want. Is it a deal?" Quinn was surprised when Draylen quickly came back with her answer.

"It's a deal." Draylen held out her hand to Quinn to shake but found herself wrapped up in her warm embrace instead. Draylen tilted her head upward to claim Quinn's mouth in a combustible lip-lock that left them wanting and ready to heed the call of ecstasy. Quinn, feeling a sense of déjà vu, tore herself away from Draylen's impermeable seal.

"Babe, you have got to stop doing that," Quinn chided. "You're in no condition to make love. Once your body heals, I promise you, there will be no stopping us. For now can we get our minds off sex?" Quinn sighed, she couldn't believe she was actually turning down the very thing she'd been yearning for the past few weeks. But somebody had to have a clear head and right now it sure wasn't Draylen, she surmised.

"Since sex is out of the question, I still need something to satisfy my appetite. You'd better call room service and fast!" Draylen demanded.

Quinn picked up the phone and started dialing. "What do you want?"

"Something chocolate, sweet and gratifying." Draylen exchanged a carnal look with Quinn that said more than any words could convey about their cravings for one another. The voice coming from the other end of the line brought Quinn's attentions back to the task at hand.

"Yes, do you have any chocolate desserts...Oh, you have seven, did you say? Great can you send one order of each to room fourteen-twenty-three? And could you hurry, please?"

18

Q uinn watched as the plane made its decent from the clouds before gliding swiftly into the airport. She braced herself, squeezing Draylen's hand as the plane finally touched ground in Chicago. She was the happiest that she had been in a while. When she left for Seattle, she was a broken woman, having lost Draylen weeks before. Draylen had made it clear in no uncertain words that she wanted to end their relationship. Quinn couldn't imagine that they would be reunited and spend the rest of the writers' conference together sharing practically every moment as a couple. Everyone else from Beacham University had left on the third day. Most had other plans for the remaining days of fall break, which left Quinn and Draylen free to express their feelings away from prying eyes.

As they waited for the 'all clear' signal from the pilot aboard the plane, Quinn smiled from ear to ear as she replayed the last few days of their trip in her mind. She and Draylen went to seminars by day and enjoyed the sights of Seattle at night. They'd even made a return visit to the quaint little restaurant where they had their first meal together—sans the shellfish. By the trip's end, Draylen had made an almost complete recovery. With the swelling gone, she had only to deal with a few patches of hives on her back and abdomen. The itching had even subsided. The thought that Quinn could have lost Draylen, settled like a ball of thorns in the pit of her stomach. She tensed, tightening her grip of Draylen's hand.

"Quinn, you're squeezing my hand," Draylen groaned, coming awake.

"Oh, I'm sorry. I was just letting you know that we've landed."

"You mean I slept the whole flight?"

"Yes, you did. You were probably tired after last night." They decided to attend the closing ceremony of the conference followed by an evening of long hot kissing and gentle caressing. They stuck to their 'no sex' agreement, deciding to wait until Draylen was fully mended, which was difficult. Quinn ached to explode with Draylen in her arms, but she remained content sharing her bed and her time. That was more than she could have possibly hoped for. She was glad that she was booked on the same return flight home, and pleased when she convinced Draylen to cancel her ride from the airport so that she could take her home instead. Everything was going so well that she didn't want to be away from her for a single minute, if possible.

Quinn had to admit to herself that in spite of Draylen's vow to spend the rest of the week with her, she was still apprehensive as they boarded the plane. She could change her mind once they arrived in Chicago, she thought. Then where would she be —right back to pining for her. No, that's not Draylen, she thought. She's true to her word. Quinn released her tension in a heavy sigh.

"Babe, stop daydreaming. Everyone's getting off the plane now."

"Here you are, home sweet home," Quinn announced as she pulled the car up in front of the apartment building.

"Yeah, here we are." Draylen made no motion to get out of the car, instead she remained seated peering at her hands. She knew the promise she made to Quinn, but now in the light of day and back on Chicago soil, doubt loomed and she hoped that she could honor her words and give them a chance. Surely she could try for the next four days to let her guard down with Quinn. It wasn't like either of them were looking to fall in love, far from it, she reasoned. Quinn had her 'one date rule,' and though they may have blurred the lines regarding the inner workings of said rule, the point was neither of them wanted commitment. They had feelings for one another and liked to spend time together, but who said anything about love, she pondered. We're just doing what feels good for now. Besides, she couldn't commit to anyone, not while she was working to rebuild her friendship with Dava.

"Are you okay, Babe?"

"Yeah. I'm great," Draylen replied.

"What time can I expect to see you tonight? I thought I might throw something together for dinner."

"No, no. We just came back. I don't want you cooking. We can order out when I get there."

"And what time will that be?"

"I'm going to unpack, make some calls, jump in the shower, then I'll be on my way. I'd say give me three hours."

"Or you can call me when you're ready and I'll come get you. That will shave a half hour of travel time off your schedule and I get to have you back with me sooner."

"Quinn," Draylen whined.

"Okay, we'll do it your way. I'll see you later. Ring my phone once, so that I know that you got in your apartment safely."

"I will." She gave a light kiss to Quinn's mouth before exiting the car, retrieving her luggage from the back seat. "I'll see you later." Draylen waved as she headed through the security gate. She worked diligently unpacking then repacking clothes for her stay at Quinn's. She had done everything on her list, making calls to her parents, letting them know that she was back from her trip and to Bradley, informing him of her decision to take the rest of the week off for some much needed rest and relaxation—of course she did not mention to him that her time away from work would involve rekindling her relationship with Quinn. Since she and Dava parted ways, Draylen found herself confiding from time to time in Bradley, at least about some things like her desire to go back to school for her master's, but definitely not about matters of the heart—for that she had no one to turn to. But maybe with time, all of that would change, she hoped.

Draylen walked purposefully to the living room to pick up her laptop just in case she came across an assignment that she couldn't pass up. Quinn and Bradley were right, she was a workaholic, she thought. Truth be told, she was in the position to purchase those two properties now, she had more than enough saved, but she figured she could always have more. Whenever she decided to retire, she wanted to do it comfortably. Satisfied that she'd gotten all of her things together, she picked up the phone to call for a cab, but was interrupted by the sound of the doorbell. She chuckled. Quinn was relentless at times, she thought. She told her not to bother coming to pick her up, but obviously she did not listen. Draylen, hung up the phone and went to the door, pressing the intercom. "Yes?"

"It's Dava."

Draylen was startled. Her pulse quickened. Dava was the last person she expected to show up at her door. She hesitated before pushing the buzzer.

"What are you doing here?" Draylen was clearly surprised to see her.

"Gee! Can't I get in the door first and then can I get a 'hello'?" Dava said as she entered the apartment."

"I'm sorry. Hey, shouldn't you be at work?"

"Sure, but a good friend of mine wanted me to pick her up from the airport today, and then changed her mind at the last minute. But I had already put in for the day off. Did you forget?"

"Well I remember it differently. I recall mentioning my trip to Seattle and then someone volunteering to give me a ride to and from the airport. I didn't know that you had to take time away from work or else I would have never agreed."

"Be that as it may, I did not work today. It was no big deal. You're my friend, I'd do anything for you."

"Aw, thanks." Draylen hugged Dava and was somewhat surprised when Dava gave her a quick peck on the lips.

"It still doesn't explain why you're here."

"I came to hang out with you. You know, spend some quality time repairing our friendship. You did mean it when you said that you wanted to work on it, right?"

"I did. It's just that I didn't know you were coming by today. I made some other plans," Draylen said.

"Plans to do what?"

"Uh...Well." Draylen didn't want to tell her that she was going to try and mend her relationship with someone else. That would make it seem as though she did not value their friendship enough. She knew Dava and if she suspected that she was not the focus of all the attention, then she'd probably give up the whole idea of reconciling, and she did not want that. Not when they were making strides in the right direction.

"I was going to go hang out with my mom," Draylen lied.

"Oh come on. Doesn't she still play Pokeno at the community center on Tuesdays?"

"Yes." Draylen forgot that Dava knew her parent's schedules about as well as she did. She knew that Debra played Pokeno on Tuesdays the same way she knew that Dava's dad played golf on Saturdays and Sundays, and that her stepmother had a standing appointment with her beautician every other Friday. Knowing these things came with sharing a life together, and no amount of absence would stop you from remembering, Draylen thought.

"Why don't you go see your mom tomorrow? That way you can get in the time with her and you won't have to interrupt her games. You know how serious she takes her Pokeno," Dava said.

"I know. She can be cutthroat," Draylen agreed.

"Exactly. Anyway, I have something for you." Dava went into her pocket extracting a thin case. "The entire Godfather saga!" Dava grinned, waving the box set in the air.

"You're kidding? One, two and three?" Draylen jumped up and grabbed the movie from Dava's hand, reading the dust jacket and smiling. The Godfather movies were a favorite of hers. Back when she and Dava were together, they'd have a Godfather night once or twice a month, where they ordered takeout and settled in for a night of mafia drama.

"I thought that we could order some pizza and watch movies. Doesn't that sound like a plan?"

"Alright. Give me a minute. I've got to call my mom and let her know that I'm not coming."

"Great, I'll order the pizza."

Draylen excused herself to the bedroom. She knew Quinn wouldn't be happy, but what choice did she have? She dialed the number and calmed herself as she waited for Quinn to pick up.

"Hello?"

"Hey."

"Hi, are you on your way? I know you said not to do any cooking but I couldn't help it. It's been a while since I've cooked for anyone besides myself and I thought it was time for you to check out my skills in the kitchen."

"I'm not coming," Draylen rushed out before Quinn could catch her next wind.

"What do you mean you're not coming?"

Draylen could hear the disappointment in her voice. "Something came up."

"What came up, Draylen?" Quinn asked incredulously.

"Look, I can't get into that right now. Just know that I'm sorry."

"You're a liar."

"Quinn, please. I said that I'm sorry. It's something that can't be helped."

"You made a promise to me back in Seattle to spend the rest of this week with me. Did you forget? We haven't been in Chicago but a few hours and already you've changed your mind. You never intended to keep your word and that makes you a liar."

"I'm going to make it up to you, I promise."

"Draylen, you've just proven that your promises don't mean anything. You know what? Do what you want to do, I don't care anymore." Quinn slammed down the phone. She was furious. She had placed too much stock in Draylen keeping her word. Quinn hated to admit that she'd seen this coming, but she had —still she was hopeful that Draylen would prove her wrong. Quinn removed the boiling pasta from the flame and tidied up the kitchen, before going to bed. She was no longer in the mood for food.

19

Q uinn pulled up to the valet parking, quickly turning over her keys to the attendant. She was twenty minutes late for her date with Sabrina. She decided that she'd given Draylen more than enough of her time—too much time wasted. She was tired of ending her days crying into her pillows. She needed to get out and get her mind on other things.

Finally after constant pleading from Jerry, she decided to take him up on his offer to fix her up with a woman he and April claimed was perfect for her. According to Jerry, Sabrina Taylor was a beautiful forty-five-year-old pharmaceutical sales rep, highly successful, who loved to have fun and enjoyed meeting new people. She'd learned not to take too much from Jerry and April's overblown descriptions. However, as the waiter led her to the table, she was taken off guard by the beauty of the woman who sat before her smiling. Sabrina was provocative. There was not a manufactured hair out of place. Her smooth mocha skin reminded Quinn of decadent chocolate. Reddish-brown wisps of hair framed her angular face. Jerry might be right about this one, she thought. She didn't want to jump the gun with her assessment—she had been wrong before.

"Sabrina?" Quinn asked, extending her hand.

"Yes, and you're Quinn?" Sabrina took the proffered hand and gave a brief squeeze.

"Pleased to finally meet you." Quinn took her seat. "I apologize for being late. The sad thing is that I really don't have a good excuse."

"That's perfectly fine. I was just glad that you didn't stand me up. I've had that happen to me before," Sabrina said.

"Oh, no, I could never do something like that. Usually I'm a stickler for being on time. If my students ever found out about this, they'd hang me out to dry."

"In that case, we won't tell them," Sabrina said smiling.

"Are you hungry?" Quinn asked reaching for the menu.

"Not really. We can order some wine and talk for a while, if that's okay with you?"

"That sounds great." Quinn signaled for the waiter after they'd decided on a bottle of wine.

"So tell me, what made you finally decide to give me a call? I know Jerry has been trying to get us to meet for some time now," Sabrina said, taking a sip from her wine glass.

"I don't know. I've been...consumed, for lack of a better word, by some things that I realize now aren't really worth my time. So I decided that I needed to get out and have some fun. It's been a while between dates, I may be a bit rusty. And what about you?" Quinn drank from her glass. "What made you agree to meet me?"

"Let's see. I have been traveling non-stop for my job. I tend to be a workaholic. It puts a real damper on my social life."

Quinn snickered under her breath.

"What's funny?" Sabrina inquired.

"I'm sorry. What you said about being a workaholic reminded me of someone." Quinn chided herself inwardly for letting thoughts of Draylen creep into her head during what was supposed to be a Draylen-free evening.

"Anyway." Sabrina continued, "When Jerry and April told me about you, I was curious and I said sure, why not?"

"I see," Quinn remarked as she worked to keep her mind focused. "What did they say about me? I often wonder about their pitch when it comes to describing me to others."

"They told me that you were gorgeous, an excellent professor who dabbled in writing. You enjoy fine food and wine, you love to travel and that you speak fourteen languages."

"Only fourteen, huh?" Quinn laughed.

"Okay, maybe I added that last part in. What did they say about me?" Sabrina braced herself, pretending to bite nervously at her well-manicured fingernails.

"That you're gorgeous. I think that Jerry may have even used the word sexy. They also said you were intelligent, loved to have fun and that you enjoy hiking. I may have gotten that last part wrong, though."

"No, that's correct. I used to live in California and I belonged to a hiking club with a group of career women looking to de-stress on the weekends."

Quinn scrunched her face. "Hiking?"

"Yes, Quinn. Its good exercise and a lot of fun. There are a lot of good trails here in Illinois. You should come with me some-time. Oh, but I forgot about your 'one date rule'."

Quinn's head shot up in surprise. She could feel the heat rushing to her cheeks as she blushed. "They told you about that too, huh?"

"Yes, they did," she said, taking a sip from her glass. "Don't be mad at them. Jerry was so interested in selling you to me, that he ended up telling me more than he probably meant to."

Quinn fidgeted slightly, running her index finger around the rim of her wine glass

"I'm not mad. I suppose that I'm shocked, more than anything that you still agreed to see me. Most women knowing that valuable piece of information wouldn't have bothered."

"Well, call me crazy, but I tend to be intuitive about a lot of things and people."

"Really," Quinn deadpanned.

"Uh-hmm. I'm a salesperson, so getting vibes off of people comes with the territory. I knew that if twenty percent of what Jerry said about you was untrue, then the other eighty percent was worth my getting to know."

"That's nice of you to say," Quinn said, smiling sheepishly. "I can't figure out why Jerry and April waited so long to set the two of us up."

"I think I can shed some light on that for you. A few years ago I was married to my husband of twenty-three years, then we divorced. I hadn't spoken with April and Jerry for quite some time. You see my ex- got most of the friends in the divorce settlement, so naturally I assumed that he'd won them over as well. I only ran into April recently at the Memorial Hospital. She was visiting a friend and I was there speaking to some clients." Sabrina shrugged. "The rest is history as the saying goes."

"So they never knew you had..."Quinn's voice trailed off to silence.

"Come out of the closet? No, they had no idea. But once I told them, it wasn't long until they were talking you up and planning for us to meet."

"Wow. That's quite a story."

"Yeah, it is. But not nearly as fascinating as the story you're holding out on."

Quinn stared with a puzzled look on her face. "I don't have a story to tell."

"Yes, you do. I told you that I'm intuitive. You're sitting here with me and you're doing an okay job of keeping the conversation going. But I get the feeling that you'd much rather be somewhere else, or shall I say, with someone else." Sabrina smiled as she raised her perfectly arched brow.

Quinn's mouth fell as her eyes widened. How could she know that Draylen was heavy on her mind? "Am I that transparent?"

"Maybe a little," Sabrina said, demonstrating with her thumb and forefinger.

"I am so sorry. I thought I was doing a good job of covering."

Sabrina chuckled. "It's okay. I may as well confess to you that I knew there would be no love connection between us the moment you came to through the door."

"How could you know that?" Quinn asked.

"You're too pretty."

"Hey, I thought that was one of my selling points." Quinn pouted.

"It is, but...Well I'm more into a...I hate to use stereotypes, but I'm more into stud women."

"Oh."

"Although, I can always use a good friend, if you're interested," Sabrina offered.

"I think that is something that I can definitely go for," Quinn answered.

"Excellent," Sabrina said, lifting her glass to toast. "Here's to new friendships." Quinn lifted her glass and clinked it with Sabrina's before taking a sip.

"I'm ready to order if you are."

"Good, so am I," Sabrina replied, opening her menu. "Have the lobster. Dinner's on me. Actually I think I'll let the company pick up the tab on this one."

"You know what? I'm going to pass on the lobster and get a steak instead." The mention of lobster took Quinn back to

Draylen's allergic reaction to shellfish and how terrified she was at the thought of possibly losing her.

"You're going to pass up a lobster dinner? You don't like seafood?"

"No, it's not that. It's a long story," Quinn said.

Sabrina studied Quinn closely before saying, "I'm not going to ask you about it now, since we've just met, but if you ever want to talk about her then I'd be more than happy to listen."

"Thank you Sabrina." Quinn was touched that Sabrina didn't pry into her problems. Her feelings were too raw to expose to anyone right now.

"You're welcome. Let me call the waiter over before I eat my way through this basket of bread." Sabrina motioned for the server who quickly came and took their orders.

QUINN CLOSED AND LOCKED THE DOOR JUST AS THE "WILD THING" ringtone began to play on her cell phone. It was Jerry calling, no doubt wanting information about her date with Sabrina. She answered after retrieving the device from her purse.

"Hey, Jerry, isn't it past your bedtime?"

"Very funny. That's Dean Galloway that goes to bed early. I'm Jerry. I defy all curfews and rules. I'm a rebel."

"Oh, right. I forgot. What can I do for you, Rebel?"

"Don't be coy. You know perfectly well why I'm calling—to get the details on your night out with the seductress, Sabrina."

"Seductress? Does April know about your filthy mouth?"

"Of course she does. She's sitting right here next to me. Oh and you're on speaker, so be nice." Just then April could be heard saying, "Hey, Quinn, give us the details."

"You guys are crazy."

"Alright, we've established that. Now enough beating around the bush. What happened on the date?" Jerry insisted.

"Will you hush," April said.

"We talked over wine, before, during and after dinner. It was a wonderful time. I must say that this time, the two of you actually picked a winner." Quinn could hear Jerry and April whooping and hollering with excitement.

"Are you going to see her again?"

"This may shock you, but we are going out again soon."

"Really?" Jerry yelped.

"Yeah. She wants to take me hiking."

"Uh...okay. It's a date, right? Who cares where you go? All that matters is you're finally saying goodbye to that crazy dating rule of yours."

"Hallelujah!" April cried.

"You guys, I hate to bring you down, but there won't be a budding romance between Sabrina and I. We decided to be friends instead." Quinn could hear the silence coming from the other end of the phone and began talking to fill in the quiet.

"I know that you two were looking for a love connection, but it just wasn't meant to be."

"What did you do, Quinn?" Jerry sounded like he was reprimanding a puppy for having an accident on the carpet.

"To be honest, as much as we had in common, we weren't attracted to each other. In fact, she said that I was too pretty for her tastes."

"Too pretty? What did she mean by that?"

"Let's just say that our Sabrina goes for a more handsome woman and I didn't measure up."

"Oh."

"I really did have an incredible time and I think we'll be lifelong friends, which will take some getting used to. Jerry, having you as a best friend all these years, it will be strange having a woman friend to talk to—not slighting you at all, April. You know what I mean."

"I'm not offended, Quinn," reassured April. "Sabrina's a terrific person and has always been a good friend."

"Quinn, do you know what I'm thinking?" Jerry asked.

"No, Jerry. We're not so close that I can read your mind. What are you thinking?"

"I'm thinking that Olga Buchannan would be perfect for Sabrina."

"Olga Buchannan? Jerry, I said handsome. I don't think that Sabrina would appreciate a burly woman and definitely not Olga."

"Maybe you're right...Hey, what about the girl that works in the theatre department. You know who I'm talking about—she has a slight build and is always wearing her tool belt. The lady that sells the cookies every year for her daughter's Scout troupe."

"Oh, you mean Jodie?" Quinn asked.

"That's her name, Jodie," Jerry remarked.

"Jerry, Jodie is a man and he's married—has been for years." Quinn broke into laughter along with April.

"A man, really? Hmm," Jerry pondered.

"Jerry, say goodnight." Quinn was still laughing when the call ended.

Quinn headed for her bedroom, quickly changing into her nighty. She was finding it harder and harder to sleep in her bed. She prayed that after having an enjoyable evening out with Sabrina, she would have a peaceful slumber without the likes of Draylen Corliss tormenting her dreams.

It was bad enough that she consumed her thoughts every waking moment of the day, but she would give no respite, even in the wee hours of the night. Quinn picked up her phone and let her index finger scroll down to Draylen's number and hovered over it, primed and ready to dial—but all too soon the thought was abandoned, as she returned the phone to her night stand. If Draylen wanted to be with her, then she'd be there, lying beside her—since she was not there, it was perfectly clear that she didn't.

Angrily she kicked off the sheet as she stared at the phone, willing it to ring. Just before dawn, she drifted off to sleep as a single tear strolled over the bridge of her nose landing softly onto her pillow.

20

Draylen was exhausted by the time she turned off her computer. Between work and hanging out with Dava, she didn't have much time for herself. It seemed that everything was going at such a rapid pace, against her better judgment.

She took on two quick turn-around assignments for Bradley, who claimed that he was desperate for help, even increasing the pay as an incentive. He always knew how to convince her. In truth she didn't mind the work, it helped her to dull the pain of not being with Quinn. In those hours when she wasn't working, Dava was commanding her time. She was constantly being dragged somewhere to do something all in the name of reconciling their relationship. Draylen thought that it was great that Dava was taking their friendship seriously, however she was relentless. There were surprise lunches and nights out on the town, a concert, movies and impromptu gifts.

Draylen was used to Dava's extravagance since they were in grade school. Her parents had money and lots of it, and they were more than generous with their children. Lavish spending was something she came by honestly. However, it was one of the major conflicts in their former relationship—Dava's use of money, the other being her sense of entitlement. Dava's idea of solving a problem was to throw cash at the situation. To her, it was a lot easier than doing the hard work required.

Dava claimed that she changed in many ways since their break up, but Draylen wasn't completely convinced. As much as she wanted to cement their friendship, she wouldn't be bought in the process. Dava was over-compensating for the terrible way in which she left things between them years ago. Draylen understood that, but she also got the feeling that Dava had ulterior motives. Then there were other times when they'd share funny moments and laughter—just like old times.

Draylen pushed back from the desk and came to her feet stretching to relieve the tension in her shoulders and back. She picked up her cell phone remembering to turn the ringer back on, before checking her voicemail. She sighed heavily. This was another day without Quinn, another day without hearing her voice. It was getting harder to pretend that she didn't miss Quinn or that her staying away was the best thing for them. She had every intention of going to Quinn that night as she'd promised but when Dava showed up unexpectedly, she had to put Quinn aside. She had planned to go to her the next day, but once again, Dava had made plans for them.

By the third day, it just didn't seem right to show up on her door step. What could she have said to Quinn that would have made her give them another chance? Nothing. What sense did it make to beg Quinn's forgiveness only to cause her more hurt down the line? No, staying away was better, but no less difficult, especially when she longed to lay with her, taste her, breathe her—love her.

Draylen collapsed into the chair as her head began to swirl. "I can't be in love with her," she cried. "It's not possible. I won't have it!" Draylen continued to protest even as she knew the truth. She loved Quinn.

QUINN SAT ON THE SOFA LISTENING TO TORCH SONGS AS SHE poured out the last of the bottle into her glass. It was not her intentions to drink a whole bottle of merlot, but nothing else seemed to dull the pain that she was feeling. It was Draylen's fault that she was in this mood. She had not heard from her in two weeks, and now here she was walking around angry enough to kick kittens. She could not believe she was allowing Draylen to have so much control over her emotions. How many times today had she picked up the phone to call her and apologize— for what, she had no idea and at this point it didn't even matter. She just wanted to hear her voice. She needed to connect with her on some level.

Quinn turned the volume up when Lena Horne's rendition of "Stormy Weather" began to play. In the past two weeks, her mood went all over the spectrum from anger to hurt, forgiveness to sadness then back to anger. How dare Draylen treat her as if she were of no consequence? Did I ever matter to her or was it just all in my mind, she wondered. She would see women like her on daytime TV, pining over someone that could care less, and she would laugh at them thinking that she was too smart to be that stupid. As she finished off her glass, those women didn't seem so stupid anymore.

"This is ridiculous!" She yelled out into the empty space. If this is the way she wants it, then fine. "I'm done." She picked up the remote and turned off the wailing dulcet tones pouring out of the speakers. "Sorry, Ella. This is my last sad song for a while. Draylen can go to h—"

The knocking on the door interrupted her thought. The clock on the wall said three-forty-three. There was only one person that would call on her at this time of the morning.

Looking through the peephole, her suspicions were confirmed —it was Draylen.

Quinn took a moment to channel her anger. She intended to let her have it with both barrels and then show her the door. No sooner had she vowed this, than she was in Draylen's arms holding, kissing and caressing her. She'd chide herself tomorrow, but at the moment all she wanted to do was indulge herself in more of what Draylen was doing to her. She knew she should be giving her grief for treating her so badly. However, for the life of her, she couldn't remember exactly what she wanted to say. Dammit! She swore inwardly. Draylen's touch was everything and more. As she continued on slowly divesting Quinn of her tank top, she could feel the heat ignite from within her woman's center. There were so many things that she wanted to...Draylen fondled her bare breast. "Oh!" she cried. "Babe, I missed you so much." "Where is my anchor?" She wondered, as her mind raced, tossing her from one emotion to the next in split seconds, causing her knees to buckle and she fell into Draylen's tight hold.

"I missed you too," Draylen said into her ear.

Quinn tried to undress Draylen, however her mind was so numb and her fingers were clumsy that all she could manage was one button of her shirt. She groaned in frustration. "Help me...please," she pleaded through labored breaths. Draylen kept her gaze locked into Quinn's as she took over removing her own clothing, leaving them to rest in a pile on the rug.

Quinn waited anxiously for her to resume her deep kissing and was not disappointed when Draylen's tongue thoroughly explored the recesses of her mouth then pulled out to suck at her bottom lip before entering her mouth again to feast on her tongue. She nearly collapsed as Draylen's hand found its way down her pajamas and silk panties and cupped her throbbing mound. She wanted them to be in her bedroom but the passion was too great—there simply was not enough time. As Draylen helped ease her to the rug, she could feel herself losing all semblance of control. She would have begged Draylen never to leave her again, to stay with her forever—if she could only find the words. She trembled when Draylen removed her bottoms along with her dampened panties, leaving her naked and wanting. She reached for her, needing to feel her heat. It had been a long time since they had made love and tonight was definitely her breaking point.

"Please...Please. I need you," she cooed.

Draylen moved with a slow hand as she kissed and caressed her way down Quinn's body. Impatient for release, Quinn attempted to change their positions and take what she'd been craving for so long. They had not made love since weeks before the Seattle trip and Quinn was out of her mind with need. However Draylen could not be hampered.

"You want to be on top?" Draylen asked in between kisses to Quinn's navel.

"Yes." Quinn panted, barely able to speak.

"Well, if you were on top," Draylen said spreading Quinn's thighs. "Then I couldn't do this..." Draylen positioned her head at the seat of Quinn's desires and began to feast greedily, titillating her engorged cherry with the tip of her tongue, before sucking it with such voracity.

"Ooooh. Don't stop," Quinn screamed as her fingers mindlessly danced through the wild wooly coils of hair on Draylen's head.

Draylen continued manipulating her love bead, fluctuating the motion and pressure at whim to elicit the strongest response. Quinn moaned aloud as her hips undulated willfully to its own rhythm. Ultimately the pleasure began to reach its summit, though she fought feverishly to contain it. Her undoing came when Draylen entered her, massaging her inner sanctum with her fingers, while still savoring her clitoris. Somewhere off in the distance Quinn heard a voice screaming "Oh, Draylen, I love you. I love you so much. I love you. I love you!" As she made her decent back into the living room, she recognized that the voice belonged to her.

A moment of clarity washed over her. This was the reason Draylen had such an effect on her. She was in love with her. When her breathing came under control, she ventured to open her eyes and witness the source of all of her sleepless nights and agonizing days. She didn't know what to expect from Draylen after such an admission of love. She waited, looking at the grave expression on Draylen's face. Suddenly there was a low snicker that built into uproarious laughter. "Was it that good, babe?" Draylen asked as she unsuccessfully managed holding back her chortle.

Embarrassed, Quinn turned her face into the floor. "Go away," she grimaced.

Draylen moved up to hold her as they spooned. "Don't be that way. I've said some crazy shameful things while in the throes of passion—who hasn't? I'm just glad that I was able to please you in that way." Quinn turned into Draylen's embrace. Still unable to look her in the eyes, she settled for burrowing her head deep into her supple breasts. If Draylen only knew that what she screamed out at the height of ecstasy was the truth in every sense of the word. The real question was, what was she going to do now? She knew that she could not withstand her rejection if she confessed her love to her once again.

"Quinn?"

"Yes?"

"It's cold. Can we please go to your bed?"

21

"Good morning sleepy head."

"Morning. Why are you so chipper?" Quinn murmured as she struggled to open her eyes.

"I woke up with you in my arms, the sun is shining. It's a special day."

"If you say so." Quinn sat up in the bed and noticed that Draylen was holding a tray. "Did you make breakfast?"

"Judging by my watch, it's more like brunch. Since I wasn't quite sure how you'd feel after downing what I'm guessing to be a whole bottle of merlot this morning, I only made a few things. I've got oatmeal, nice and soupy, greasy sausages—you know the kind with the hard gristle thrown in, and some eggs, sunny side up. Yum!"

"Oh yuck! Please be kidding. I don't think that my stomach can take it."

"I am kidding. Here..." Draylen placed the tray across Quinn's lap and smiled.

"Croissants, marmalade, Danishes and coffee. Aw thanks, honey." Quinn wasted no time taking a sip of coffee. "Mmm, you got my favorite blend. How was everyone at the café?" Quinn teased.

"Café? I'll have you know that I kneaded the dough for the croissants and Danishes by hand, right here in your kitchen. The marmalade's also done in-house."

"Don't tell me you blended and roasted the African and Columbian coffee beans as well," Quinn said biting into the pastry.

"Yeah, well the coffee...that was a bit tricky. I'd like to tell you about it, but it's a trade secret. Lives have been lost or at least put in harm's way trying to find that out."

"I see. I'm definitely not going to meddle with proprietary secrets, especially when I'm being spoiled like this," Quinn said.

"You're a very wise lady," Draylen said as she grabbed a Danish from the tray and took a bite. "Are you busy today?"

"I need to go over this article once more before I submit it to the magazine," Quinn said. "Other than that, my day is free. Did you—"

"What's it like?" Draylen interrupted.

"What's what like?"

"To be published in a magazine."

"It's thrilling. I guess that's the only word I'd use. The very first time something of mine was published, I was on cloud nine. I didn't make one red cent from it, but I felt like I'd won a million dollars-make that ten million, to account for today's inflation."

"What was the article about?"

"It was a story about how my family came to New York from the Dominican Republic. When my grandparents, mom, and her siblings arrived, it was a different time. Things were harder. Anyway, I got published in this rinky dink magazine that possibly a handful of people actually read. But I felt like I was a writer. I was then published in a few other places until finally I got into a national publication. That's when I felt like I had arrived. Then I got rejection after rejection—I refer to that time as the Dark Ages, but I came out of it. Like I said, Draylen, rejection comes with the territory." Quinn placed her hand on Draylen's and was pleased when she did not move her hand away.

"You've had a lot of things published. Do you still get excited by it?"

"I'd like to say that, at this point in my career, I take it all in stride, but I don't. I'm as thrilled as the very first time. The only thing I take in stride are the rejection letters. That's why the Writer's Club is so important because we're all there for each other, especially during those times when our good work goes unnoticed or pushed aside." Quinn's gaze fell on Draylen's intense expression and knew that her words were sinking in—at least she hoped.

Instantly Draylen's mood changed and she smiled. "I want to take you out to dinner on this special day. The weather is nice with no forecasts of rain or snow. What do you say, you want to go out on the town with me?"

I'd go anywhere with you because I love you, Quinn wanted to say. "Yes, I'd love to go out on the town with you. It should be fun. I've felt like a hermit for the past few weeks." She stared into Draylen's eyes trying to get her meaning across that she had been miserable without her and that she never wanted to experience her absence again. It was too painful to bear.

"I know," Draylen replied before bowing her head. Message received, she thought. "So, here's what you need to do—"

"Do? You mean there's instructions that I have to follow? I thought that we'd just go out and let the night unfold." Quinn pushed the tray aside and listened.

"No, dear. This plan comes with a simple set of instructions. You see, it's all about preparation. I know that it's hard for a free spirit like you to grasp, but it is what it is." Draylen kissed Quinn on the cheek. "Alright, I'm gonna' go home and work on the plan—"

"Go home?" Quinn intervened. "How long are you going to be gone?" Suddenly the idea of Draylen being out of her sight for any length of time did not appeal to her. "Draylen, why don't you run home, get your clothes then come back over here and we can work on your plan together." Quinn anxiously chewed at her bottom lip. The last time Draylen promised to come back to her, she stayed away for two weeks. They still hadn't talked about what happened. They had spent the early morning making love until the sun came up and once more after. "Can't you do it my way?" She pleaded.

"I can't. It won't work that way. It's my plan. I'm taking you out. Besides I've got some things to do at home."

"You're not going to work, I hope. Whenever you get on that computer, you always lose track of time. And I'll be here dressed to the nines while you stand me up." Quinn sighed. Already she had a dislike of this plan.

"I'm not going to do any work, I promise. All you have to worry about is wearing something extremely hot and make sure you're ready by exactly six. You got that—exactly six p.m." Draylen pointed to her watch for clarification.

"I've got it," Quinn said giving Draylen a salute.

"I've got to run." She kissed Quinn on the lips before leaving.

22

"**D**ammit! I knew this would happen," Quinn fumed as she wore a path in the living room floor. Draylen said that she'd be there at exactly six o'clock and now it was exactly eight forty-five p.m. She glanced at the cell phone clutched tightly in her hand. There was not one text or voice message from her —nothing.

"She must have placed a dozen calls. She didn't like being helpless. She prayed that Draylen had not been in an accident. This night out with Draylen was supposed to be wonderful. Even though Draylen would have decided where they went and what they did, Quinn had a few plans of her own later this evening. She had decided to express her true feelings to Draylen, once again. This time she'd make her understand that what she blurted out in the grips of a sensuous release wasn't happenstance, but the truth. However, as she removed the last hair pin that held together her sleek chignon, releasing her springy shoulder length curls, she knew that the moment had passed.

Quinn looked at herself in the full-length mirror. The wine colored slip dress hugged her slender frame in all of the right places. She had since removed the matching four inch sandals with crystal inlaid ankle straps. She had taken every preparation from the lavender scented bath, the mani/pedi, to her flawless make-up, and favorite perfume, Tungsten. At six o'clock she sat on the sofa, a faux fur shawl and evening bag lay across her lap as she waited for Draylen to arrive.

Hours passed, and the fear that something may have happened to Draylen suffused her body. She had to go by her place and see if she was there. Maybe her phone was not working, or maybe Bradley called her with a last minute assignment and the money was too good to pass up. She didn't know, but she decided that the not knowing was driving her crazy. Quickly she removed the frock, exchanging it for a light sweat suit and some tennis shoes. She grabbed her car keys from the accent table and rushed for the door.

"Baby, why aren't you dressed? We don't have much time."

"Draylen! You're okay?" Quinn stood in the door way, her stomach doing summersaults.

"I'm fine. Now can I come in?"

Quinn moved back and let her enter the house. She swallowed the lump in her throat. Draylen was fine. She exhaled but before she could release her feelings of worry, they had now been replaced by anger. "Where the hell have you been? You said for me to be ready by six, did you not?"

"I know, the time got away from me. I just wanted to make sure things went according to my plan. Now hurry up and get dressed." Draylen urged her forward with her hands at the small of her back.

"No! I was dressed, three hours ago. And as far as your plan goes, it sucked. I'm going to bed. Lock the door before you leave." Quinn's effort to walk away was halted by Draylen's firm grasp of her arm.

"Wait. I know you're extremely pissed at me. I get that and

you have every right to be. But I'm asking...no, I'm begging you, please get dressed. If you want to read me the riot act later into the wee hours of the morning, I promise to be receptive, no matter what you have to say." She gazed at Quinn with childlike pleading in her eyes. "Please?"

After a moment of inner counsel, Quinn headed for the bedroom. "I'll be back in a minute." She chided herself for obeying Draylen so easily. Love is making me stupid, she thought as she slipped back into her dress, and quickly re-primped for the last time.

"Well, here I am all dressed up and—" Quinn's jaw dropped.

"Draylen, what is this?" Quinn was completely taken aback. The dining room table was elegantly set for two, complete with roses and candlelight. A wait staff of three aligned the wall nearby.

"I wanted to do something a little different. I had planned for us to go out for dinner and dancing, but then I realized that what I wanted more than anything was to have you all to myself. Do you mind?"

"No, this is better than anything I could have imagined. I love it." Quinn beamed her approval as she took in every detail.

"Come here. I will seat you." Draylen held out the chair and helped her slide it up to the table.

"Thank you," Quinn said as their eyes locked.

"You're welcome," Draylen placed a quick kiss on her lips.

One of the wait staff assisted Draylen with her seat. As the women placed their cloth napkins in their laps, the sommelier introduced the chosen wine pouring each of them a glass.

"This is delicious," Quinn said as she enjoyed the fruity

flavor. She was familiar with this vintage South African wine and knew that it was far from cheap.

"I'm glad you like it. I got another bottle for later, or maybe you can keep it for a special occasion. By the way, you look stunning. It's so weird to see you like this. You look amazing." Draylen especially liked the plunging neckline that left very little to the imagination. There was no way in hell that she would let her go out on the town in that dress, and have others ogling her like she was the last meal at fat camp. No way, she thought as she stared intently at Quinn's hardened nipples protruding the delicate fabric. "Mmm," She said aloud.

"Excuse me, what did you say?"

"Nothing. I was just appreciating every stitch of that dress."

"I was sitting here thinking the same about your dress. Teal looks great on you," Quinn stated.

"Thanks, but do you like the dress on me?"

"I do. I'm just shocked. In the time that I've known you, I've never seen you in a dress. I didn't think you wore them. You should wear them more often, it boosts your sexy up to mega status."

"Mega status, huh? Okay, that's good to know. Actually, I do wear dresses and I have quite a few in my repertoire. I'm just more comfortable in pants. When I'm in a dress, I feel awkward. That is why I reserve dresses for special occasions and church. I don't know how to incorporate them into my everyday wardrobe."

"I can help you with that." Quinn thought that there were so many things she wanted to do for Draylen but most of all she wanted to love her and to have that love returned. Maybe one day.

∽

"OH MY GOD! EVERYTHING WAS SO DELICIOUS," QUINN SAID pushing her plate forward. I haven't had a meal like that since Seattle. I'm nearly stuffed. I'm just going to put it out there, babe...When I get up from this table, you may notice that my dress will fit a little different right around the midsection." Quinn rubbed her protruding stomach for emphasis.

"Don't worry, I feel the same way, Draylen moaned as she watched the wait staff quietly remove the dinner setting and excuse themselves into the kitchen.

"Where did you find them? The food and the service has been top notch." Quinn took a sip from her water glass.

"They're students in their senior year at the culinary school not far from the university."

"Really? How did you find out about them?"

"A client of mine. One day she mentioned to me that her daughter attended the school and that many of the seniors did catering on the side to make extra money and get experience—it looks good on a resume as well. She gave me her daughter's card and I took it just to be polite, never thinking that I'd ever use it, but..." Draylen hunched her shoulders.

"This was your plan all the time, huh? How sneaky." Quinn wiggled her finger at Draylen.

"Actually, this was not the plan. We were going out for dinner and a night on the town, but...well...there was this..."

"What?"

"I know I promised I wouldn't, but there was this assignment that was supposed to be quick but as it turned out required more time to complete. Before I knew it time had gotten away from me. That's when I called the culinary school. It wasn't easy but I managed to convince them of just how important today was and once Jenny, our chef for the evening, found out that I knew her mother, things kind of tipped in our favor."

"I suppose I should be upset with you for working, but if you hadn't then I wouldn't have ever had pan roasted squab, asparagus drizzled in herb-infused olive oil, mashed potatoes and leeks, so you're forgiven."

"Thank you," Draylen sighed pretending to wipe her brow. I've never had squab before either. What did you think of it?" she whispered.

"It tastes like chicken," Quinn whispered back.

"I know. I was thinking the same thing." They laughed aloud before abruptly ceasing when the wait staff returned with dessert.

"Happy Birthday and please enjoy our molten lava cake," Jenny said.

Quinn looked at the delectable confectionary creation with a look of surprise and a hint of confusion. As the staff returned to the kitchen, she decided to confess. "Draylen, I love this, but I need to tell you that it's not my birthday."

"I know, it's mine. Surprise!" Draylen removed the 'Happy Birthday' skewer from the dessert, licking the chocolate filling from it.

"Draylen, I had no idea." Quinn's head sank into her chest. "How could I not have known? We've been intimate for Christ sake. I should have at the very least known that today was your birthday." She shook her head.

"How would you know that today was my birthday? I've never told you. To be honest, it just never came up."

"But don't you see, it should have come up. We've...we have been together—all this time and it's like we barely know each other."

"C'mon. So we don't know everything about each other—"

"But we don't even know the basics. What kind of foundation is that?" When Quinn raised her head, her eyes were filled with unshed tears.

"Quinn, if it makes you feel any better, I wasn't even going to celebrate my birthday. In fact, I haven't celebrated it in the last three years. It's just...this is my fortieth, so I decided that maybe I should do something. I mean I would hate to look back on my life with regret because I didn't celebrate this milestone in my life."

"Oh God, It's your fortieth. I feel like such a heel." Quinn covered her forehead.

"Quinn, please. Like I said, this is a special day. I want to enjoy it with you. I don't want you upset on my special day. You don't want me to look back on this as the day I devastated Quinn, now do you?" Draylen reach out and Quinn placed her hand in hers.

"You know I don't want that." Quinn dried her tears and presented a smile that grew wider by degrees until she was beaming.

"Great. Now can we please get off into this molten lava cake? It looks delicious."

"Baby, you had me at molten lava," Quinn said. The two shared a lascivious smile before eating their dessert.

Having sent the catering crew on their way with high praises and a generous tip, Draylen and Quinn stood in the middle of the living room swaying slowly to the melodic jazz tunes coming from the surround sound speakers.

"Draylen, this was the perfect evening. I couldn't have asked for better." Quinn placed a gentle kiss behind Draylen's ear.

"I'm glad you liked it," Draylen murmured into the bountiful curls that rested on Quinn's shoulders.

"Did you enjoy tonight, seeing that it was your birthday feast?"

"I did. I'm happy that I got to be here with you. I'm also grateful that you didn't kill me when I first walked in here this evening, or else I would have been eating squab out on your front stoop with a dumb look on my face." Draylen cringed at the thought.

Quinn chuckled. "Draylen, Happy birthday. I promise that I will make it up to you."

"Shh," Draylen pressed a finger to Quinn's lips silencing her.

"I am going to make it up to you. That's all there is to it," Quinn said defiantly. She removed Draylen's finger from her mouth and gave her a long sensuous kiss that left them both absent of breath in their lungs.

"Okay, you win. No need to pull out the secret weapon," Draylen said

The deep smoky voice of Laylah Hathaway singing "Forever, For Always, For Love" surrounded them as they became lost in each other's arms.

"May thirty-first," Quinn whispered, seductively into Draylen's ear.

"What's May thirty-first?"

"That's my birthday. That's next year. I'll be forty-five and I want to share that day with you." (And the next birthday, and the one after that into infinity, Quinn thought).

"I've got it and I'm locking it away in my mental vault."

"What's your middle name?"

"Elizabeth."

"Draylen Elizabeth Corliss. That's nice."

"Thanks. And yours?"

"Ayala. It's my mom's maiden name."

"Quinn Ayala Kendall. I like it."

"Tell me, what's your favorite color?"

Draylen dipped her backwards. "I don't have a favorite color." She smiled.

"I don't either," Quinn remarked, completely astonished. "What's your favorite dessert?"

"Quinn Kendall." Draylen looked at Quinn and quirked her brow before breaking up into laughter.

"Draylen, you're so crazy," she snickered trying unsuccessfully to maintain her resolve.

The rest of the evening was spent getting to know one another, each new fact bringing them closer together.

23

"Ouch," Quinn yelled after hitting her toe on the large cedar chest. "I hate this stupid thing. Why don't you move it?" Quinn limped her way over to the settee. Sitting down, she massaged her foot, inspecting it for injuries.

"Why don't you slow down and pay attention to where you're going," Draylen reprimanded from her perch in the center of the bed.

"I can't slow down, thanks to you." She quickly put on her trouser socks. "Now, I'm going to be late for class. Quinn rushed through the task of dressing.

"You're not going to be late, and even if you are, I'd say that after what we did this morning, it was well worth it, wouldn't you?" Draylen grinned as their gazes locked into each other.

"I'm not saying that I didn't enjoy it."

"Then what are you saying, Quinn? That you would have preferred it had we made love at a more suitable time—a time of your own choosing? Well I'm sorry. I don't work like that. I woke up, saw you and I reacted. If you were so concerned, you could have stopped me. Your hands weren't tied, although the thought had crossed my mind. Why didn't you stop me?"

"Because...You know why." Quinn's fingers were trembling as she attempted to button her white cotton shirt. Memories of this morning's love making replayed in her mind.

"No, I don't know. Why don't you tell me," Draylen said as she got up and stood before Quinn assisting her with the buttons.

"I loved the way you made me feel and I didn't want you to stop." Quinn exhaled deeply, embarrassed by the admission.

"Now was that so hard to say?" Draylen kissed the tip of her nose.

"I just don't want to let my students down that's all."

"So what if you're five minutes late," Draylen exclaimed, rolling her eyes.

"What will they think?" Quinn agonized.

"They're gonna' say, 'thank God she's late, because I didn't finish my homework,' or 'I was late too and I didn't want to be stuck on the other side of the door because of her stupid tardy policy.' Who knows what they'll think and who cares? By the way, is there any chance that you'll ever put an end to that crazy attendance rule of yours, or at least relax it some? I mean give a student a break."

"I did relax it a few times, for you, but where did that get me? You still ended up dropping out." Quinn held Draylen captive in her stare until the hurt she wanted to convey was received.

"Touché," Draylen said as she helped Quinn pack her satchel.

"What are you going to do today? Do you have a lot of work?" Quinn went to the fridge and removed the orange juice container, pouring herself a small glass.

"This may surprise you, but I don't have any work today. I've got the whole day to myself."

"What are you going to do?"

"I don't know. Maybe I'll go visit my mom and hang out with

her for a while. She's always so busy at the community center with her friends, and we haven't really had much time to spend together." Draylen grabbed a banana and an apple from the fruit bowl on the table and the sandwich she'd made earlier and place them in a brown paper bag along with a bottle of iced tea.

"Draylen, I'd really like to meet your mother. Maybe we can invite her to dinner or something." Quinn waited for Draylen's response. She had to gauge where she fit into her life. Until she knew that Draylen's feelings matched that of her own, she decided that there was no way she could confess her love to her again.

"Quinn, I'd love for you to meet my mom and for us to invite her to dinner, but if my dad found out, and trust me, he'd find out—I could not deal with that Vietnam, and trust me, neither could you. Here..." Draylen placed the satchel on Quinn's shoulder and walked her to the door. "I know you like locking your door because it amuses you to see some poor student with their face pressed up against the glass looking pitiful. Even I have to admit it is kind of funny—that is unless you're the one standing on the outside. However I do implore you not to be a speed demon on the road just so you can get to class in enough time to punish some student because they overslept this morning."

Quinn debated in her mind before saying, "Alright, I promise not to speed. I will drive safely."

Draylen exhibited a look of scrutiny towards Quinn before she unbolted and opened the door. "I guess that will have to do," She said with up turned lips. "Go on. Have a good day." She kissed her lips.

"Oh, I almost forgot. Don't stay at your mom's too late. Remember the Writer's Club meets tonight."

"I did forget," Draylen grumbled and sighed as she scratched her head.

"Well, I'm glad that I reminded you—and you're coming. No excuses. I've got a surprise for you."

"What is it?"

"Sorry. Can't talk about it. I'm late. See you tonight and be on time, please."

THE RESTAURANT WAS ABUZZ WITH FIFTIES MUSIC COMING FROM the jukebox. The clanging of plates and cutlery could be heard over muffled conversations from diners left behind from the afternoon rush. Draylen sat at the back of the space with her mother talking over a late lunch.

"You must have read my mind," Debra Corliss said as she added sweetener to her iced tea. "I was thinking about you and was gonna call but I wasn't sure if this was your busy day."

"Mom, I told you the last time that my schedule varies. I don't have one day where I'm busy. That can be any day. That's why you have the number to the house phone. You can call me at any time." Draylen took a bite of her garden burger.

"I thought that was for emergencies only."

"It's for emergencies and for my mom and dad."

"Speaking of your Dad, did I tell you that he had the nerve to walk up in the church with that woman on his arm?"

"Yes, Mom. You told me."

"I thought, of all the nerve. I can't believe him," Debra sucked her teeth as she shook her head. "I tell you, I had half a mind to go up to them and slap—"

"Mom!" Draylen interrupted. "Why are you so upset? My God, you two have been divorced for well over ten years. And look who's talking, you've been in another relationship and on a few dates with other men, I seem to recall."

"Yes but they've all been age appropriate. Not like that preteen your Dad is snuggling up to."

"Margie is not a preteen, she is fifty-five. If we're going to sit here while you say mean things about Daddy then I'm going home."

"You always were a Daddy's girl. Fine. I'll stop talking about his tired a—"

"Mom," Draylen said with a look of warning.

"Okay, okay." Debra rolled her eyes as she took a long sip from her glass.

"Thank you, I know that was hard." Draylen sighed. "Besides whenever I'm with him, he accuses me of being a Mama's girl when he feels that I'm siding with you about something."

"I'm sorry, Bunny Chops. You're right about your Dad and me. I guess that our problem is that we still love each other on some deep...deep...very deep level." Debra cringed as she speared her blackened shrimp.

"Forget about it. Can we please change the subject?" Draylen asked.

"Of course we can. Tell me, how is your girlfriend?"

"I don't know what you're talking about. I don't have a girlfriend." Draylen chewed her food intently but suddenly her appetite was gone. The last thing she wanted to do was to have a conversation regarding her relationship with anyone. She appreciated that her parents had been very accepting when she first decided to come out to them. Debra and Edward Corliss had always been supportive of her lifestyle and her choices in partners. The only time that they'd ever gone against her was when she opted not to pursue her master's degree. Even with that, they managed to forgive her. She knew she was blessed to have them for her parents. Although they had a close bond, she never felt comfortable discussing the intimate details of her love life. She had made that mistake three years ago and she promised never to do it again. Her parents had taken her break up with Dava about as hard as she did. She wasn't ready to open them up to meeting someone new in her life, especially when she was not sure about where she and Quinn were headed.

"Draylen, when good things happen to you, you're supposed to share that with others."

"Mom, if I had some good news to share, then I would. But since I don't, I can't."

Debra sighed, a look of defeat unveiled on her face. "I'm your mother, not some stranger off the street. I know you, and you're different. Are you aware that you've smiled several times since we've been in this restaurant and it's definitely not because of anything I've said or done?"

"Mom I—"

"No," Debra said with a wave of her hand. "You listen. It's okay to be happy again. You've got to stop fighting against your true feelings. Let love take its course. Your Dad and me...Our marriage is over, but I wouldn't take back a moment of those thirty years and I'm certain your Dad feels the same way." Draylen watched as her mother dabbed unshed tears from the corners of her eyes with a napkin.

"What if there were someone in my life but there were obstacles?" Draylen spoke just above a whisper. She looked at her plate of burger and fries, avoiding her mother's all-knowing gaze. She had lost her appetite.

"Bunny Chops, when it comes to love, real love, there are no obstacles unless you create them. Now, come on. It's been a long time since I've taken my baby shopping. You feel like going shopping with your mama?"

Draylen put some bills along with the check into the billfold and placed it in the center of the table. "Yeah, I could go for a little shopping."

"You think you can keep up with me? You know I'm a beast in the stores," Debra said as she slipped into her leather jacket.

"So am I. Where do you think I got it from?"

DRAYLEN SCRIBBLED HER SIGNATURE ON THE SIGN-IN SHEET, AND ran down the hall. She knew she shouldn't have let her mother talk her into going to yet another mall. She was pressed for time when they left the second mall. However her mother assured her that they would stay only a minute. That was lie and now she was extremely late for the meeting. She'd have to slip in discretely and sit in the back, she decided. She took the seat nearest the door and was pleased that she did not cause a stir. In fact no one even noticed that she had entered the room. Everyone's attentions were focused on Quinn, who was front and center reading a short story. She didn't tell me that she was working on a new piece, Draylen thought.

Quinn's story had everyone riveted to their seats. Draylen hated that she showed up late. How much time had she missed, she wondered. As she listened, she began to take notice of the words and how familiar they seemed.

'It had become clear. They were drifting apart, becoming strangers, offering up forced pleasantries for the time being. But how much longer could they keep this up before decisions had to be made, Kaitlyn wondered.'

The story was a little too familiar, Draylen thought. Just then it registered. This story was hers. Draylen saw a flash of red before she jumped to her feet. "What the hell are you doing?!" She yelled. Quickly the room turned its focus on her, but all she could see was Quinn with a surprised look on her face. "Where did you...How could you do this? I can't believe you!" Draylen ran from the room. Looks of shock accompanied low chattering and curious whispers as the room came to a standstill.

"Draylen, wait!" Quinn went after her. By the time she reached the front desk, Draylen was walking out the exit door.

"Draylen, stop," Quinn yelled. Draylen stopped in the entryway of the lobby, but she did not turn to face her. Quinn came to her. "Do you mind telling me what that was all about?"

"No, I don't mind. What gives you the right to read my story to everybody? I'm not okay with that. You didn't even ask me."

"Technically I did ask you, and you said that I could read your stories."

"What I said, I do recall is that you," Draylen pointed her finger into Quinn's chest. "I said that you could read them. I said nothing about your reading them to the masses. That's my personal stuff and you had no right to take it upon yourself and do something so calculated."

"Oh, come on. Aren't you being just a little dramatic? Jeez, we're not talking espionage here. I read one of your stories, big whoop! I didn't tell you about it because I wanted to surprise you."

"Well then, I guess you got the reaction you were looking for, because I was definitely surprised. I gotta go."

"Alright. Let me take you home, and we'll discuss this some more."

Draylen reached into her pocket and pulled out a set of keys dangling them before Quinn in her customary fashion. "No thanks." She walked briskly towards the parking lot with Quinn following close behind.

"Draylen, can we please talk about this. I don't want you angry with me."

Draylen unlocked the door and quickly got behind the wheel, starting the engine. Quinn held onto the door preventing her from closing it.

"Draylen, don't leave things like this. I never meant to upset you."

"I need to return this car. Will you please let go of the door so I can leave?"

Quinn reluctantly released the door and watched as Draylen drove away. "Damn! Why am I always getting it wrong with her?"

"WHO IS IT?"

"Draylen open the door," Quinn was relieved when she heard the buzzer sound. She pushed the entry door and made her way to the stairwell. She didn't look forward to yet another argument with Draylen, but it seemed to be the only way they ever made progress in their relationship. She reached the top of the landing to find Draylen standing rigidly in the doorway.

"What's all that?" Draylen asked upon seeing Quinn bogged down with her hands full.

"It's work, a change of clothes for tomorrow and in case you haven't eaten, I've got Chinese. I also brought a very big apology from me to you." Draylen stood a moment blocking the entrance as she contemplated her next move. Finally, she stepped aside and Quinn walked into the apartment. She followed Draylen into the kitchen and watched as she took plates and silverware down from the cupboards and placed them on the table.

"Do you want to eat first or talk? I don't want to do both," Draylen said coarsely.

"I'd rather talk first even though I run the risk of not having an appetite later," Quinn replied.

"That's fine by me," Draylen agreed as she walked into the bedroom and sat on the reclining chair.

Quinn sat on the settee. "Draylen, I'm sorry about reading

your story at the Writer's meeting without asking. I guess I didn't see anything wrong with what I did."

"You could have asked me. The stuff that I write is personal and not for everyone to hear. I determine what I want read in that meeting and there's a lot that I do not wish to share with anyone, and that story was one of them."

"But it doesn't make sense when what you write is so good."

"Have you ever kept a journal or a diary?" Draylen asked.

"You know I have. You've seen me write in it."

"Suppose I printed copies of it and passed it around to the faculty and your students without your permission, would that be okay?"

"Alright, I got it. It's just that when I read it, I fell in love with the story. The characters, Kaitlyn and Ava were so raw and in your face. They practically leaped from the page. I felt like I knew them personally.

"I don't want to talk about the story. I'm quite familiar with it. I want to talk about you, and your inability to stop meddling when it comes to my writing. If I choose not to pursue this writing thing, then that should be enough for you."

"But—"

"But nothing. Don't fight me on this because you're going to lose every time. Can I have your word that you won't interfere anymore?" Draylen studied Quinn, watching her inwardly weigh the pros and cons of making such a definite promise.

At last, accepting defeat, Quinn let out a heavy sigh before saying, "Fine. If this is what you really want."

"It is," Draylen retorted.

Quinn was right, she thought to herself. She no longer had an appetite. The disagreement had been settled and still it felt as if nothing was resolved. Draylen was still angry with her—she could see her cloak of negativity shrouding the space. Tonight may have set them back further than they'd ever been.

"I'm gonna' go take a shower," Draylen said as she got up to leave the room.

"I've got some papers to grade." Quinn grabbed her satchel and went to the living room.

It wasn't until the wee hours of the morning that Quinn slipped quietly between the covers. She had finished with her papers an hour before but wanted to make certain that Draylen had fallen asleep before she came to bed. She wanted to make sure that the tension levels had dissipated some. However judging from Draylen's shallow breathing, she was wide awake. She had waited for her.

"Babe, I know that you're still upset, I don't want you to be. If I could take it all back, I would. I'd do anything to keep you from feeling like this towards me," because I love you, she yearned to confess. "Can't we just hold each other and put everything else out of our minds?"

Draylen wasted no time when she turned quickly into Quinn's arms and nestled her head against her breast. Quinn sighed, relieved in knowing progress had been made, though it was but a small step forward.

24

Q uinn could barely contain her excitement when she heard the news this afternoon. Two of Draylen's literary pieces had been selected for the new upcoming edition of 'The Write Off,' the university's highly acclaimed annual journal publication. She could have phoned Draylen and told her the wonderful news but decided that it would be even better if she could share in the excitement with her. To be published in 'The Write Off' went very far in the literary scene. There were professors that had not gotten the pleasure of such an accomplishment. Perhaps this would give Draylen the confidence boost she needed to really pursue writing as a career, she thought.

Quinn had made a promise only a day ago to never meddle in Draylen's writing career, or lack thereof. However, technically, she had already submitted the two short stories weeks prior to making said agreement. Also Draylen had given the stories to her "as parting gifts" after she dropped out of school. Therefore since the stories were hers, she could do with them as she wished—this would be her reasoning should Draylen explode on her again, though she seriously doubted that she would.

Quinn was fortunate to find a parking space a few doors down from Draylen's building. She removed her satchel and a bag from the back seat before pressing the key fob. She walked briskly, anxious to get to Draylen and deliver the good news. As she got closer to the front gate, she noticed a woman leaning on a blue sports car, smoking a cigarette. She recognized the car immediately—this was the car that Draylen frequently drove. The woman made eye contact with Quinn, so she spoke. "Hello." She thought that she should probably keep going, but found herself intrigued by this woman and wanted to know why she had taken it upon herself to casually lean on this particular car.

"Hello," the woman replied in between puffs of smoke.

"Is that your car?" Quinn asked while she studied the woman. She was about her height, with close-cropped curly hair, and of medium complexion. She clearly had a masculine presence. From the reflection of the streetlight casting a modest glow, Quinn could tell that she bound her breast beneath her tailored men's suit. She was quite attractive and gave off a cocky air.

"Yes, it's my car. Do you like it," she asked beaming proudly at the tricked out car with regulation tinted windows, two-toned metallic shimmering blue paint color and twenty-four inch rims complete with spinners. Ghetto, Quinn thought.

"It's a nice car. I was really asking because one of my students drives this car. So you must be friends with her."

"Yeah. Draylen and I go way back. I let her use my car a lot because I usually drive a company car."

"Oh, I see," Quinn said. She didn't know why but she was starting to feel uneasy about this woman. "I'm sorry. I didn't mean to be rude. I'm Professor Kendall. I teach at Draylen's university."

The woman took a final drag from her cigarette as she did a slow assessment of Quinn from head to toe, before returning her attentions back to her face. "My name is Dava," she said flicking the cigarette butt into the grass. She stuck out her hand and Quinn stepped closer accepting the extended gesture of greeting.

"Pleased to meet you, Ava."

"No, it's Dava, with a 'D' at the beginning," Dava corrected.

"Oh, I'm sorry. I thought you said—" Then Quinn remembered the story. Draylen's private story that she read yesterday at the Writer's meeting. Ava was the character in the story that had broken Kaitlyn's heart. The woman that Kaitlyn could never seem to get over. Ava was the woman that—as Kaitlyn put it— she would love forever. Things were finally coming clear as a feeling of dread began to pervade Quinn's mind.

"Are you okay?" Dava asked.

Quinn, returning from the fog, realized that she was still holding Dava's hand. She quickly released it. "I'm sorry about that. I just remembered something I should have done earlier. Don't mind me." Quinn smiled though that was the last thing she felt like doing.

"No problem. Don't worry about it. You're fine. Forgetting things is just another way of saying that we're human."

Just then Draylen walked through the gate. She immediately got a sinking feeling at the sight of Dava and Quinn talking to each other. "Qui— Professor Kendall. I didn't expect to see you here." Draylen had nearly blown it by almost calling Quinn by her first name. She could tell by her stone cold expression, that Quinn was enraged, but was holding it together nicely, she didn't want Dava figuring out their relationship any more than she did. They'd exchanged a knowing glance before Draylen turned her attention to Dava.

"Here you are," she said handing Dava the car keys. "I put the gas hand back to full for you." She smiled timidly.

Dava pulled Draylen into her embrace and planted a long

kiss on her lips. "Thank you, baby. Are you going to need it anymore this week?" she asked, still holding on to Draylen.

"I don't think so," Draylen replied freeing herself from Dava and stepping to the side. She didn't have to look at Quinn to know she was angry. She could feel the fiery darts being shot at her from her glaring eyes.

"Baby, didn't you tell me that you quit school?" Dava inquired suspiciously while cutting an eye towards Quinn.

"I did quit." Draylen looked at Quinn briefly then back to Dava.

"Good. Like I told you, you've already got a degree. There's no sense in racking up student loans for a little hobby. You can write those little stories in your spare time and that doesn't cost you anything." Dava looked over to Quinn challenging her to refute her words.

"I told you that I quit, Dava. End of story," Draylen scolded. She hadn't meant to snap, but Dava had a way of turning the screw a bit too tight at times. She surmised that this show was all for Quinn's benefit. She may not have known exactly what was going on between her and Quinn, but Draylen knew that Dava suspected something.

"Alright, sorry Baby. I'm gonna' get on out of here." Dava hugged Draylen and tried to kiss her mouth, however Draylen anticipated the move and quickly turned her head leaving the kiss to land on her cheek, which did not go unnoticed by Dava.

"I'll call you later," she said, clenching the muscles in her jaw. She made her way to the driver's side of the car and opened the door, giving one more scathing look at Quinn then Draylen, she got in the car, fired the engine, revving it a few times before pulling off, tires screeching hurriedly down the street.

As the sound of the car gradually faded in the distance, Draylen and Quinn stood in silence until it became unbearable.

"What brings you here tonight, Quinn? I didn't expect you."

Draylen closed in the distance. "You should have called. You didn't, but you should have."

"I've never known you to call before you come to my house. You always just show up whenever you want—most times at an ungodly hour."

"Whatever, Quinn."

"So, that's Ava," Quinn stated harshly through tight lips.

"Dava. Her name is Dava."

"You know perfectly well what the hell I mean. She's the one you wrote about in your story that I read. She is Ava, the woman you'd always love. Ava, the one that owns your soul. That is what you wrote."

"Quinn, it's a book of fiction."

"Really? I don't think it is."

"I'm not having this conversation with you on the sidewalk in front of my building. That's not going to happen." Draylen made an attempt to walk away, but Quinn caught her by the arm and pulled her back.

"Are you still in love with her?" Quinn could feel the blood boiling in her veins as she awaited Draylen's reply. When there was no response, Quinn continued. "She's using you."

"What? You don't know a damn thing about what's going on with us. You don't even know her." Draylen paced Quinn like a caged animal ready to pounce on its prey.

"Oh, she's using you alright, and if you took a moment to think, you'd see it for yourself."

"I don't have time for this crap." Once again Draylen tried to leave but Quinn blocked her path.

"She holds you right where she wants you, using that damn souped-up car. What else? Does she give you other things, money or gifts, like that new watch that you've been sporting around?" Draylen looked up in shock, her jaw dropping slightly.

"Yeah, I've noticed the watch." Quinn said.

"So what? I can't control whether or not she decides to buy me things. She's a grown woman," Draylen fumed.

"And so are you. Stop acting like a spoiled child. My God, can't you accept the fact that she is using you? Are you still sleeping with her too?" Quinn's heart sank as she watched Draylen turn away from her.

"I'm not answering that. You have no right to ask me that. It just proves that you don't know a thing about me."

"Okay, since you're not helping me to understand what is really going on between the two of you, then I'm left to my own devices and I have to assume that this, whatever it is, is how you want things to be. She dumps you, treats you like garbage, then turns around and dangles little trinkets for you to jump at, and all at her whim. Where does she go when she's had her fill of you? Does she still have a girlfriend like in the story? If so I feel sorry for her, because she's probably as clueless as I am. You cannot be this stupid, Draylen." Quinn turned Draylen's head to face her. "What hold does she have over you? Does this do it for you, getting scraps from the table, instead of a full meal? Is this enough for you? What about us? I thought we were trying to—" Quinn watched as Draylen crossed her arms over her chest moving her hands up and down to stave off the chill in the night air.

"If this is how you like it, then so be it...Here..." Quinn reached into her satchel and pulled out a large envelope and slamming it into Draylen's chest, and then handed her the beautifully decorated bag. "It's the other bottle of that South African wine. I brought it to celebrate your two short stories being selected for the next publication of 'The Write Off.' I had submitted them weeks ago and they were chosen. Congratulations," Quinn said, void of emotion. She took hold of Draylen's face and kissed her, infusing all the hurt, anger, frustration, disappointment and love into her mouth, hoping that it would spread like wildfires to the deepest points of her soul and lay like a heavy weight in her heart. Maybe then Draylen would have an idea of how she felt at that moment. She ended the kiss and walked away. As she drove off, Quinn for the first time since their relationship began, had lost her appetite for Draylen Corliss.

25

Draylen woke in an evil mood. It had been a week since Quinn stormed off leaving her to ponder what happened. It was never her intentions to hurt Quinn, which is why she tried to keep distance between them in the beginning. Why did she have to kiss her that very first time? She cursed. Why didn't she drop Quinn's class the moment she realized that she was falling for her? There were far too many questions why and not nearly enough answers.

It wasn't all her fault. Some of the guilt lay at Quinn's feet. She pursued her at every turn, so why was she the one feeling bad? Quinn needed to assume a portion of the blame, Draylen decided. For the past week she attempted to contact Quinn, but all of her calls went unanswered. She would not come to the door when Draylen went to her house, even though her car was parked in the drive way and she was clearly at home.

Already she had dismissed Draylen from her life without so much as a thought. No way was she going to continue to allow Quinn to treat her this way.

Draylen walked through the after hour entrance and signed in on the registry that sat atop the security guard's desk. She flashed him her student ID and was granted access. She opted for the stairs instead of taking the elevator, feeling the need to expel some of the tension that built up on her way to the university. She had some choice words for Quinn and needed to clear her mind of excess dribble. When she got to the English department, it was dark, save for the soft white light that emanated from Quinn's office.

Draylen stood outside of Quinn's office trying to gain her composure. She gave a few raps on the door.

"Come in," Quinn answered. She figured that it was the cleaning staff needing to get in and remove the trash. However when she saw Draylen peek her head around the door, she froze. It had been the hardest week of her life. She vacillated between apologizing and remaining distant. Finally deciding on the latter, she forced herself to ignore Draylen's calls and visits. Draylen was a part of her past now, she reminded herself. That's the way things had to be.

"What are you doing here? You're not even a student. You know, I could have you arrested for trespassing."

"I need to talk to you," Draylen said as she moved further into the room, closing the door behind her. She walked over to Quinn's desk, looking down at the English textbooks sand-wiched between two heavy precious stone bookends. Neat stacks of papers lay in front of Quinn as she continued the task of grading assignments.

"I tried to talk to you a week ago. Don't you remember? You weren't feeling it, I seem to recall." Quinn kept her mind focused on the paper she was grading, writing comments in the margins as she went along.

"That was then. This is now," Draylen said. "And right now I want to talk to talk to you."

Quinn ignored Draylen and continued working, placing the

completed paper in the graded stack and pulling another paper from the ungraded pile.

"Why didn't you answer any of my calls?" Draylen huffed.

Avoiding Draylen, Quinn read the paper looking for grammatical errors before she began to grade for the content of the student's work.

"I called you several times and each call went into voicemail." Draylen crossed her arms over her chest and jutted out her hip.

"I was busy then, like I am now," Quinn stated, never losing focus of her task. She could feel the heat of Draylen's glare, but refused to acknowledge her.

"Fine. If this is how you want to do this, okay. I tried to apologize to you for what happened that night, but since then, I've had time to think, and I feel that you owe me an apology."

Quinn was appalled and suspended her work. In an instant she stood before Draylen, staring vehemently at her. "I owe you and apology, for what? Tell me and please make it good." Quinn placed her hands inside her trouser pockets and gave Draylen her undivided attention.

"I'm not going to even talk about the scene you caused in front of my apartment building for all the neighbors to see..."

"So, don't. Now what do I owe you an apology for?" Quinn asked keeping her on subject.

"For doing everything possible to screw up my world."

"What!" Quinn laughed aloud.

"That's right. You pursued me every chance you got and the more I tried to keep you at bay, the more you turned on the charm. I never encouraged you. So how dare you get upset about Dava, she's been in my life a hell of a lot longer than you."

"You're right about one thing, I did try to pursue you because I saw something special in you. I thought, here's someone with promise who could do extraordinary things if only she could get out of her own way. I wanted to help you and do whatever I could to foster some sense of confidence in you—that's all I wanted." Quinn's voice softened. "However things began to happen, my feelings for you started to change and turn into more than concern. I began to care for you." Quinn's hand came up of its own volition and stroked the smooth surface of Draylen's cheek. "For that I'm sorry, but that's where it ends. My feelings about Dava remain intact, she's taking advantage of you. You said that you've had time to think. Well did you think about that?"

Draylen struggled to hold on to her rage even as she felt herself melting into Quinn's touch. This is not what she had in mind when she decided to pay Quinn this visit, she thought.

Quinn continued seducing Draylen, caressing her cheek, allowing her hand to slowly and methodically trail down the nape of her neck. Draylen closed her eyes to the ecstasy as she reveled in the splendor of Quinn's assault. Aching need set off an awakening of pure delight as Quinn replaced her sense of touch with that of taste, kissing and sucking behind Draylen's ear.

"What does she do for you, Draylen?" Quinn slowly unzipped Draylen's hoodie, removed it and tossed it onto her desk chair. She let her hand graze Draylen's nipples as they protruded the thin fabric of her top. Draylen trembled as she let out a shuddered cry. "Quinn, please, don't—" She shivered as a white heat of passion began to ignite within her.

"Don't what, Draylen?" Quinn whispered. "I'm only asking you a question—what does Dava do for you?" Quinn grabbed hold of the bottom of Draylen's top lifting it up over her head, tossing it too on the chair. She then tongued a path down the swells of Draylen's breast before teasing the engorged peaks through the fabric of her satiny bra, using her teeth. Draylen moaned in dizzying rapture. The sheer aching need knocked her off balance and into Quinn's arms. Quinn held fast to her, keeping her from falling.

Draylen tried to escape the gravitational pull seducing her mind and body into submission, but Quinn would offer no reprieve as she undid the clasps of her bra, letting it fall to the floor.

"Quinn...please," Draylen begged when Quinn's nimble fingers gently tugged at her nipples before taking each one into her mouth.

"Oh...God," Draylen cried as she nearly collapsed. Exercising her quick reflexes, Quinn caught her, then with a sweep of her arm, sent every book, paper and incidental object on her desk crashing to the floor. Carefully she laid Draylen across the smooth surface then resumed her interrogation.

"Does Dava do this for you?" Quinn tantalized Draylen's nipples, taking them into her hot mouth applying the right amount of suction to incite a whirlwind of emotions—causing her to spiral out of control.

"Quinn, please don't make me feel like this," Draylen pleaded unconvincingly. Her cries fell upon deaf ears as Quinn moved forward with her plan to drive her crazy. She thought that it was high time they had a meeting of the minds, feeling that it was long overdue. She let her tongue dance playfully down to Draylen's belly, giving her a preview of what was in store for her.

Draylen writhed in anticipation when Quinn took her time sliding her pants down her shapely legs and onto the rumpled pile on the floor. Her panties soon followed. She placed them in her pocket—a keepsake, she thought.

"Draylen, look at me," she demanded

Draylen could barely hear Quinn, she was too far gone, drowning in the splendor of true ecstasy. Never had she been so arrested. She had no choice but to surrender and hope that she came out on the other side unscathed.

Quinn dipped a finger between her wet fleshy folds. Draylen bucked upward at the delightful invasion, opening her eyes. When Quinn knew that she had her full attention, she began her masterful ministration, worrying her love bud, applying the right amount of pressure and rhythm. Draylen tossed and turned as moment after moment of unyielding pleasure consumed her.

"Do you feel what I'm doing to you?" she asked. Draylen nodded as she writhed in agony.

"Does she make you feel like this? Does she?" Quinn knew that Draylen was reaching the pinnacle of rapture, but she would not let her get there until she made her understand something very important—she belonged to her. Quinn coaxed and manipulated the sensuous bud, setting a pace that drove her to frenzied undulations. She danced wildly to the rhythms Quinn orchestrated. When Draylen had the movements to memory, Quinn changed the score, sending every nerve ending off course.

"Please...I can't take anymore." Draylen begged for the release that only Quinn could give her.

"Does Dava do this for you?" Quinn repeated as she continued her torment, refusing to let up.

"No!" Draylen cried out, using the last vestiges of breath. "I need you. Only you!"

Quinn smiled feeling that she had accomplished what she'd set out to do—get Draylen to realize where her heart truly lay—with her. Quickly she replaced her hand with her mouth. Ravenously, with her skillful tongue, she devoured Draylen's clitoris, giving it her undivided attention. Draylen moaned as her body was catapulted on an atmospheric rise to eternal bliss and the sweetest release.

Draylen lay depleted, trembling from the aftershocks of the most earth-shattering explosion she had ever experienced.

Quinn grabbed her jacket from the hook on the door. She took one more look at Draylen's glistening naked body, savoring the image. "When you're done getting dressed and straightening up the office, make sure you lock up before you go." Quinn exited the office, leaving Draylen to stew in her own juices.

QUINN SAT IN THE TEACHER'S LOUNGE EATING PRETZELS AND mindlessly thumbing, for a second time, through a magazine that held little interest. She had not heard from Draylen in days and it was killing her. She fought the urge to call her out of fear that she would not answer. She figured that she was probably upset with her for seducing her and then leaving so abruptly. Quinn admitted that what she did was not the best way to handle things. She was ashamed of herself. She had no right to use sex as a bargaining chip in order to get her to confess her feelings. It was a cheap move, she thought. The last thing she ever wanted to do was disrespect Draylen. Yet in spite of her actions, she had hoped that Draylen would come to her and that together they could work out their differences. It looked as though her plan to drive a wedge between Dava and Draylen served only to bring them even closer.

Maybe it was time to cut her losses and wish her all the best, she reasoned, though she knew Dava was definitely not what was best for her. Even as she tried to convince herself that giving up was the right move, she found it unfathomable—she loved her, and had come to the conclusion that she always would. "Damn you, Draylen," she swore softly—"Damn you for stealing my joy."

"You're not doing the happy dance this semester?"

Quinn looked up to find Jerry seated across from her at the table. "What are you talking about, Jerry?"

"The end of the semester. It's almost over and you haven't done the dance yet. Remember I was going to join in this time. A bet is a bet, and I lost."

Quinn vaguely remembered the silly bet that they had about the delivery date of the Chancellor's granddaughter. She guessed December third and was right on the nose. As was the agreement, if Jerry lost, then he had to do the end of the semester crazy dance on the steps of the student union with her.

"I'm going to let you out of our bet. I absolve you." Quinn tapped Jerry on his shiny forehead then returned her attentions to the magazine.

"I was actually looking forward to it. You always seem to have so much fun doing it, and I wanted to join in," Jerry said with a tinge of disappointment.

"I'm just not feeling it this semester." Quinn thumbed again through the magazine barely glancing at the pages.

"Okay, let's talk." It was more a demand than a suggestion, as Jerry got up from the chair and took Quinn by the arm, bringing her to her feet.

"What are you doing? Where are we going?" Quinn asked.

"We're going to my office, so that we can get some things out into the open." Jerry led Quinn as they walked arm and arm to his office.

"Have a seat." Jerry sat on the edge of his desk waiting for Quinn to be seated in the chair facing him. "Now, tell me."

"Tell you what, Jerry?"

"You know."

"All I know is that I feel so blah. I'm seriously thinking about taking next semester off. I need to figure some things out." Quinn massaged her temples, sighing deeply.

"Quinn, that's not it, and you know it. Tell me what's

going on."

"Jerry, I don't know what you're talking about. Tell you what?"

"What's going on between you and Ms. Corliss?"

"What? What makes you think that something's—"

"Spare me," Jerry interrupted. "I've known almost since the beginning. If you two were trying to be discreet, then I'd hate to burst your bubble, you weren't." Jerry quirked his brow as he watched Quinn squirm in the chair. "Hell, anyone could have figured it out, all they had to do was look. Some days, at the Writer's meetings the vibes emanating from the two of you were so strong that it was almost palpable. Watching the two of you firing each other up, I nearly got heat stroke—really I did. The secret glances and subtle touches when you thought no one was looking. I tell you, it was quite a show."

Quinn found herself blushing as she listened to Jerry. Sure she was embarrassed but everything he said was the God's honest truth. It was hard to be in the same room with Draylen and not touch her smooth skin. Even the slightest touch was enough to feed her soul, if only for the moment. "I didn't know we were so obvious."

"Well you were. Thank God Mildred Vance is a talker and not a gawker, or else you'd have no business at all, because she would have told it."

Quinn's eyes grew wide. Did anyone else know about them, she wondered. Reading her expression, Jerry said, "Don't worry. No one else knows and if so, they haven't let on. Now are you going to tell me what's been going on with the two of you?"

"What can I say? I made a mistake and fell in love with someone who did not feel the same way about me. I thought she did, but I was wrong. She made no advances toward me in the beginning—that was all me. I couldn't stop myself—even after I saw where I was going with my feelings. She kept putting up road blocks between us, skipping classes, avoiding my calls, and finally quitting school. Still I didn't take the hint, I couldn't. My mind was on one thing and one thing only—Draylen." Quinn slumped down in the chair, the weight of her admission was too heavy for her to shoulder.

"Quinn, just because she kept her distance, that doesn't necessarily translate into her not caring for you," Jerry reasoned.

"Oh, but it does. You see, you haven't heard the clincher. All the time I'm thinking that she was keeping her distance out of concern for me and my job, the reality is that she didn't want me to find out about the woman she's been in love with this whole time. A woman who couldn't care less about her—and yet Draylen loves her." Quinn stood and began pacing the modest-sized office. She could feel her blood boiling with every step. "Do you remember when I read those pages from Draylen's story and how incensed she became? It turns out that the story was a personal telling that detailed her relationship with this woman."

"Ava," Jerry said, recalling the character from the story.

"Huh?" Quinn said, surprised that Jerry remembered the character's name so easily. "Yeah, Ava," Quinn replied. "Oh Jerry, I was such a fool. I feel stupid just telling you about it. How could I let myself be taken down like this? I'm a professional woman, for goodness sake. I should have known better than to get involved with one of my students. I could have gotten in deep trouble for that. Thank God Draylen had the foresight to end things or else I'd still be with her, possibly putting my academic career in jeopardy."

"Oh, please," Jerry scoffed with a wave of his hand. "If this university fired every professor who got involved with one of their students, over half of the faculty would be on the unem-ployment line—myself included."

Quinn looked to Jerry in utter shock, letting her jaw drop.

"You mean to tell me that April was your student?"

"Yes, my wife was once my student. It was my very first year teaching here. Our eyes met, and the rest is history."

"And no one knew about the two of you?"

"Sure they did," Jerry said. "But who was going to point fingers when they were doing the same thing? So we all kind of turned a blind eye and continued to love whomever we loved. That tradition holds true to this day. For example, Dr. Baxter and her TA Dave Connelly, you know the one she only brings out to private engagements. He was one of her students and twenty years younger to boot. They're engaged now, but that's on the hush-hush."

"They're together, and you know all about it?"

"Girl, everyone knows. You're the only one who didn't, and that's because your mind has been elsewhere. Quinn, your mistake wasn't falling in love with your student. Draylen brought passion and excitement to your life. Celebrate that. I know you're hurting now, but don't beat yourself up for having a human emotion. Besides, I don't care what you say, I've seen the two of you together, and trust me, Draylen was not faking her feelings for you. There was definitely something real in the way she gazed into your eyes. Maybe she doesn't know what or how to communicate those feelings to you. Have the two of you talked, I mean putting everything out on the table?"

Quinn's chuckle was void of amusement.

"What's so funny?"

"Nothing. It's just that she is the hardest person to talk to. It's like pulling teeth."

"Jerry laughed boisterously. "Then it sounds like you've met your match."

"Can I tell you something?" Quinn whispered, though no one was within earshot.

"What is it?" Jerry asked.

"Never in my life have I wanted anyone so much. I crave her body, I smell her scent and it hurts that I can't have her." She could feel a tear trailing down her cheek.

"Then go see her," Jerry insisted.

"I can't, because if we see each other, I'm afraid that she won't tell me what I need to hear from her—that she loves me and only me. If she can't say those words to me, then I'll know that it's really over. I could never look at her again. I think it would destroy me. Why did I have to read that damn story? I could have gone on blissfully ignorant."

"Speaking of that story..."

"Yeah, what about it?"

"The night you read it at the meeting and Draylen stormed out with you running after her..." Jerry hedged impishly.

"And?" Quinn asked impatiently.

"Well you left the story behind and so I took it home with me, you know for safe keeping, and to see how it ended..."

"And then what? Come on spit it out, Jerry."

"I loved it so much that I let my April read it. She loved it as well and took it to work and showed it to an editor at Couver Publishing. They're interested in it, I mean really interested, like let's make a deal."

"Really, that's unheard of, isn't it?" Quinn asked.

"It's a fluke, but no less a fantastic opportunity."

"I think that's great. I doubt that she'll want it published though. It's too personal for her. She made that perfectly clear to me."

"I'm sure you can convince her of what a chance this is—"

"Wait a minute. Me convince her? Didn't you hear what I've been saying? I can't talk to her—not about us, not about this book, not anything. I'm sorry Jerry, but if you and April want her to know about this, then you're going to have to be the ones to tell her."

26

"Dray, it's your turn."

"What?"

"The game. You're up," Dava said pointing at the TV screen.

"Oh," Draylen pressed the start button on the controller and with it firmly in her grasp, sliced carelessly through the air inciting the animated player to just miss making contact with the tennis ball. After three failed attempts at hitting the ball, the words 'Game Over' flashed on the screen with her animated opponent laughing at her and calling her a loser.

"That was pitiful, just pitiful," Dava said. "It's like you didn't even try. My niece plays this game better than you and she's only three."

"I'm happy for her," Draylen said, returning to her perch on the floor next to Dava. "But as I said earlier, I didn't want to play. I don't even like video games." Draylen tossed the controller on the coffee table with more force than was intended causing it to skid off the edge and onto the floor.

"Since when don't you like playing video games? You used to —we used to play all the time. Your memory must have lapsed or something."

"I didn't forget, but I was a kid then, and the games were more interesting and fun. I don't enjoy the games out now. I'd prefer the vintage titles to all of this high definition extreme stuff. I'm not a fan."

"We used to play video games when we were a couple just a few years ago," Dava remarked, getting perturbed.

"I only played because you liked to, but I didn't care for it."

"So why didn't you ever say anything?"

"I did, but you have a way of convincing people to do things they don't necessarily want. I just went along to appease you."

"Alright, what's this about?"

"What is what about, Dava?" Draylen asked as she stared mindlessly at the TV.

"You have been in a crappy mood all day and it doesn't have anything to do with video games," Dava said turning off the television with the remote control.

"I'm not in the mood for anything today. That's all."

"Lately, you're not ever in the mood for anything. I make suggestions and you either shoot them down or are so disinterested that it sucks the fun right out of it. I don't understand. You said that you wanted to improve our relationship but you're sure not acting like it."

"I'm sorry Dava. You're right. It's just that I've been under a lot of pressure with work," Draylen said.

"Hey, I sell cars all day long. You don't think I'm under pressure every day? But I still make time for us and it's a little hurtful when you don't want to participate. Do you really want this or are you doing this to appease me again?" Dava got up from the floor, retrieved her jacket from the winged-back chair and slipped into it. "I'm gonna go. I don't want to upset you any further."

"I thought we were going to order take-out and watch the Scorsese movie," Draylen said coming to her feet.

"I just remembered I have an early day tomorrow, so I should really get some rest."

"Dava, please don't leave like this. I apologize for being such a drag and you have every right to be upset with me. I haven't been keeping up with my end of the deal. I need to get my priorities in order." Draylen looked at Dava who didn't seem convinced of her words. "I tell you what, the next outing or activity will be on me. I'll plan everything. You'll see, and all you'll have to do is have fun and enjoy. How does that sound?"

"You're going to plan everything," Dava repeated for clarity.

"Yep. You got it. So is it a deal?"

Dava came with a ready smile as she nodded her head. "Okay, you have got a deal."

"Cool." Draylen smiled. "You're sure you won't stay? I know how you love De Niro."

"Nah, you go on ahead and watch it without me. I brought it over for you anyway. I'll call you later." Dava gave Draylen a warm hug, closing her eyes briefly, losing herself in the moment before releasing her and making a quick exit from the apartment.

Draylen sighed heavily with her back against the door. It was a relief that the evening with Dava wasn't totally soured by her gloomy mood. She had made every effort to cheer up and get on board with Dava's game night but it seemed senseless trying to have fun when her insides were breaking, yearning for Quinn.

When she went to see Quinn that evening and was seduced, her body pulsating from a most exquisite release, she wanted to be angry with her and to curse her for manipulating her sexually and robbing her of all resolve, but she couldn't. It was just Quinn's passion—coarse yet gentle, exacting but simple—for that, she couldn't fault her, only thirst for more of what she had been given. Quinn had left her in a precarious state as it was becoming challenging to keep her distance, even at the height of deep-seated fury.

Quinn was becoming an essential part of her life regardless of any efforts she may have conceived to excise her. To the detriment of her budding reunion with Dava, Draylen had floundered seeking Quinn out at the risk of causing irreparable damage to an already flawed friendship. She had seriously considered explaining her feelings for Quinn to Dava, thus relieving herself of this impossible inner turmoil that devastated her. However she had seen evidence of Dava's intolerance during peculiar times and therefore decided against it.

It was getting harder to keep this information under wraps. At some point the truth would come out if she was not more careful at concealing her emotions, and she definitely could not afford for that to happen. Dava's friendship was vital to her existence, and she would do anything to foster its growth.

Her mind traveled back to their childhood and some of the crazy antics they pulled like the time Dava stole her dad's brand new Cadillac so they could go to a concert in Indiana in style. Neither of them had a driver's license, only a newly issued permit. The concert was great and they probably would have made it home with their parents none the wiser had they not run out of gas one mile outside of Chicago. When the police discovered them and notified Dava's dad, he was livid and grounded her for a month. Of course, she did not fare as well. She was confined to the house for the entire summer, with the exception of going to church.

Draylen laughed aloud when thinking about how Dava had climbed up to her bedroom window and snuck in, bringing with her all of the interesting gossip and other happenings from life on the outside. They would stay up until late, laughing and talking about everything and nothing until an hour or so past

Dava's curfew. Then they'd do it all again the next day. The year of her fifteenth birthday, Dava was Draylen's summer vacation. It was one of the high points in her life. Many years later, in a conversation with her mom, she learned that both her parents had been aware of Dava's nightly visits, but chose not to make a fuss.

QUINN TOSSED AND TURNED UNTIL HER BEDDING LAY IN A JUMBLED pile on the floor. She couldn't sleep. Every time she closed her eyes, Draylen was there making love to her, burning her up with every touch. She looked at the clock on the night stand, it was four minutes after three in the morning. There was no way she was going to make it to her first class. Quickly she put in a message to Jerry, certain that he would get it first thing when he arrived to his office. She went to the bathroom and opened the medicine cabinet and grabbed the bottle of sedatives. She hated taking them, but times such as these called for drastic measures. She popped the lid just as the doorbell rang startling her and sending little pink pills spilling out onto the floor.

Quinn's body trembled. She knew that Draylen was on the other side of the door. Making her way to the living room, she could feel her heart pounding in her chest, as her body ran hot and cold simultaneously. She reached the door, and as a precautionary measure, looked through the peephole—bracing herself as her hand grabbed hold of the handle. Opening the door, she immediately locked eyes with Draylen.

"I couldn't sleep," Draylen said.

Quinn took one look at Draylen's wild wooly coils, puffy eyes, rumpled pajamas and fluffy bunny rabbit slippers then welcomed her into her house and into her awaiting arms. They walked to the bedroom leaving a trail of discarded clothes in their wake.

Quinn was a quivering ball of nerves as Draylen kissed the hollow of her neck. She closed her eyes, losing herself in the glory of her touch. She didn't think she'd ever see her again. After that night in her office when she made love to her, Draylen had not called her or come by. She had just about given up all hope of them ever being together. But now, when Draylen was sucking her earlobe and fondling her supple breast, was there a chance for them, Quinn wondered, or was this their ritual coming together for sexual fulfillment after a heated exchange, where appetites are indulged yet no problems are ever solved. Now she wasn't so sure.

Even as her inner thighs began to liquefy under the onslaught of nourishing kisses, Quinn began to question what it was they were doing. Why hadn't Draylen come to her sooner, she asked herself. Didn't her feelings count for anything? Where was Draylen while she was alone crying and pining for her? Where had she been while I was climbing the walls aching for her, desperate for her beautiful love making, she pondered.

"I missed you so much," Draylen murmured between tonguing Quinn's other earlobe and nibbling her neck and shoulder. Instantly she felt herself being forcefully push backward until she fell clumsily to the bed. "Babe, what are you doing?" Draylen asked, scooting back onto the mattress.

"You missed me, really?" Quinn said sarcastically.

"Yeah, of course I did." Draylen registered the tinge of anger in Quinn's expression, before she mounted her and began kissing her mouth, pressing her lips hard against hers.

When Draylen moaned from the pain, Quinn softened the kiss before breaking their seal. "If you missed me so much, then where the hell have you been?" Quinn didn't give her time to answer before she covered her mouth once again in an urgent kiss that sent them both to a heightened sense of being.

Draylen grappled to change their positions but was quickly pinned to the bed by Quinn's manacle-like hold on her wrists. "My bed, my rules," Quinn said as she stayed Draylen with a piercing gaze. She tantalized the curve between her neck and shoulder before biting down on the soft flesh she found there.

"Quinn, you're hurting me," Draylen cried out.

Quinn released the pressure, marveling at the slight imprint left by her teeth—she then kissed it soothingly, nursing it back to health before gently trailing down to the swells of Draylen's breast. She stared wickedly at Draylen's terror-stricken face before taking a taut nipple into her mouth, sucking it savagely. Draylen screamed in pleasure, the earlier pain already forgotten. "Don't stop, Baby. Please don't stop."

Quinn chose that time to detach abruptly from her breast. She wanted to punish her for all of those lonely nights she spent tossing and turning, burning up the sheets with desire and penned up need for her. "Beg me," She crooned.

"What!" Draylen squirmed helplessly. It was essential that Quinn complete what she started, less she'd implode and cease to exist.

"You want more, then beg me." Quinn teased her other nipple with her teeth, eliciting wonton cries escaping Draylen's lips.

"Please, Baby. Don't leave me like this. Please, I need you." Draylen held her breast to Quinn in offering. Quinn took both breasts to her mouth and sucked voraciously. She wanted to please Draylen, but more importantly she needed to feed her own hungry soul. She didn't know if this was the last time that they'd ever make love, therefore she wanted to gorge herself on Draylen, savoring her, preserving her delectable passion.

"Open for me, she commanded as she kneaded Draylen's glistening breast squeezing her nipples exacting moans of ecstasy. Deliberately she began to move against her slick mound as the two of them cried out in reckless abandon. Without warning Quinn found herself flat on her back as Draylen straddled her, giving her a nefarious grin.

"Set me free," Quinn yelled, shivering with fury and sexual desire. "Let me go, I said!" Quinn thrashed about though it was useless. She realized that she'd found a worthy opponent in Draylen, who was strong and unyielding. She held both of Quinn's wrists firmly to the bed with one hand while spreading her legs with the other. She rode her with all the vigor of a prized stallion. She grabbed Quinn's curvaceous behind squeezing it to her, creating a moist seal uniting their pleasure filled buds in an electrifying heat. Quinn found herself in a battle of wills with herself as her body defied her mind, surrendering against her better judgment. She mustered one last endeavor to overpower Draylen, kicking wildly from side to side which only served to heighten the intensity of their rhythm. Even as she felt she was approaching a most exquisite climax, she found herself pleading, "Draylen, let me go. Set me free, I'm begging you. Don't make me feel this way."

"I can't, Quinn," Draylen said between labored breaths. "Don't you know by now that I can't let you go?" Draylen quickened the movement of her hips and Quinn quickly caught up to her rhythm and together they screamed out in a most power-exploding release.

"Quinn, I'll never let you go."

"Damn you, Draylen...Damn you." Quinn cursed as she clung to Draylen's quivering body.

THE BRIGHT SUN BROKE PAST THE SLITS OF DRAYLEN'S EYES causing a disturbance. Frowning, she woke gradually raising her eyelids until finally she was reluctantly able to greet the morning and Quinn who lay besides her staring intently.

Immediately Quinn was a prisoner of the deepest, richest dark brown eyes she had ever witnessed. She would not give Draylen the satisfaction of blinking. Her only movement came with a slight quirk of her brow.

Draylen gazed in awe at the grace of the woman before her. She was beauty by design, from her expressive bold eyes, her prominent nose, her pouty lips and her round chin that dimpled ever so slightly whenever she was in deep thought or on the verge of uncontrollable laughter. God, what she wouldn't give to see her laugh, or show any emotions other than the blank expression she was giving her.

Quinn had been awake for an hour and in that time she had been to the bathroom, picked up the clothes they had left behind in the living room, put on a pot of coffee and called Jerry to see if he could handle her first class of the day. She had been relieved when he said yes, no questions asked. She had spent the next forty-five minutes watching Draylen as she slumbered, wondering where they stood. Would they be together forever or would this be the last time they shared a bed—a lifetime? She had waited with baited breath. Everything hinged on what happened after Draylen opened her eyes.

Quinn took pause at the idea of something as simple as the raising of one's eyelids determining how she lived out the rest of her life. She needed Draylen to say the magic words, "I love you and only you." It didn't have to be those exact words, but she definitely had to confess her love and desire for exclusivity, otherwise it wouldn't work for her. She needed to hear the words or else her soul would fracture into a million pieces. How could she recover from that, she wondered as Draylen began to come awake. She could have said 'good morning,' but since that remained to be seen, she decided that silent communication was the best course of action. They may have been together for only a short spell, but in that time they had both become adept at reading each other's body language, learning sexual needs and feelings. That information had been coded mystically and embedded deep within their cerebral cortexes, making the use of words a rather crude practice. They were on a much higher plane.

Quinn caressed Draylen with her piercing gaze. In that one look, she expressed her undying love and affection. She promised to always respect and care for her. She communicated her need to be the only woman in her life from which she drew satisfaction, strength, passion. She raised her brow asking Draylen if this was something she could handle. Was she capable of loving her only, accepting the vows that she'd put in place, or was this beyond her abilities. She waited for her answer.

Draylen wanted to give Quinn what she asked. She bit her bottom lip as she searched for the mental words to convey her feelings, but fell short, deciding it best to leave things as they were—unanswered. She tore her eyes from Quinn and turned her back. Quinn rushed from the room, her insides numb, her heart crushed and in disrepair. She ran to the bathroom locking the door. Turning on the shower, she quickly removed her robe and stepped into the two-person stall and collapsed under the powerful spray of water cascading down on her. She let the impatient tears flow though she never made a sound. She lacked the strength it took to cry aloud. She felt her world crumbling before her and all she could do was watch as it happened.

Draylen lay in the bed unable to move. She never meant to hurt Quinn. She loved her. She was her first thought every morning and her last thought at night. The truth was that Quinn scared her. Quinn had the power to ruin her with one word. She also knew that loving her, gave Quinn the ability to hurt her and turn her world around until she lost sight of who she was. She'd gone through that already with Dava and was still trying to pick up the pieces. She didn't know if she could endure that pain again. It's better to leave things as they are, she reasoned, and save ourselves from the impending doom that a serious relationship can bring.

When Quinn emerged from the bathroom, she quickly dressed. Draylen ventured a glance and saw from her puffy red eyes, that she had been crying. She ached desperately to console her but what could she say to her when she was the source of her sorrow. Draylen closed her eyes and swore inwardly, regretting that she'd ever decided to come over this morning. She fought against it and even as she flagged down a cab, still dressed in her pajamas, she knew she should have stayed away.

It was that inner need that insisted she come to Quinn. A need so all-consuming and powerful that it obliterated any justifiable rationale she had for keeping away from her. This need propelled her to react. When Quinn opened the door, all thinking went out the window as she rejoiced, deeply cocooned in her embrace. She knew that until then, she had been existing on the fumes of their last love making—she was barely living. And when Quinn opened to her, she was once again right with the world. Without Quinn, she was living on crumbs, but with her she could feast forever. If it were only that simple.

"When you leave, please lock up behind you," Quinn croaked, as she slipped into her jacket. She kept her back facing Draylen as she spoke. Walking to the door she stopped abruptly. "By the way, Dean Galloway wanted to speak with you. If you have the time in your schedule then maybe you can get in touch with him."

"Okay," Draylen said softly, staring at Quinn's back.

"Draylen?"

"Yes, Quinn?"

"Have a good life." Quinn rushed from the room for a second time that morning, needing to leave before the first tear began to fall.

27

Draylen went over the notes from her editor regarding the changes that she requested to her manuscript.

The list was somewhat sizeable but not impossible. She had not expected that she would have to make changes to the simplest things. The editor was a stickler for details and if she wanted to see her book sitting out on shelves then she had to toe the line.

When she spoke with Dean Galloway and his wife April, they had told her about Couver Publishing's interest in her untitled manuscript. Thrilled as she was, she did have reservations about having it published. It would be different if it were one of her purely fictional stories conjured from her vastly imaginative mind, but it was not. This was a slightly fictionalized telling of her troubled relationship with Dava, warts and all, and she didn't know if she was prepared to relive that time in her life.

Some parts of that period had not completely healed, like her feelings of self-doubt and insecurity. Years of loneliness left a huge void that had changed her—and not for the better. Instead, it made her incapable of trusting.

After Dava was no longer a part of her life, she gave up on

the possibility of finding anyone to care for her and anyone for whom she could care. It made more sense to cut herself off from the world than to experience hurt again, she reasoned. If Dava, the only person who knew her well besides her parents, was capable of causing her so much pain, then her heart was not to be trusted with anyone ever again—lesson learned.

Then as time passed and she began to break free from the loss of Dava, she entertained thoughts of moving on with her life, getting out, re-acquainting herself with the outside world, experiencing new things, meeting new people and seeking new relationships. She managed to do just that though fear was ever present in the recesses of her mind.

As far as the subject of love was concerned, she felt that she lacked the tools necessary to carry off a successful relationship with anyone—Dava 's leaving had shown her that. However being with Quinn had taught her something valuable and dispelled a long-held belief that she was incapable of loving. She did love, deeply and it was the truest feeling she had ever experienced.

Loving Quinn had opened up her world, breathing new life into her existence. Suddenly she wanted to feel things rather than numb herself to life. She wanted to love and to be loved by someone who was willing to accept and care for her without question. She wanted to matter to someone, and thanks to Quinn, she was able to get a sense of what that felt like.

Though neither of them expressed feelings of love to one another, if Quinn could love her just a tenth as much as she loved Quinn, then that would be more than substantial. But as it stood, she was in a one-sided love, she couldn't even call it a rela-tionship because they were no longer together. Through lies and omission, she had managed to ruin the best thing to come into her life.

Even though she and Quinn had not gone the distance, she

was all the better for having known her. The question was, now that she had all of this love for Quinn welling up inside of her, what was she going to do with it? She came out of her deep thought at the sound of knocking. She took her time getting to the door. Whoever it was, they could wait, she grumbled.

"Dava, hi. I wasn't expecting you, was I?" Draylen asked as she followed Dava into the living room.

"Since when have I needed an invitation to come over and see you?"

"No, I'm not saying that. I just couldn't remember if we had plans to do something today."

"Relax. We don't have any plans. I was in the neighborhood and thought that I would pay you a visit." Dava plopped down on the sofa and rested her foot on the edge of the coffee table, which always annoyed Draylen, but she refrained from asking her to move it onto the floor.

"What were you doing in the area?"

"I took the car to get detailed and some other things. You'll see," Dava said with a haughty grin.

"Dava, I don't understand why you spend so much time and money upgrading that car. You work for a dealership. Instead of adding all the extra bells and whistles to a car that's at least ten years old—"

"Twelve years-old. It's twelve years-old," Dava corrected. "And I don't see you complaining when you're asking to borrow it." Dava crossed her arms over her chest and put her other foot on top of the table.

"Look, I'm just saying, why go through all of that when you can just buy a car where all of these features come standard. I'm sure it's got to be a lot cheaper in the long run."

Dava rolled her eyes. "It's not about the money. It's about me doing what I want because I can. I happen to love my car, but I can see how you wouldn't understand something as simple as that."

"What are you trying to say?" Draylen asked putting her hands on her hips.

Dava looked at Draylen who was riled and ready to fight, and decided it best to change the subject. "I didn't mean anything by it, Dray. You know how I get about that car, it's my baby and I want it to have the best. Let's not argue over something so silly. How about you take your hands off your hips and I'll take my feet off your coffee table, because I know how you hate that. We can silence this crazy noise" Dava said.

Draylen's stern expression gradually softened into a slow smile. "You're right, it is silly."

"Very," Dava chuckled.

"Okay then, we're both forgiven."

"I have an excellent idea. Let's go to Nipples and Such, have some drinks and shoot some pool, you know, like we used to do back in the day."

"I'd like to Dava, but I can't. I have a deadline to meet."

"Again with work," Dava said exasperated, "Dray, you work for yourself and you can set your schedule to suit you."

"Oh, and I suppose that you can sell cars only when you feel like it?" Draylen countered.

"You know I can't," Dava replied.

"My job is no different. I am responsible to my clients just as you're responsible to your boss. And by the way, I'm working on my book, not my job."

"Goodness and mercy, not that again," Dava said coming to her feet, "You're blowing me off for a little hobby? You have got to be kidding me."

"Well I'm not. That little hobby, as you so lovingly put it, has been accepted by Couver Publishing and is going to be made into a book," Draylen said, beaming with pride.

When Dava made no utterances to the news, Draylen walked up to her and said, "I believe 'congratulations' is the word you're searching for, but save it. You never believed in my talent as a writer."

"A writer, really? Just because someone finally took an interest in something you wrote? That doesn't necessarily make you a writer. You're delusional. It's nothing more than a hobby, some pointless words on a page."

"It's not pointless to me," Draylen mumbled. She hated when she let Dava put her in this place. Always the shade tree never the sun, unless it was something that mattered to her.

"You went to that school and they filled your head with nonsense. They've got you believing that you're the next Terry McMillan or Barbara Taylor Bradford, and you've decided to run with it. I admit that you tell a good story from time to time and maybe you'll make a success of this one book, but that don't make you a writer. It just makes you lucky."

"It does make me a writer. Why can't you support me on this?"

"Why can't you support us? You go around listening to these other people who don't even know you like I do, thinking that they know what's best for you, when all the time I'm here for you. I've got your back, not them. I'm the one that loves you." Dava caressed Draylen's neck, gazing into her eyes. "Doesn't that mean anything to you?" Dava guided Draylen's face into hers until she was able to exact a kiss from her soft lips.

Draylen recoiled. "What did you do that for?"

"Haven't you been listening? I love you and I thought that you felt the same way, at least you did once—that is before the sexy siren professor started making house calls."

"You don't know what you're talking about."

"Don't I? How stupid do you think I am? At first it was you and me, back together again. Then she shows up and all of a sudden, my calls start going straight to voice mail. I stop by and you're not home but its way past what's considered a respectable hour. Or I'll drive by and see her foreign made car parked in front of your building. Well shame on you for thinking that I'm not intelligent enough to figure out that you've been sleeping with your professor. I'll bet that Beacham University would find that bit of news interesting. Perhaps, I'll enlighten them."

"You wouldn't."

"What makes you say that?" challenged Dava.

"Because I know you. It wouldn't suit you to be so cruel. Besides, I'm not her student anymore, so trying to ruin her career would be a wasted effort."

"The two of you will never make it," Dava said arrogantly.

"How would you know?"

"Because I've met her. I got a real good look at her too. She's a cross between high society, old world charm and sophistication. You're neither of those things and when two people are that far apart on the love spectrum, those opposites just don't attract, no matter how much you want them to. Sorry to be the one to break it to you, but you're just not good enough for her."

"That's funny because she said the same thing about you— that you're not good enough for me. She got your number from the beginning, but since you were my best friend, or so I thought, I defended you to the point of letting her walk out of my life."

"Better that she did it now than to walk out on your later, like I did," Dava spewed.

"I told myself that I would never ask you about that, but since you brought it up, why did you leave me three years ago?" Draylen inquired.

"Wh-what? You already know why I left. I met someone else. I'm not proud of it, but what's done is done," Dava said as she looked to the floor.

"What was her name?" Draylen asked suspiciously.

"Why do you want to know that?" Dava stammered.

"Since you've been back in my life, you haven't so much as mentioned her name. At first I thought that it was out of respect for me, but now...You were with her for three years, yet her name has never passed your lips. It seems a little strange to me. Was there ever another woman, Dava?" Draylen closed in on Dava causing her to flinch under the pressure.

"Of course there was. I-I don't see what this has to do with anything," Dava said shifting from one foot to the other.

"It's one thing to leave me because you found someone better, but it's another if you left because you didn't want to be with me anymore. Which is it? Did I not measure up to your standards any longer? Tell me the truth. You owe me that much for the hell you put me through." Her eyes were focused and her face was hard and unforgiving as she waited for Dava's response.

"Dray, baby you don't understand..." Dava reached a hand out pleadingly, but Draylen stepped away.

"I knew it," Draylen said. "There was no other woman. You just couldn't stand me. I was the problem all along." Draylen could feel the tears forming in her eyes as she watched Dava shrivel up—her earlier bravado now gone.

"We were constantly fighting about something," Dava said, approaching her with caution. "You had made up in your mind that you wanted a better life for yourself. You became obsessed with making it happen—working from sun up 'til sun down. You barely had any time for me. You completely factored me out of the equation."

"Dava, you worked hard, too. You didn't get as far as you did by clocking out at five p.m. every day, so don't try and pin this all on me. You were equally ambitious."

"The point is, we stopped being close and we were starting to resent each other for not being who we needed the other person to be."

"I never resented you," Draylen yelled, leaning against the bookshelf, hands balled at her side.

"Didn't you? You never wanted to become involved romantically with me—that was all my doing. I convinced you that we belonged together and you went along with it only to, as you put it, appease me. You loved me, sure, but were you in love with me?" Dava shook her head as the tears flowed recklessly down her face meeting at the point in her chin before falling ever so lightly to the hardwood floor. "I've been in love with you since grade school." Dava watched as the blood drained from Draylen's face.

"Dava."

"I never said anything to you because I always thought that one day you would realize that you were in love with me too. So, I waited and waited until reality stepped in and showed me that you were incapable of seeing me as anything other than your best friend. That was when I decided to leave you. It wasn't what I wanted to do, but I couldn't stay and risk your one day hating me. How could I recover from something like that?" She asked.

"I loved you Dava. We could have worked things out. But you do what you always do when things don't go your way or if situations become too difficult—you either throw money at the problem or you run. Since you couldn't buy your way out, you ran. But what I don't understand is why you decided to come back."

"Isn't it obvious?" Dava said, bracing Draylen by the shoulders. "I'm still in love with you. I needed to have you back in my life in any way that I could."

"You said it was because you wanted us to be the best of friends again. That was all a lie though, wasn't it?" Draylen asked, as the truth finally fell into place.

"I was desperate to have you back so I said what I thought you wanted to hear, but I was always hoping to win your love and unlike the last time, I'm willing to wait until forever if I have to because that's just how much I love you, Draylen."

Draylen broke free of her hold and collapsed into the winged-back chair, unable to withstand the heaviness that weighed upon her any longer. "I can't believe what you're saying. All this time I thought that you walked away because you had found someone capable of loving you the way you needed, and therefore you no longer wanted me. You really hurt me. When you left nothing was ever the same for me again. I lost the ability to trust. You made me feel like I was unlovable and worthless."

She fingered a lock of hair while mulling everything over in her mind. "Since you've been back, you have done your best to discourage me from writing and furthering my education. You have tried to buy my affections with gifts and the use of your car —but I fault myself for accepting without question what you gave freely. Dava, you have tried to break me. You knew how important it was to me that we reconciled our differences and restored our friendship—our true foundation. I lost someone special to me, while trying to preserve what you and I used to have."

"I used to be special to you," Dava remarked softly, standing over Draylen. Draylen pushed to her feet, side-stepping Dava's intentionally blocking frame. She needed air. She wanted to escape.

"I was naïve to think that we could move into a new understanding and re-establish that thing between us that made our relationship so wonderful. Remember how close we used to be and how we were always there for one another. I miss that, Dava. But it's time for me to grow up. I can't believe that I let you hurt me again. Fool me once, shame on you, but fool me twice..." Draylen sighed letting her words linger in the stale air.

"You're in love with her—the professor. You're in love with her aren't you?" Dava asked, staring deep into Draylen's eyes.

"It doesn't matter what my feelings are at this point." Draylen said staring off into space. Quinn was gone and her world was empty once again—nothing else mattered anymore, she reasoned. How did things get this bad, she wondered.

"I know that I've caused you a lot of pain, but it was because I love you and was afraid of losing you. We were growing apart and I could do nothing to stop it. Hopefully in time you will see things my way and understand why I've acted the way that I have. Maybe you will see your way to loving me again. I wish that I could change the way I feel about you, but I haven't been fortunate in that regard. I've loved you and been in love with you for most of my life, and that simply cannot go away with a snap of my fingers. I'm begging you to try not to hate me. If given the chance, I would undo the last eight years, that way our friendship would still be intact and right as rain."

"I think you'd better go," Draylen said heading to the door.

"I'm sorry, Draylen I really am," Dava said, a fountain of tears bathing her cheeks.

"Dava, I still love you and I always will, but I need to put some distance between us for a while."

"What is it about her, Dray?" Dava asked.

"Dava don't." Draylen admonished.

"Have it your way then. Goodbye Draylen." Dava chanced a kiss on her cheek then walked through the open door as a conflicted Draylen watched her life-long friend walk out of her life for a second time. Closing the door, she slid to the floor hugging her knees to her chest as she sobbed.

28

"Draylen for the last time, no. I will not give you an assignment. It's Thanksgiving. What would people say if they found out that I had one of my best workers toiling away over a manuscript on Turkey day? I can be a taskmaster sometimes, but even I am not that heartless. I cannot believe that you're calling me when you know how stressed I am about preparing my first dinner for Michael's parents. I've got my turkey in the oven, and I'm sweating bullets hoping it turns out alright. I've got to make a good impression."

"Bradley, I'm sure everything will be fine. You're just obsessing. Maybe you should ask your hubby to help you and take some of the pressure off."

"Fat chance of that happening. I asked him to watch the stuffing while I grabbed a few winks of shut eye and I woke up to the smoke alarm going off like crazy, all because he was so engrossed in the football game. He couldn't tear himself away for one minute to check on the food. I had to make more stuffing; lucky for me I had enough leftover ingredients. I've opened all the doors and windows to air the place out before the in-laws get here, which will be any minute now. Why aren't you at your mom's eating one of her famous ninety course meals?"

"I wasn't feeling in the spirit of the season, so I told her that she didn't have to go through the trouble because I was going to stay home and relax. Although, if someone would give me a short assignment to tide me over, then I'd be forever in his debt."

"Well as tempting as that sounds, my answer is still no. And to save you the trouble of asking me on Christmas and New Year's, the answer is no then as well. Draylen, when are you going to learn to stop using work as a distraction for living your life? It doesn't solve anything, it only puts things on hold. Don't put life on hold. And that's the lesson for today." Just then the doorbell rang. "Oh no! They're here and I haven't changed. I look like a hot disaster. The house still smells like smoke...wait, that's my turkey! Draylen, I'm gonna get you for this..." The call ended and Draylen still had nothing to fill the void left by Quinn's absence. She couldn't bring herself to work on her book; it brought back too many memories of Dava and Quinn.

She thought when they made love two nights ago, it was the mark of their getting back together and that all of their differences had been resolved. But how could that be, when she refused to tell Quinn about Dava, or what was in her heart? She caused the problems in their relationship and until she was able to right the wrongs, then she deserved to be out of Quinn's life. She picked up the remote control, hit the power button and began going through all the channels in search of anything that had nothing to do with the holidays. Finally she decided on the home improvement channel. Since property ownership was in her future, she thought that maybe she could pick up some pointers.

During the commercial break she quickly ran to the kitchen and tossed a bag of popcorn in the microwave oven and waited until the last kernel popped before removing it and returning to the sofa to settle in for a day of home renovations and do-it-yourself programming. When the doorbell rang, her heart sank to her feet. She sighed Quinn's name as she made her way to the intercom. "Who is it?" she called out, but there was no answer.

She sulked. It was probably somebody ringing her bell by mistake, she thought—a pitfall of living in a multi-unit apartment dwelling—someone was always ringing the wrong bell.

She walked back into the living room, but before she could curl back up on the sofa, there was a knock at the door. She returned to the door with thoughts of Quinn in her head. "Who is it?"

"Your Mama."

"Mama?" Draylen said, perplexed as she unlocked the door.

"Hi Mama, what are you doing here? You didn't tell me you were coming." She gave her a big hug, kicking the door shut in the process.

"Watch the bags. I carried this food hot from the oven of my house to the car, from the middle of your block and up two flights of stairs and I've managed to not spill anything on me. I would like to keep it that way."

"Oh, let me get those from you. Mama I smell an entire turkey dinner complete with desserts in these bags. You promised me that you wouldn't cook today." She took the bags into the kitchen and began removing the contents, with a big smile on her face.

"You know me. When have I ever not cooked on Thanksgiving? Or any holiday for that matter? I can't help it. Besides, I can't have my baby sitting here eating..." Debra sniffed the air. "Is that popcorn?"

"Yes, I just popped it. I was about to watch the home improvement channel and pick up some pointers. After all, I will be a property owner soon."

"Well you just leave all the hard work to your father. He can do all of that rehab work and you know that he can't wait for you to get them keys in your hand. I wouldn't be surprised if he asked to come along with you on closing day. And please believe me when I say, he'll have all of his tools and anything else he can think of in the back of his truck. He lives for that stuff."

"You love being a property owner too. Don't try and put it all on Daddy." Draylen washed her hands and got plates and flatware, setting the table.

"I loved bossing him around and telling him what fixtures I wanted in each of our properties. Of course I also love the income. That's why we made such a good team, we each had our own jobs to do, and it worked." Debra was silent as her mind went off to happier times. Draylen stepped in to bring her back from revelry.

"I know I said that I didn't want you to make a fuss, but I'm glad you did," she said while piling her plate with food.

"Mm hmm, I know you. One day you're going to realize that, stop fighting and just accept it. I'm your Mama." She grabbed Draylen's hands and said a quick blessing before continuing. "Now what's going on with you and this girlfriend that you claim you don't have?" She added potato salad to her plate.

"Mom?" Draylen whined.

"Draylen Elizabeth."

"Yes Ma'am. Well her name is Quinn Kendall and she's a professor at Beacham."

"A professor, you say?"

"Yes, she was my instructor for my Creative Writing class— that is until we became involved. Which is why I dropped out."

"I see. But did you have to leave school?"

"I couldn't see any other way. I didn't want to cause trouble with her job. I was also trying to work things out with Dava, forge a new friendship. Things just didn't work out right. I didn't know how to juggle the two. So now Dava and I aren't friends and will probably never be again and Quinn wants nothing to do with me, and I can't blame her. I made such a mess of things." She picked at her food with her fork.

"That's a shame. Could you please pass me the macaroni and cheese?"

Draylen scrunched her face as she handed the bowl to her. "All this time you have been begging me to open up and bare my soul to you, then when I do, all you have to say is 'could you please pass me the macaroni and cheese?' I mean, where are your words of wisdom that you always love to give whether I want to hear them or not?"

"You don't want or really need my advice, Dorothy. You've already got the ruby red slippers and everything that you need to make things right."

"Mama, I am not Dorothy and this is not The Wizard of Oz. I can't click my heels and go home because there is no one there, not anymore." She let the fork fall onto the plate and pushed it away.

"Okay, I will say this and then I'm going to leave it alone. Sometimes you can't force things, like your relationship with Dava. They have to evolve organically, but then there are other times when need to put forth every effort to make things work. So it's up to you how you're going to handle your mess and eventually when you've had enough time spent moping and suffering, and when you're ready to open that heart up wide enough to let some love come in, then you'll be fine. Now did you get all that?"

"Yes, Mama."

"Good. Now go put that plate in the microwave for a minute and get back to eating, or else no peach cobbler or sweet potato pie."

Draylen did as instructed. She then came behind her mother and gave her a hug and kiss on the cheek. "I love my Mama."

"And I love my baby."

QUINN WAS BUSY ALL MORNING MAKING SURE EACH DISH WAS prepared to her exacting standards. For many, Thanksgiving dinner was the one time of year where true culinary skills were called upon to impress friends and loved ones, but for Quinn she gave no less than one hundred percent every time she stepped into the kitchen. She loved to create lavish meals and wished that she could do it more often. Coming from a family of men and women who prided themselves on their talents and often competed with each other for bragging rights, she came by it naturally.

At the sound of the timer, she opened the oven door and smiled upon seeing four perfectly baked Cornish hens. She had thought about doing a turkey, but it seemed like such a waste and therefore opted for the hens instead.

The doorbell chimed just as she was placing the roaster on top of the counter. "Coming!" she said as she fashioned a tent out of aluminum foil and placed it over the roasting pan. She made haste getting to the front door.

"Hi, I hope I'm not too early." Sabrina hugged Quinn, kissing her on the cheek.

"No, you're just in time. I only took the Cornish hens out a minute ago." She helped Sabrina remove her coat "Make yourself at home. Would you like a glass of wine?"

"Sure. It smells delicious in here," Sabrina said. "I hope you didn't go to too much trouble."

"Oh not at all. Do you want to follow me to the kitchen? I just have a couple last-minute details to tend to while the meat rests." She led the way from the living, past the elegantly set table in the dining room, and into the kitchen.

"You can uncork and pour the wine, if you don't mind," Quinn said, as she continued slicing tomatoes for the salad.

"Not at all." Sabrina cleaned her hands in the sink before moving over to the large island.

"You can choose whatever you want in the wine cooler right behind you. The glasses are in the cabinet above and the opener is in the middle drawer."

"Okay," Sabrina said, following Quinn's instructions. "Are there other people coming?"

"No. I'm afraid that it's just you and me."

"It looks like there is enough food in here to feed a small army."

"I know. It started out with just a few dishes and before I knew it, it turned into an eight-course meal. So I hope you're partial to take-away bags because I'm sending you off with most of this."

"Well seeing as how I'm rarely home long enough to make anything that doesn't require a microwave, I'd say I'm more than appreciative." Sabrina poured a glass and handed it to Quinn.

"Good."

"So what's on the menu?"

"I wasn't sure what you liked so I have some traditional dishes like baked mac and cheese with a little kick. It's very spicy. Then, of course, the Cornish hens, sweet potatoes, green beans, and black bean soup, which is like a staple in my family. Homemade dinner rolls, heart of palm salad and for dessert, raspberry sorbet and bread pudding made with brioche bread. That's basically it."

"Wow, I'm glad that I wore my stretch denim with the elastic waistband. I'm going to need it."

"I set the table, but if you want, since it's just the two of us, we can eat in here. It's less formal."

"I was going to suggest that. Why waste a fabulous island like this?" Sabrina said as she sat in the stool opposite Quinn. "Did you renovate this house?"

"Yes, about five years ago. Why do ask?" She said as she began serving up the various prepared dishes.

"I know a great deal about Chicago bungalows. It's not customary to have this much space in the kitchen area."

"Yes, that was a problem for me since I love to cook. So there used to be a den over where the table and chairs are. One day I realized that I rarely if ever used that room, it was just wasted space. That's when I decided to make this into my dream kitchen—new open front cabinetry, stainless steel appliances, quartz countertops, and of course, this gigantic island. I then did the living and dining rooms, opening them up and making them a little more contemporary without taking away the character. I needed to add more of my style to it."

"I think it's wonderful. It's not what I expected at all when I walked in." Sabrina said grace before diving in fork first into the macaroni and cheese. At the first bite, her eyes rolled to the back of her head as she moaned out her pleasure. "This is so good. I would ask for the recipe, but I won't even entertain the thought of trying to make this on my own. I would be crushed the moment it didn't turn out right. That's my way of saying that you can make this for me anytime." She continued eating purposefully enjoying everything on her plate.

"Thank you for that compliment. You're the first person that I've cooked for in two or three years."

"You're kidding. You mean to tell me that you never cooked like this for Draylen?"

"Never. We usually ordered in or went out for meals."

"I'm sure if she knew that you could burn like this in the kitchen—and when I say burn, I mean it in a good way—then I'm sure she would've never let you go." Sabrina froze, staring at

Quinn with regret. "I'm sorry. That was an insensitive thing to say. I just meant that—"

"I know what you meant, and its fine. Don't worry about it." Having lost her appetite, she moved food around on her plate.

"Have you heard from her?" Sabrina asked delicately.

"No. A few times I came close to calling her but I just couldn't go through with it. I said goodbye and I meant it. It serves no purpose going backwards. All the same issues would be there waiting for us to pick up where we left off." She sighed before reaching for her glass.

"I know all about reliving the same thing over and over again. I loved Christopher and we had what I think was a beautiful marriage—until it wasn't. He started wanting more of everything, more material things, money, status, attention. Suddenly our marriage was no longer good enough and when I saw that we were drifting, I tried everything that I could do to reign us back in, but it was too late. He was practically out the door. Then one day, I just helped him the rest of the way. I asked him to leave and he didn't put up a fight either."

"He almost ran from the house. I mean he packed in ten minutes flat—give or take a few. It was as if it were planned. So we were separated for about a year and in that time I mourned the loss of our love and then took a look at myself. That's when I decided that I was going to live my truth and I came out shortly after signing the divorce papers. The ink was barely dry. The next thing I knew, Christopher had bad mouthed me to all of our friends, saying that I had relations outside the marriage with women. It became unbearable dealing with everyone's scrutiny. I could not believe some of the things that were said to me by people who had been my closest companions for over twenty years. Finally I made the decision to move back to the Midwest. I dusted myself off, found me a new job, and now I'm living life on my terms."

"Gee, that was an awful tale of woe," Quinn said, looking on sympathetically."

"Wasn't it? I'm just saying that one way or the other, you'll get through this. From everything that you've shared with me about Draylen, I know that you may not want to hear this but, it just feels like this thing between you, is not over. You love her and I bet money that she feels the exact same way."

"Then why didn't she tell me? I gave her every opportunity. Time and again I took her back each time, hoping that things would be different, but they never were." Quinn could not stop her runaway tears. "It hurts, Sabrina. Some days I can't see my way to make it through another day without thinking of her. Yesterday I left school and the next thing I knew, I was parked in my driveway. I don't even remember starting my car, much less driving home. I could have killed myself or someone else. I miss her so much." She put her head in her hands as she wept. Sabrina came from around the island and held her as the weeping changed into gut-wrenching sobs.

"It's okay Quinn. Go ahead and cry it out. You've held this in for far too long."

"But that's the thing, it's only been two days since I last saw her. How can I be this distraught? We've been apart from each other longer than this and I didn't behave this way. What's changed?"

"You honey. You've changed. You're loving her harder which makes the pain all the more intense. Now that you've resigned to yourself that it's truly over, you're missing her terribly." Sabrina gave her cloth napkin to dry Quinn's tears.

"I'm so sorry. I didn't mean to ruin your Thanksgiving with all of my blubbering. I guess I've been trying to act like I'm fine when I'm really a basket case." She sniffed.

"Hey, we all can use a good blubber every once in a while, but we can't always pick the time when the tears flow. As far as ruining my Thanksgiving dinner, my plate is clean and I've got enough elastic in these pants for another helping of everything, with just a little room left for dessert. So you don't mind if I help myself do you?" Sabrina was already refilling her bowl of black bean soup and moved onto the rest of the dishes.

"Eat until your heart is content, or at least until your elastic gives out on them jeans. Honestly, you're so tiny, I don't see where you put it."

"I've been blessed with a fast metabolism."

"I hate you." Quinn made a squinting face.

"Don't you just?" Sabrina snickered as she brought another fork-full of sweet potatoes to her mouth.

"Watching you eat is bringing my appetite back." Quinn speared green beans on her plate.

"Great, dig in before I eat it all."

"Have you been on any new dates lately?" Quinn asked.

"Yes. One of Jerry and April's fixer-ups with someone named Millicent Upshaw."

"Oh no! They set you up with Miss High Society even after I distinctly told them the type of woman you're looking for. That cannot have been a fun evening for you."

"No, it was an absolute bore." Sabrina shook her head. "All evening she name dropped about what new celebrity her law firm represented and blah, blah, blah. I wanted to ram a rusty fork through my eye. I mean, what is with this sorority that April belonged to?"

"I don't know, but it had a high concentration of lesbian snobs—a bit of an oxymoron if you ask me. But to be fair, it was an all-girls school."

"Now they want to set me up with an Angela—"

"Angela Douglas Esquire?"

"Yeah, that's her."

"Do yourself a favor. Just say NO."

29

After what seemed like hours of debating and delaying, Draylen decided that it was now or never as she rang the doorbell. The door opened almost immediately.

"Draylen, come in, come in. It's good of your to come. Merry Christmas! Unfortunately, you just missed Dean Galloway, but it was way past his bedtime," Jerry said.

"I'm so sorry that I missed him. Gee, it seems that his bed time gets earlier and earlier every time you speak of him. Do give him my best season's greetings the moment he awakes." Draylen smiled, giving a wink and a nod.

"I will do that," Jerry said escorting her into the decorative home, complete with a beautifully adorned seven foot tree. Two gingerbread houses sat on display in the foyer, trays of sweets and hors d'oeuvres were at every corner of the room. Christmas music chimed in from recessed speakers throughout the house.

"Just about everyone is here and you know most of them. If you come across some that you have not met before, then chances are those are my close friends and neighbors, all harmless. There is plenty of food and spirits everywhere."

"Oh, this is for the occasion." Draylen handed over two bags. Jerry quickly opened them like a little kid opening Christmas toys.

"Wine. Excellent. I thought that it might be more fruit cake. Would you believe we already have ten of them? What the heck are we supposed to do with ten fruit cakes?"

"I hear they make great door stops."

"No, we're good on door stops." Jerry thought a moment before saying, "I have been meaning to replace the missing cobblestones on the walkway. Maybe I can use them for that. They're the perfect dimensions."

"It could work," Draylen said. "If you leave them out to dry in direct sunlight, they should be ready by spring time."

"Yeah." The two of them were silent as they each pondered the idea before breaking into a fit of laughter. "I'm gonna take these into the kitchen and have April put them in the cooler. Go mingle and have fun. Merry Christmas."

Draylen moved about the spacious rooms darting in and out of various conversations all while looking for her reason for coming in the first place—Quinn. After searching through every social area on the main floor, it became obvious that Quinn had not arrived yet. She patiently waited, holding conversations that normally she would never engage in, but she had to keep her mind from drifting back to the last day she and Quinn were together and how she sent her body and soul into orbit with her intense caressing and intoxicating kisses. She could think of nothing else since and it had driven her to come out to the Christmas party when she would have otherwise stayed home. With each ring of the bell, her head turned towards the door seeking her out to no avail.

Two hours had passed and still she was hopeful that Quinn would come in at any minute, even as her heart sank gradually with each passing moment.

"Hi, Ms. Corliss. Have you been enjoying yourself?"

"Sure Jerry. You really know how to throw a fantastic party. I love the decorations. It must have taken you and April hours to do this."

"Yeah, but we love doing it. We sing Christmas carols, drink apple cider by the fire, and just spend that time together."

"That sounds wonderful." She made an effort to put a bright smile on her face, but it didn't quite make it.

"Ms. Corliss, can I speak with you for a moment, in private?"

"Of course."

"Follow me." Jerry took her to the very back of the house and into a small room just off the sun room. "Welcome to my little writing nook. This is where all good ideas come to die."

Draylen could tell that Jerry was stalling. "What did you need to speak with me about?"

"She's not coming." He said.

"What? Who's not—?"

"Quinn. She's not coming. I'm only saying this because I've noticed you watching the door for most of the evening and I thought that if you were waiting for her, then you needed to know."

"What...Why didn't she come? Was it because of me, is that the reason she's not here?" She leaned against the antique writing desk, letting it catch the weight of her grief. She couldn't put on the fake face any longer nor keep up any pretense with Jerry. Besides she was certain that Quinn had taken him into her confidence, judging by the gentle way in which he spoke to her. But how long had he known, she wondered.

"I think that she just needed some rest. You know, being a professor can be a grueling and demanding task. You're speaking to one who knows."

Draylen heard his words but more importantly she heard what he was trying not to say; it was because of her that Quinn had opted not to come to the party. She couldn't bear to be in the same room with her. But she needed desperately to see her, the constant aching was tearing her to shreds. "Maybe I'll stop by her place, you know, just to check on her."

"She's not there, Draylen."

"Where is she?"

"She went to spend the break in New York with her family. She won't be back until classes resume. I'm sorry. I wanted to tell you when you first got here but I couldn't bring myself to wipe away that pretty smile of yours."

"I see...Uh, do you mind if I slip out the back. I need to make stops at a few other places and spread some Christmas cheer before it gets too late."

"Well okay, honey. Again, I'm sorry about this. I wish that—"

"Hey, don't think about it," Draylen, interrupted. "I'm fine. I'm just gonna head out and let you get back to your party. Goodbye Jerry, and merry Christmas." Instantly she was swept up into a brotherly hug. She allowed herself a brief moment to lean into his comforting warmth before quickly making her exit. As she wiped away hot tears that rapidly cooled in the Chicago winter's frost, she came to one final conclusion. It really was over.

QUINN SAT AT THE KITCHEN TABLE SURROUND BY THE WOMEN FOLK in her family shouting in order to be heard over the blaring music and animated conversations spilling in from the next room. New Years' was always a festive time for the Ayala and Kendall family. Everywhere she looked, people were laughing and enjoying themselves on the last day of the year. She loved this time and spending it with her family made it all the more special.

When she decided to stay her entire break in New York, it wasn't a decision made lightly. She needed to put some distance between her and her thoughts of Draylen. It wouldn't be safe for her heart if she remained in Chicago; not while she was aching terribly to be with her again. So on the last day of class, she had her bags packed and waiting in the trunk of her car, that way she could head straight for the airport. She didn't trust herself with three weeks of free time and not enough activities to fill it with. Draylen was her drug and if left to her own devices she was afraid that she would run right back into her arms.

She was thankful that Sabrina had kept her weekends occupied with visits to art galleries and mindless shopping, things that she would never do with Jerry. But even that was not enough to quell her need for Draylen. She left an indelible print on her soul making it difficult to move on. This time away was proving to be the medicine she required. Getting through Christmas was hell. Wanting to pick up the phone and call Draylen, just to hear her voice, was a constant struggle. Somehow being in the company of family, helped to take her mind off the loneliness.

If she could only get a handle on her feelings. As it stood they were unpredictable. Some days she would be fine, then the next she'd have to excuse herself and leave the room before the water works started.

"Everyone, it's time for the countdown," her uncle Orlando announced. Quickly, everyone filed out of the kitchen and into the large open spaces of the Brooklyn brownstone. Quinn and her mother went around passing out champagne glasses and just as the last person was given a flute, the countdown began on the television and everyone joined in until the clock struck midnight and the ball in Times Square reached its final descent.

"Happy New Year!" Everyone yelled out. Noise makers blared. The sound of paper streamers shooting into the air exploded on impact and rained down on the room of people, as everyone hugged and kissed each other, happy that they made it to another year.

Quinn watched as her parents slow danced together, lost in their own world amidst the joyous merriment and the sounds of firecrackers and fireworks bursting in the sky just outside—and at that moment, she felt more alone than she had ever been. She managed to quietly steal away upstairs to her childhood room which was now reserved for guests. Closing the door behind her, she let the tears have their way, staining her cheeks and summoning a cry from deep within. She was able to suppress it long enough for her to run into the connecting bathroom, locking the door.

She turned on the shower full-force to drown out her wailing. When she could cry no more, she splashed her face with cold water from the sink and admitted to herself that she could not escape Draylen, no matter how much she tried. She yearned to hear her voice. Removing her phone from the pocket of her jeans, she dialed Draylen's number, counting down the moment when she would lose herself in sensuous melody. After the fifth ring, a generic automated voice invited her to leave a message. She intended to hang up before the beep, but was in such a state that she had not been quick enough to end the call, and was left to ponder what her next move should be—either hang up or leave a message.

"Uh, hi Draylen. I just thought that I would wish you a happy new year. You're probably with...I mean, you're probably out celebrating and everything, so I totally get why you didn't answer. Anyway, again happy New Year..." She paused wanting to say more, but decided against it. Startled by the loud knocking on the door, she lost her grip of the phone causing it to fall into the sink of running water. "Shoot!" She cursed. "Who is it?"

"Quinn, it's Papa. Are you alright?"

Quinn unlocked the door, holding the dripping phone in her hand. "I'm fine, Papa."

"Oh sweetie, did I make you drop your phone in the water?"

"No, it's my fault. I shouldn't have had it so close to the water in the first place, no big deal. What did you want?" Quinn sat the wet phone on top of the dresser then took a seat on the side of the bed.

"I came to check on you. I know that you're hurting and you've been trying to hide it from your Mama and me."

"Papa, how do you get over loving someone? I have done everything that I know to do and still I'm no better off—not really."

"Quinnie, sometimes love is...well it's like a paper cut."

"A paper cut?" Quinn raised her brow.

"Yeah, hear me out... You know how sometimes you get a paper cut and it stings? Then you get one that really hurts like hell and you almost want to cry... But you think, what am I gonna do, cry over a paper cut, who does that? So you just suck it up and suffer in silence until the pain eventually subsides, then when it does you look back and wonder how you were able to get through the hurt."

"Yeah, but this hurt is far worse than any paper cut that I've ever had and I do cry—all the time. The pain isn't getting any better. I'm just getting better at covering, that's all. So I'm afraid that I'm going to have to shoot down your analogy."

"You haven't told me much about this person, but I can tell that she means a lot to you. Listen to me, Quinnie, being in love is a struggle sometimes. Just because your mouth declares that your relationship is over, it takes time for your insides to adjust to the loss, and there is nothing you can do to speed up the process. But the point is you will come through this. I'm sorry that I never had the pleasure of meeting your girlfriend, but she must be something special for you to take notice and want to be with her. Once you started that crazy dating thing you were up to, your mother and I had given up hope of you ever finding someone to love."

"Papa, she's everything that I could ever want. But, I wasn't enough for her."

Anton sat down next to his daughter and cradled her head to his shoulder.

"Papa, I want what you and Mama have. I want forever. I've spent the past few years trying to convince myself that I was content being on my own and I guess that maybe, on some level, I thought I was, but all that went out the window the moment I fell for Draylen."

"I wish that I had a magic wand that could take away all of your suffering, but this isn't a fairy tale is it?"

"No, it isn't."

"Quinnie, your Mama and I went through a lot to get to where we are now. I could tell you stories that would blow your mind. Just know that every relationship requires work. When you love someone and decide that what you have with them is worth putting forth the effort, that's what makes it a success. I have a feeling that you're going to find out what I'm talking about real soon."

"Really, what makes you so sure?" Quinn asked.

"Because you want it. Quinnie it's a new year that we're in and I believe that good things are coming for you. But first, you have to do some work."

"Okay, I'm going to try and get through this without rushing the process," she smiled at her father, wiping away a tear on the sleeve of her shirt.

"That's the spirit. Now let's go back to the party. It's a brand new year baby. Say goodbye to the past and look forward to the future." He brought Quinn to her feet and twirled her around until she started laughing like when she was a child.

As they headed back down to the New Year's celebration, she decided that Draylen was in her past now and she was glad that she hadn't answered her call. It was time to move on.

IT WAS THE LAST DAY OF THE YEAR, A TIME FOR PARTY PREPARATIONS and resolution making. But none of that appealed to Draylen. She was invited to a get together at her next door neighbor's place— although she knew that it was more to do with them wanting to party for as long and as loud as they wanted without disturbing her peace and quiet. A few times in the past, she had to ask them to keep their five children's noise to a minimum because it was interfering with her work. Normally, she wouldn't have said anything. She thought, kids will be kids. However it was usually very late in the evening and always when she was working against deadlines.

Let them have their party, she harrumphed. She could care less. She had plans of her own—an entire day of cleaning. She had put off tidying up her apartment for far too long. With the new year coming right around the corner, it made sense to get a jump on her household chores by purging all of the rubbish that had been collecting over the years. Starting in the kitchen, she threw away food that had reached its expiration date weeks before and Tupperware that had seen better days. She spruced the apartment from top to bottom until she was satisfied that every nook and cranny sparkled and smelled spring time fresh.

Next, she did her wash. She could remember her mother saying that it was bad luck to go into a new year with dirty laundry, so she never did. She went about the apartment looking for things that needed washing until she had amassed three good loads for the downstairs laundry room. She was glad that no one else in the building shared her mother's superstitious beliefs because she had all the machines to herself and was therefore finished quickly.

By the time she had completed her chores, every channel on television had begun to televise its New Year's Eve celebrations from all over the country. She decided to kick back with a nice glass of wine and watch until the ball dropped.

She was ready to see this year come to an end. So much had happened that, as far as she was concerned, her life couldn't get any worse than it already had. Losing two people that meant the world to her was the icing on the cake and she was more than ready to put this year behind her. She only hoped that next year she would fare a lot better.

The party next door was well under way, yet surprisingly the loud thumping of the music didn't faze her—in fact, she found it soothing. She put the TV on mute rather than try to compete with the noise coming through the walls shared by her neighbors. She sank deep into the sofa, letting the wine lull her into a comfortable cozy state. Resting her wine glass on the top of her stomach, she fell fast asleep.

DRAYLEN WOKE WITH A RUSH, TIPPING HER GLASS AND SPILLING ITS contents all over her, as the loud banging at her front door and the ringing of her phone simultaneously confused and annoyed her. She must have fallen asleep, she gathered. Carefully she rose, mindful not to let her sopping sweatshirt make contact with the camel colored sofa.

She searched for her phone remembering that she had left it on the kitchen table, then decided to handle the more immediate knocking first. When she opened the door, still rubbing sleep from her eyes, several of her neighbors and their friends tossed confetti at her and stuck a glass in her hand—instantly someone else was filling it with champagne.

Before she could thank them and make her excuses, she was whirled into a stranger's arms and caught up in a meringue on the landing of the second floor as others clapped and cheered. It didn't even matter to them that she had not dressed for the occasion or that her white sweatshirt was covered in red wine. Everyone was feeling good. Last year was behind them and they were already looking to their futures. She decided right then to follow suit.

As she danced, laughed and talked into the wee hours of the morning, she could feel the effects of the alcohol on her practically empty stomach. After saying her goodbyes, she headed back to her little hovel. Taking a quick shower, she felt refreshed and slipped into a clean nighty, then headed to the kitchen for a nosh—the last thing she needed was to wake in the middle of the night with a hangover. As it was, she had taken celebrating to a new height, and was not standing on steady legs, she thought—this after bumping into stationary fixtures in her apartment, including the wall, the door, the baker's rack.

Leaving the kitchen, she remembered to grab her phone. She tapped her touchscreen to check the time and saw a missed call message. It was not a number that she easily recognized, at least not in her present state, she thought. Nevertheless, she let the message play and sobered the moment Quinn's voice reached her ear. All ready unsteady, she sank to the floor of her bedroom as she closed her eyes and allowed Quinn's message to wash over her for a second time.

"She cares," Draylen said as she touched the call tab and waited while the phone rang. When she was transferred to voice mail, she hung up and dialed again and again continuously until just before the sun came up, but there was no answer—and maybe that was the answer, she thought. Maybe Quinn had second thoughts about having called her and that was her reason for not picking up the phone. She didn't bother to leave a message. Instead she slipped under the covers and willed her mind to forget the last twenty four hours.

30

D raylen sat at her desk re-editing her manuscript for what seemed like the thousandth time since she had gotten the official contract agreement from Couver Publishing. Her life had changed drastically. She was forced to admit to herself just how little she really knew about the industry; she was finding it more complicated than she'd imagined. The past few months had been nothing more than a series of meetings, rewrites and endless edits and still the book was in its infancy stages of being published.

Several times during the process, she wanted to chuck the whole idea of becoming a writer and instead continue her safe obscure job proofreading—it was easier, she was good at it, and it paid well. But was it rewarding? This was a question in Draylen's mind that required little thought.

There was nothing like putting words together in various combinations, shaping and forming them into stories that touched other people, making them think and feel. She enjoyed being able to do that. It fed her soul and there was only one other thing that compared to this—loving Quinn. Draylen jumped at the sound of the phone ringing, it was the landline, reserved for emergencies and her parents. She picked up on the first ring.

"Hello?"

"Hey, Bunny Chops."

"Hi, Daddy. How are you doing?"

"I'm good. Just checking up on my daughter."

"Oh, that's nice." Draylen knew her dad had something he wanted to get off his chest. She had just seen him. It was not his way to contact her twice in one week, that was more her mother's speed. She'd be lucky if she spoke to him twice a month by phone or in person. Since he discovered social media, he preferred to keep up with her that way. She was convinced that he had something. She decided to wait him out until he was ready to share.

"So, how's Margie doing?" Draylen asked as she cleaned under her fingernails using a pen top.

"You know, I will never understand women," Edward Corliss said.

And there it was, Draylen thought. Her dad had women problems. "What's going on, Daddy?"

"You know your mother is seeing Reggie Winston?"

"You mean Mr. Winston that used to live at the end of the block?"

"That's him."

"He's nice. I can see the two of them together. So, what's the big deal?"

"The big deal is that she doesn't need to be mixing with him. She's going from bad to worse. She's just doing this to get a rise out of me—bringing him to Bible class and showing him off to everyone."

Draylen rolled her eyes and shook her head in exasperation. When her parents decided to divorce, she was not happy about it, but respected their wishes and even managed to come to terms with it, in time. However, it seemed that, these days, the only ones not adjusting to their divorce were her mom and dad.

"Daddy, Mr. Winston is a fine upstanding man in the community. He's a lawyer and he's active in his church. I don't know what more you expect of him. He treats Mom with respect and they enjoy each other's company."

"How long have you known about the two of them seeing each other?" he asked.

"Mom told me a couple weeks ago."

"But did you know that he's had two wives already?"

"Yes, Dad. Mom told me. He married when he was seventeen after he'd gotten his girlfriend pregnant. They stayed married for ten years before divorcing. Then he married again to his second wife and they'd probably still be married if she hadn't passed away. So what is your point, Dad? You're with Margie. Why can't Mom date Mr. Winston? Neither of you have ties to one another anymore. I say date who you want. I'm just getting tired of the two of you laying your love burdens at my feet. I've got my own issues and I'm trying to write a book."

Draylen heard her dad's heavy sigh before he said, "I'm sorry, Bunny. I saw them together and I just saw red. The idea that she could possibly end up in love with him! Those other men she dated, I knew they didn't have a chance, but Reggie...he might. When someone you still love...I mean, used to love..." Edward's voice grew silent, his thoughts left incomplete.

"Daddy, if you're still in love with Mama, then you should let her know. Then be honest with Margie. She loves you. Don't string her along, she doesn't deserve that. Let her go so she can move on with her life."

"You're right, Bunny. I've got a lot of thinking to do. Sorry to bother you with this."

"It's okay." It wasn't okay, but she could tell her dad was in the midst of a battle with his heart—something that she could strongly relate to. It can be difficult when you have no one to help you sort things out. She envied her dad. At least he had her to come to. She had her mom's ear, but even she was dealing with her own love life. The last thing she wanted was to be a burden to either of her parents.

"Draylen?"

"Yes, Daddy?"

"Do you want to talk about your...issues?"

Draylen chuckled. He had read her mind. "No, I'm good."

"Are you sure? You can tell me anything."

"No I can't, Dad, but thanks for being a willing ear. I love you."

"I love you too. Take care."

"Alright, bye." Draylen hung up the phone. She wished that her parents could get their lives straight, but whatever their choices, she'd love and support them, no matter what. She looked at the clock on the computer. Once again, she let the day get away from her. She had worked far longer than she'd intended, which annoyed her. Since she ended her relationship with Quinn, she had decided to make some changes in her life, one of which was devising a work schedule and adhering to it. In the past she had been accused of working too hard and too long. What did it mean to have a fat bank account and no life? There is a whole world outside of these four walls that I know nothing about and I need to get out and be a part of it, she thought. But how, she wondered—she hadn't a clue where to go or what to do.

Draylen's eyes fell upon the stack of unopened mail sitting atop her desk. She began to sort each piece, discarding the junk into the nearby trash can. The last letter was from Beacham University addressed to Ms. Corliss Extraordinaire. Draylen snickered. There was only one person crazy enough to send out a letter like this—Dean Jerry Galloway.

When she opened the envelope to remove the letter, a card along with what looked to be confetti fashioned out of colorful hole-punch chips, fell to the floor. She picked up the card and saw that it was an invitation to the end of the academic year's Writer's Club celebration, with the days date stamped at the bottom.

Draylen unfolded the handwritten letter, which read, 'Dear Ms. Corliss, while I do recognize your efforts in getting your first novel published, we would love it if you could spare a few hours and celebrate with us. I hope you like Karaoke—Jerry, P.S. don't tell Dean Galloway. He's a stick in the mud.'

She stared at the letter and was suddenly struck by a moment of clarity. "Maybe it's time I took my own advice," she said to herself as she made her way to the bedroom.

EDGAR ALLEN POURS SPORTS BAR AND GRILL, A LOCAL establishment near the university, was abuzz with laughter, celebration and song. It was packed to capacity. Two hours in, the celebration was still running at full steam. At the end of the last karaoke rendition of "I Will Always Love You," Jerry called everyone to the front of the stage.

"Now comes the part that we all enjoy—our awards ceremony, otherwise known as the Scribblers."

Everyone applauded, cheering loudly.

"Before we get underway, I must first bring up my beautiful and trusty presenter for the evening. Would you please give a round of applause to Quinn Kendall, also known around the university as Dr. Quinn, Tardy Assassin?"

Quinn came up on stage bowing to the audience and blowing kisses. "Our first Scribbler goes to the most improved writer, Dana Shores, for her piece, "Writing Under the Influence…"

All totaled, Jerry and Quinn had presented nine awards to various members of the Writers' Club leading up to the last award of the evening.

"And now for the final category. This person wins hands down as the most talented all round writer of 2015. Voted unanimously by everyone in the Writers' Club. This prestigious Scribbler Award, which also comes with a gift certificate for two at the posh Vincent Supper Club, this gold-plated plaque," Jerry showed everyone the plaque, receiving oo's and ahh's from the crowd. "And this fine handcrafted pen goes to none other than Ms. Draylen Corliss."

Applause rang out. It died down when no one stepped forward.

"Well, it looks as though she was unable to make—" The clapping resumed, interrupting Jerry's talk and gaining momentum as Draylen weaved through the crowd to make her way to the stage.

"I was going to accept this award on her behalf but I don't have to, she's here, everyone." The crowd continued to applaud.

Draylen waved to the audience. Jerry gave her a big hug, wishing her congratulations.

As she went to accept her award and winnings from Quinn, their eyes locked immediately, blurring everything and everyone around them. For that brief moment in time, they were the only ones in the room.

Quinn's heart pounded as Draylen moved in and faced her. Aware of the crowd, she forced a plastic smile on her lips, though it never reached her eyes. She raised her arms robotically as she handed Draylen her award and gifts. Draylen took the proffered items, letting her finger skim the surface of Quinn's hand. She wanted desperately to plant one soul-stirring kiss firmly to her petal soft lips. Awkwardly she motioned to shake Quinn's hand, but her body had something altogether different in mind as she wrapped her arms around Quinn's pliant frame and squeezed. That simple gesture awoke a need in her so strong that she grew dizzy and had to cling even tighter to Quinn to keep from falling. Fleetingly, she closed her eyes as the feelings assaulted her, reminding her of everything she'd been missing since Quinn walked out of her life and she wanted them back. Dammit, she needed her back.

"You feel so good," she whispered into Quinn's ear before pulling away from their embrace.

Soon a rallied cry from the audience called for a speech.

Jerry handed the microphone to Draylen.

"Hello everyone. I'm going to make this quick. Thank you all for voting for me. Being in the Writers' Club has truly changed my life. As you know, I am soon to be published—hopefully by the end of the year and coming to a bookstore near you. I need to thank Dean Galloway, I mean, Jerry, for passing my manuscript off to his wife April and getting my career the kick start that it needed. Thank you April, for working diligently with me and showing me the ropes. Finally I have to thank my former instructor, Dr. Kendall for believing in my work and in me, even when I didn't believe in myself."

Draylen's glassy gaze amidst the applause sent shivers down Quinn's spine. Draylen's speech ended thus bringing the ceremony to a close, much to Quinn's relief.

The music resumed and once again the floor opened for more dancing. Draylen stood off to the side watching as faculty members and friends alike all got down on the dance floor. She laughed when the crowd surrounded Jerry as he did a silly dance with his wife. She glanced to her left just in time to see Quinn sharing in the merriment. Their eyes collided and Draylen gave a friendly nod, but was disappointed when Quinn turned her back to her and walked away. She was set to follow her but was halted by a tap on her shoulder.

"I haven't seen you out on the floor, Draylen," Dr. Gall said. He was smartly dressed in his signature brown slacks, white short-sleeved button down and red bow tie. He swayed to the up-tempo beat. "Don't tell me that you have two left feet."

"Well actually, I do," she lied.

"Great, then you'll be the perfect partner for me. You see, I have the same problem. Come on, let's see how many of these people we can clear off the dance floor."

Draylen didn't have a chance to refuse. Dr. Gall had her on the dance floor before she even realized it. For the next hour she was swept up from one partner to the next until finally she decided to hang up her dancing shoes for the evening. Besides she had something more pressing on her mind—finding Quinn. She let her eyes travel the expanse of the room until she spotted her sitting alone at the bar.

"Hi," Draylen said with more enthusiasm than was intended.

"Hello," Quinn stared down into her shot glass, avoiding any visual contact with Draylen. Her closeness was making Quinn feel things that she did not want to feel. She took a drink from her glass just as the bartender approached them.

"Hi. What can I get you, this evening?"

Draylen was caught off guard by the question. She had not prepared a drink order. Instead she looked at the shot glass in Quinn's hand before making her decision. "I'll have what she's having."

Quinn asked the bartender to place the drink on her tab.

"Thanks," Draylen said smiling timidly.

"Think nothing of it."

"You guys really know how to throw a party. I didn't think it would be this large a turnout. Is it always like this?" Draylen asked as the bartender returned with her drink before moving on to the horde of other thirsty people at the bar.

"Yes," Quinn said. "It tends to grow each year. Many of the faculty and members bring their spouses and friends. Some people just come because they want to get out and unwind after a hectic semester."

"I see," Draylen didn't care for small talk, most of the time she preferred silence, but she knew that mindless conversation might be the only way through Quinn's outer shell at this time. Draylen was desperate. She thought back on all the lonely nights when she ached to hear Quinn's voice, if just for one last time, and now here she was with her. They may not be solving any problems, but at least they were talking.

"I thought you were going to dance with everyone in the place. Every time I turned around, you were dancing with someone new." Quinn lamented, doing little to hide her jealousy.

Draylen couldn't help herself, she blushed at the thought of Quinn watching her—that meant she was interested. Could there still be hope, she wondered.

"What can I say? Once I got started, I turned into a dancing machine. But now I'm exhausted. This drink definitely comes in handy." Draylen took a hearty gulp from the shot glass and was quickly sent into a coughing frenzy as the amber liquid burned in her throat.

Quinn panicked upon seeing Draylen gasping for air and her body convulsing. She immediately came to her aid by patting vigorously on her back.

"Draylen, are you alright?" Quinn asked, concerned.

Draylen nodded, giving one final. "I'm good," she strained out. "Was that Whiskey? Good God! Is that what you're drinking?"

Quinn unable to contain her relief and her humor, cackled.

Soon Draylen became infected and shared in the hilarious moment. "Now you know the one drink that I can't seem to stomach," Draylen said as she took the glass of water from the attentive bartender.

"Stomach? You couldn't even swallow it." As the laughter died down, Quinn resumed her icy demeanor.

Draylen felt defeated seeing the joy seep from Quinn's face, knowing that she was the cause of it. She searched her mind for another way back into Quinn's good graces, but came up short, so she returned to small talk, trying again to chip away at her granite-like exterior.

"You look—" The quick cut of Quinn's eye told her to steer clear of giving out compliments of any kind. "Uh, I'm having a great time tonight. I'm glad that I came," Draylen said.

"Then that makes one of us." Quinn rose from the stool, downed the remaining liquid from her glass, threw some bills on the counter and hurried out the exit.

Draylen handed the money to the bartender and set off after Quinn. She caught up to her just before she crossed the street.

31

"Quinn! Wait, please." Draylen held her back with the slightest touch to her elbow.

"What, Draylen?" She bristled, trying to diminish her uncontrollable quaking.

Draylen's stood with her mouth open and completely tongue-tied. Now that she had Quinn's attention, she couldn't seem to find the right words to convey what was in her heart.

"What, don't you have anything to say?" Quinn asked mockingly. "Do you need pen and paper? I find you to be a much better communicator when you write things down. It's the one on one exchanges that you seem to have trouble with—at least where I'm concerned." She knew that last dig cut to the quick. A tinge of guilt welled up inside her. "Dammit, Draylen, why did you come here tonight?"

"I came because I was sent an invitation in the mail, same as you. I wanted to get out and have a good time just like you. I know you may find this hard to believe, but not everyone hates me."

"You could have stayed away. It would have been the right thing to do."

"I had just as much right to be here as you. I'm tired of planning out how best to avoid Quinn, day in and day out. I haven't been to the bookstore in months." Draylen cursed in frustration. "This is ridiculous. The truth is, I came out because I needed a break. I've been cooped up in my one-bedroom apartment, racking my mind with grief over you, over this damn book. I decided that I've punished myself enough—time served. I also came because I wanted to see you. It may have been a reckless decision, but I couldn't help myself." Draylen chanced lifting Quinn's chin so that she could see her eyes. She needed to know if her words were getting through.

Quinn, sensing Draylen's intent pulled away from her. "You've seen me now, you should be satisfied. You've accomplished what you set out to do. If you'll excuse me, I'm no longer in a festive mood. I'm going home." Quinn stepped off the curb and got half way across the street before stopping. She chided herself. Why couldn't she harden her heart towards Draylen, she wondered. She had spent the past few months erecting walls of steel around her heart and purging every memory of her from her mind—and for what—for all her barriers to liquefy with just the slightest touch of Draylen's hand? She felt like she was fighting a battle that couldn't be won.

Quinn retraced her steps until she was standing before Draylen again. "Do you need a ride home?" The words seemed foreign to her even as they came out of her mouth. This was the complete opposite of keeping one's distance. Was she really volunteering to share an enclosed space with Draylen, she asked herself. She had already proven to herself that she was incapable of being in a warehouse-sized sports bar with Draylen without her vulnerability showing. Nevertheless, here she stood tensely waiting for her reply.

Draylen slowly shook her head, smiling sheepishly as she removed a set of keys from her pocket.

"It figures," Quinn fumed with a look of disdain. Draylen was still using Dava's car, she surmised. Quinn checked for traffic before crossing into the street.

"Quinn, wait!" Draylen said running after her. "They're mine...They're my keys, to my own car!"

Quinn stopped just short of reaching the parking lot. "What did you say?"

"I said these are my keys. I thought it was time that I had my own mode of transportation."

Quinn was incredulous. "Really?"

"Really. I got tired of borrowing. The repayment plan was a bitch." Draylen raised her brow and smirked.

"Well good for you." Quinn didn't know what to make of this change but she had to admit that it was a definite step in the right direction.

"Maybe I can give you a ride one day, I wouldn't mind. I'd be more than happy to do it. God knows you've given me enough rides in the past," literally and figuratively, Draylen thought.

"I don't need your damn gratitude." Quinn turned to leave but this time Draylen blocked her path.

"I'm sorry. I didn't mean for it to come out that way. I'm just... grasping at straws here. Look, I'm winging this. I don't know what I'm saying. I am trying to..." She cried out in frustration unable to complete her thought. She paused to regain some semblance of nerve before she started again. "Quinn, can't we go somewhere and talk? It doesn't have to be your place or mine, just somewhere neutral where we can sit down and have a polite conversation, please?"

Quinn, snorted softly, shaking her head. It was criminal the way Draylen could always persuade her to do the polar opposite of what she wanted. "Fine, follow me," she muttered as they headed for the parking lot.

"THIS IS A GOOD CARAMEL MACCHIATO," DRAYLEN SAID JUST before taking another sip, "I wouldn't have expected it in a dive like this." She glanced around the drab practically empty diner that, from the look of things, had seen better days.

"The food is good too and for a fraction of what we'd pay in the city. Bedford Park is a really thriving community," Quinn added.

"It's amazing the difference ten blocks can make," Draylen said."

"Yeah. Are you sure your stomach can handle that sugary drink so soon after choking down that shot of whiskey?"

"I think I should be alright. I didn't finish all of it. I didn't know you drank Whiskey."

"There's a lot you don't know about me." Like how much I love you, Quinn thought.

"I would like to know more about you. We had gotten off to a good start on the night of my birthday," Draylen captured Quinn's attention, holding her hostage with her gaze.

Quinn freed herself and took a drink from her coffee mug. She was thankful that the flavorful beverage was as strong as it was rich. She needed all of her faculties alert and working at capacity when dealing with Draylen, lest she find herself on her back, being made love to, repeating a painful history with her. She'd rather vacation in hell than go through that again.

"You mentioned the book earlier. How is it coming along?"

Draylen noted the clever way Quinn changed the subject. Draylen had to give it to her, she was cunning. The switch was almost seamless. A less experienced person wouldn't have noticed the way Quinn spun them like a top. Luckily for Draylen, she too was a master in the art of avoidance. In fact, she could teach her own class on it.

The low buzz from the industrial fan added to the dull ambiance of the space. Quinn's attention was taken up with watching the plump middle-aged waitress replenish the dessert display with plated wedges of cakes and pies. At the sound of Draylen's voice, she withdrew and put her focus on Draylen's mouth and then her eyes.

"The book is good some days and frustrating others. I've edited so much that I've begun second guessing myself. I just want to do a good job. If it's going to sit on shelves in bookstores with my name on the cover, then I want to make sure that I've created something that I can be proud of. I know I sound extreme, but I can't help it when I become passionate about something." Or someone, she thought to herself.

Quinn placed a hand on top of Draylen's, giving a reassuring squeeze. "Babe, at some point you've got to trust that you've done your best and then let it go. That's all you can do."

Draylen couldn't ignore the electricity that surged through her when Quinn's soft hand made contact with her skin, yet she decided it best not to bring attention to the intimation. She wasn't sure if Quinn was aware of her actions. "I know you're right. I'm going to send it off tomorrow then hopefully we can move forward in the process. I want to thank you for your constant support. If it weren't for you, I'd still be trying to convince myself that being a writer was nothing more than a pipe dream."

Quinn removed her hand, stood up and slipped into her jacket. "You know me. I'm nothing if not supportive." She reached into her inside pocket for her wallet.

Draylen stopped her with a wave of the hand. "I've got this," she said placing bills on the table. She could tell by Quinn's detached aura, that she had stuck her foot in it for the umpteenth time this evening.

"Draylen, I need to get home. I've had my fill of polite

conversation for one evening. We should leave things as they are."

"But we've barely said a handful of words to each other." Draylen was crestfallen.

"Look, you asked to go somewhere to have polite conversation, and we've done that."

"But Quinn, we haven't solved anything," Draylen said, rising from the chair.

"The problems we have can't be solved in polite conversation, over a relaxing cup of coffee. We are way beyond that. Get home safe." Quinn rushed out of the diner, as Draylen fell back into the seat trying to make sense of what had just taken place.

WHEN QUINN ENTERED THE HOUSE, SHE HEADED STRAIGHT FOR the shower. The heaviness of the day had gotten the better of her. She decided to make peace with it the best way she knew how. Adjusting the dual massaging shower heads, she relaxed under the full force of tepid water pelting the tension from her body. She sighed as the weight of the day went down the drain, leaving her refreshed if not renewed.

Seeing Draylen tonight was the last thing she had expected. Even though she knew in advance about Draylen's award, she didn't think she'd have the nerve to show up. Saying goodbye to her after their last love making encounter months ago was the hardest thing she had ever done. But, what choice did she have? Draylen never loved her, instead she preferred to stay in a decayed relationship with someone that didn't love and respect her—not the way or to the extent she that Quinn did. There was no one on the planet that could love her the way she did.

Had she gotten the slightest indication from her that Draylen wanted them to have a life together, Quinn never would have ended things; she would have fought for Draylen's love. But things didn't happen that way, and she was alone now. Memories of their time together played mockingly like a loop inside her mind. Quinn pounded the white subway-tiled shower stall with her fists. Her frustration with Draylen had reached its saturation point. Too many tears shed during quiet times. Too many unfulfilled nights. How she had managed to get through this last semester was a testament to her strength. She looked forward to tonight's bash. She needed a spirited release. She wanted to relax and celebrate going through months of hell and coming out on the other side still breathing, albeit a bit worse for the wear.

A party was the perfect way to exorcise the demons of her past and move on into her future. She deserved a party, she thought. Everything was going great. She talked happily with other club members, something that she had not done in a while. She danced a little and even laughed. How she missed laughing, remembering how it was, feeling such a life-giving freedom.

Since things had ended with Draylen, she closed up her emotions and hid herself. She had even stopped going to the weekly club meetings—when asked why, she'd simply say that she had too much work to do or some other lame excuse. The truth was that she no longer saw the point of attending. It only brought back thoughts of Draylen's absence from the club and her life. Nothing that she used to enjoy made sense anymore, so she just stopped doing them and focused on work, the only thing constant in her life.

She began writing more, not necessarily for the thrill of it, but rather for the self –discovery and mental growth. It was her way of filling up the emptiness within. And just when she felt that she was on her way to a newfound peace of mind, in walks

Draylen Corliss looking every bit as beautiful as she did the last time they made soul-shattering love.

As Draylen had approached the stage, it was all she could do to keep from crying out her undying love for her. Draylen's overpowering presence had consumed the room, leaving her no place to escape and she found herself faced with a dilemma—she could stay and try to fight against her resurging feelings or she could run for her life, accepting that she'd never be free of Draylen.

She had decided to stay. She didn't want to give Draylen the satisfaction of ruining her good mood at the party. Besides, hadn't she proved that she was a strong woman with the ability to rise from the ashes of lost love?

Even as Draylen had stood before her caressing her with her eyes, she was absolute in her decision to remain at the celebration. Then Draylen had done the unthinkable, she hugged her. She knew that it hadn't been a planned act, yet the brief contact held in it supernatural powers capable of unlocking feelings and secrets Quinn had since hidden away for safe keeping. But now they had resurfaced and her resolve was wavering.

It had never been her intention to leave the celebration with Draylen. If anything she was trying desperately to get as far away from her as possible, if for no other reason than to preserve what remained of her sanity. Draylen was driving her crazy making her think and feel things, and she was helpless to do anything about it.

As they had sat across from each other drinking coffee in the all night diner, it seemed liked the most natural thing in the world to do. Had she allowed it, she could have easily suspended reality and all of her hurt just to exist for a moment in time with her. She had forgotten herself briefly when she'd reached out to comfort Draylen over the grief she was experiencing in writing her book. She didn't think, merely reacted to her suffering and knew instantly that she was in trouble. Frissons of heat settled deep inside and seized her heart.

She had been compelled to dash her feelings of despair and invite Draylen back to her place and beg her to make slow sweet love to her. She had felt herself teetering on the verge of a brand new hell, ready to jump in feet first, and she would have were it not for Draylen and her damn gratitude. How many times tonight had Draylen expressed to her eternal appreciation for one thing or another? No thanks, she thought. She could give a damn about that. What she wanted...needed, no, demanded from her was something more substantial—her love. Why was it so difficult for her to give it, she wondered.

Quinn emerged from the shower and slipped into her robe, securing it about her waist. On the way from the bathroom, Quinn stopped in her tracks remembering that she had not locked the door when she came into the house. Her mind had been preoccupied with thoughts of Draylen. Come to think of it, she hadn't checked the mailbox either.

She made her way to the living room. Maybe it was a good thing that Draylen was out of her life, Quinn thought because she tended to toss all logic aside whenever Draylen was around. Quinn opened the door and as she stepped out to her mailbox, she came face to face with the object of her desires and the torment of her heart.

32

"What the hell are you doing?" Quinn raged upon seeing Draylen's hand inside her mailbox.

"You once told me that I communicated better when I wrote things down. I thought I'd try it—I wrote you a letter." Draylen removed the letter from the box, holding it out to Quinn.

"I'm not in the mood for your literary prose," Quinn vented, taking the letter and ripping it in two. "I'll wait until the book comes out. Since you're standing there, would you please hand me my mail?" Quinn extended her hand waiting impatiently.

Draylen felt around inside the box for the pieces of mail pulling them out, but held them away from Quinn's grasp. "Quinn, we need to talk."

"My mail, please?" Quinn placed a hand on her hip, while tapping her bare foot on the cold cemented porch.

"Quinn."

"You know, it's a federal offense to withhold someone's mail. I could have you arrested." Quinn glared.

"Say that you'll talk to me."

"I'm not bargaining with you to get something that's rightfully mine."

"Here, take it," Draylen said.

"Thank you," Quinn snatched the mail and walked back inside the house ready to slam the door, but Draylen wedged part of her body in between the jamb preventing it from closing.

"Draylen, I don't have time for this. Move out of the way." Quinn stood by the opening with her arms crossed, secure in the knowledge that Draylen would make no move to cross the threshold without invitation. Regardless of their disagreement, they did respect one another.

"You don't want to hear what I have to say," Draylen began, "I understand that, but I'm sure that there is a lot you want to say to me. Don't you want to get it off your chest? Aren't you tired of carrying this anger around?" Draylen's eyes bored into hers, pleading.

"That ship has sailed," Quinn said bitterly through tight lips. "When I tried to talk to you...Draylen, I can't do this." Quinn walked away from the door and further into the living area, leaving Draylen to stand at the point of entry unsure of whether to remain there or come inside. She decided to take a chance and step in, closing the door behind her. She was relieved when Quinn didn't protest her presence.

"Quinn, despite what you may believe, talking to me, just telling me how you feel, will go a long way to making you feel better."

"I doubt that," Quinn contested, slowly pacing the living room.

"It will. I'll even help you get the ball rolling," Draylen treaded slowly into the room, "Okay, let's see...You want to tell me how much you hate me. How you rue the day I walked into your classroom and how I've caused you nothing but grief from the moment we met. You wish that you had a reset button that would erase me from your life. Your turn."

"No," Quinn turned to meet Draylen's gaze.

"It's okay. I can take it."

"I mean, no. The things you said, those are neither my words nor my feelings. I've never hated you. I could never do that. If you don't know that about me, then it's good that we're apart."

"I'm sorry," Draylen was pleased that Quinn didn't hold any hate in her heart for her, which meant that there was still hope, "You do, however, wish that you never met me."

"Draylen, I don't want to play this game with you anymore." Quinn hugged herself, slowly moving her arms up and down.

"I'm just trying to help you—you know, get some closure."

"Help me?" Quinn screamed. "You're trying to help me get some closure? Oh, how good of you. You don't give a damn about me. This...thing that you're trying to do is not about me—it's about you and your selfishness."

"What do you mean?" Draylen asked with a puzzled expression.

"When I told you in the beginning that my feelings for you had changed and that I was falling for you, instead of being honest with me then about you and Dava, you chose to exploit my feelings, leading me on and making me think that we could have a future together."

"I exploited you? That never happened," Draylen refuted. "I kept my distance and I did it time and again, but it was you that continued to pursue me, which I still don't understand, considering that being involved with me clearly went against your stupid 'one date rule'." Draylen paced in front of Quinn.

"You once called that rule genius. I told you why I created that rule. But it has nothing to do with us. It never applied."

"Why didn't it apply?" Draylen asked.

"Because I—" Quinn snapped her mouth shut.

"Because what, Quinn?"

"Where's Dava?" she asked changing the subject. "No doubt at home waiting for you in your bed." Quinn spewed her words like venom as she closed the distance between them.

"We're not talking about Dava or Sabrina or anyone else. It's just me and you."

"Sabrina? What has she got to do...Have you been following me?" Quinn asked after hearing Draylen mention Sabrina's name. How else could Draylen have known about her if she wasn't keeping tabs on her.

"No, I haven't been following you. Jerry let the cat out the bag one night when he and April had me over for dinner. It was an obvious slip of the tongue. I'm sure they were so used to discussing you openly. He tried to clean it up. Unfortunately the damage had already been done. But we're not talking about that."

Quinn could believe that Jerry spilled the beans about Sabrina. Holding secrets was simply not Jerry's forte. He'd be the first to admit that he couldn't keep a secret—he always said that his body rejected them, she had to give him credit for being consistent, at least.

"Quinn, you haven't answered me."

"You haven't answered me," Quinn counterpointed, with a raised brow, waiting for Draylen to come clean.

Draylen stared back defiantly, challenging Quinn to answer first. The clock on the wall ticked away the minutes until finally Quinn gave up and decided to speak. "This has been a waste of time. I've been down this road with you before, trying to get the truth out of you. I know how this story ends," she turned away and began walking from the room, "Let yourself out. You remember how."

"Dava is not my girlfriend," Draylen blurted out, stopping Quinn in her tracks.

"What did you say?" Quinn turned retracing her steps.

"I said that Dava is not my girlfriend."

"I don't believe you."

"It's true. We were in a relationship three years ago, but she decided that she didn't want to be with me anymore, she had found someone else—at least that's what she told me. Before she was my girlfriend, she was my very best friend. We've known each other since the first grade. We shared everything. We laughed and cried together—kept each other's secrets. Of course you know most of this from reading the manuscript. You can imagine how devastated I was when I lost her. I do wish that I had a reset button because I would have never allowed myself to become involved romantically with my best friend. In time I realized that it was the friendship that I valued most. But it really didn't matter, because she was gone."

"I'm sorry about that." Quinn felt her outer edges softening against her will.

"I'm sorry too. That break up caused me a lot of pain, which is why I vowed that I wouldn't let myself become that close with anyone again." Draylen was uncertain whether she had said too much to Quinn.

"You may have made a vow to yourself, but the truth is that Dava is back in your life and you moved heaven and earth to be with her and not with me." Quinn couldn't stop her pain from showing, nor the tears from welling up in her eyes.

"I was wrong, but I didn't see any other way."

"Really," Quinn said sarcastically.

"Yes."

"Draylen, I feel like I'm always asking you this question—why are you here?"

"What do you mean?"

"You said that you and Dava broke up, but she's back in your life and you pushed me aside to keep her there. So why are you here at two in the morning talking to me?" Quinn wiped at a defiant tear slowly falling down her cheek.

"Quinn," Draylen asked softly, "Do you still care for me in the slightest?" She moved close to Quinn, leaving just enough room for air to flow between them but nothing more.

"How could you ask me that question? Why would you ask me that?" Her voice cried in a quivering whisper, as the tears began to flow in a steady stream.

"Because..." Draylen's hand reached up and smoothed away the tears—the simple act starting her insides roiling.

"Because, what?"

"Because this..." Draylen ran her fingers through the damp curls at the base of Quinn's neck, bringing her head forward to meet her in a hunger-filled kiss.

Quinn pulled away slowly moaning under its power, even as she accepted Draylen's lips again in a more penetrating union. Each kiss lasting longer than the next. Quinn tore her mouth from Draylen's, resting her head on her shoulders, while she came to grips with her traitorous emotions.

"Draylen, we can't." Quinn said breathlessly.

"We need to, Quinn. I cannot walk out that door knowing that I can never have you. I just can't do it—I love you."

33

"What?" Quinn blinked rapidly, trying to process Draylen's words.

Draylen gently separated them, putting Quinn at arm's length so that she could read her expression as she repeated herself. "I am deeply in love with you. That was one of the things I wrote in my letter that you tore up. I didn't think I was strong enough to tell you to your face—I was afraid of your response. I just wanted you to know."

"Draylen," Quinn whispered. "I..." Hearing Draylen finally confess her love was unexpected and overwhelming, leaving her speechless.

"Quinn, I didn't tell you that to put you on the spot. I don't know what your feelings are for me. I do know that we're attracted to each other. I know that right now I want you so bad that it hurts. But if you like me, just a little, then that's something that I'll cherish. I couldn't stand it if you hated me," Draylen sighed while her heart pounded loudly, as she waited for Quinn's words to eat up the silence in the room.

"I told you that I loved you a long time ago, but you laughed at me. I kept promising that I'd tell you again and make you believe me, but there never seemed to be a right time."

Draylen searched her mind trying to recall Quinn's confession of love until it finally came to her. "Quinn, when you said that you loved me, my head was between your thighs and you were in the midst of an orgasm. I couldn't hold you to that, no matter how much I hoped that it was true. A lot of time has gone by since that evening. Have your feelings for me changed?" Draylen stood on pins and needles while Quinn took her time answering.

Quinn wanted to avoid this question. There was a time when she would have gladly answered Draylen without consult, but now that admission of love could do her more harm than good. She wanted to protect what was left of her heart. However she yearned to tell Draylen her true feelings. She held her tongue for far too long, she couldn't do it anymore, she decided. This time she decided to lead with her heart, accepting whatever pain might come.

"My feelings for you have not changed—if anything, I love you more." Quinn sighed aloud, nervously wringing her hands.

Draylen opened her arms to Quinn. "Can I hold you again?"

Quinn rushed to her embrace and was soon planting kisses all over Draylen's face and neck. She cried out when Draylen stilled her mouth, taking it in one mind altering kiss that left her wondering how she had managed to stay away from her for so long. Draylen's touch was everything. Their tongues intertwined, healing and promising forever while they nourished one another. Draylen skillfully released the belt of Quinn's robe giving her access to her luscious unbound breasts. With a slow hand, she eased the robe open and cupped them.

"Ohhh," Quinn cried out at the exquisite pleasure. There was no way that she could prepare for Draylen's carnal appetite as she trailed her tongue down to her breast laving them entirely.

"Babe, I need to make love to you." Draylen reached for Quinn's hand and was surprised when she pulled away. "Wh-what is it, don't you want to make love with me?"

"I know that you love me and you know that I love you, but I still don't know where I fit in your life."

"I don't understand. I love you. What more is there? I want you in my life, Quinn Kendall. It's that simple." Draylen held her breath. Things were going so well and now she found herself on shaky ground yet again. She didn't mean to rush Quinn, but her head wasn't exactly in control of the situation. Had her brain sought counsel with her body, she would have let Quinn have some more time to consider the direction of their relationship instead of steering her right to the bedroom.

"What about Dava? I may be generous about some things, but not when it comes to this. I'm not willing to share you—not with anyone. So you need to let me know now where I stand with you and what your endgame is."

Draylen walked the expanse of the living room, before sitting on the edge of the sofa, head in hands.

"Dava and I were trying to reconcile our friendship—at least this is what I thought. She spearheaded everything. She decided what we did, where we went, how we spent our time together. I went along with it because getting my friend back meant everything to me at the time. I thought we were on the same page, but I was wrong."

"She's still in love with you." Quinn stated, taking a seat beside her.

"Yeah. She confessed this to me not long ago. She told me that she's always been in love with me long before we ever became involved, only I didn't know it."

"If she loved you then why did she leave you in the first

place?" Quinn's brow furrowed as she waited for Draylen's answer.

"At the time we had been arguing a lot, about any and everything. Looking back now, I can see that part of it was my not being truly happy in the relationship. We started finding fault in one another until one day she said that it wasn't working between us and that she had met someone else. I was so hurt. Three years later and here she was apologizing and saying that she wanted to rebuild our friendship. I jumped at the chance. I was so stupid. I wouldn't entertain thoughts that she was using me and that all this time she was looking to get back together with me romantically. I was foolish. But you took one look at Dava and summed her up in no time at all. How did you know?"

"I saw the way she looked at you when you weren't paying attention. I find myself looking at you the same way," Quinn said, gazing warmly into her eyes.

"Is it the look you're giving me now," Draylen asked with a slight smile.

"Uh-huh. It is." Quinn moved in close wrapping her arm about Draylen and placing a probing kiss to her lips, re-igniting the fire simmering just below the surface. She broke away before things got out of hand again and she lost control.

"Quinn, I realize now that my relationship with Dava is over. I've wasted time that I should have been spending with you. It will never happen again. My endgame is to spend my life with you for as long as you'll have me."

Quinn brought Draylen's mouth to hers as she picked up where she'd left off, with a hungry kiss, bringing their passions to new heights. "I need to make love to you. I can't hold out any longer."

Draylen came to her feet grabbing Quinn's hand and took a step towards the bedroom, before Quinn halted, pulling her back towards the sofa.

"Quinn, you're driving me crazy," Draylen cried.

"I want us to make love here, right now."

"You're sure, you're not going to stop and change your mind again."

Quinn rose and began removing Draylen's clothes tossing them haphazardly around the room until she was standing nude before her. She sucked air through her tightly clenched teeth, exhaling willfully as her inner thighs tingled in anticipation. God, how she missed her, she thought as she carefully laid Draylen on the thick fluffy, crème-colored rug.

"Are you ready for me," she purred softly into Draylen's ear. Draylen took one look at Quinn's heavy hooded eyes, drunk with a sexual desire that matched her own, and nodded. Quinn intended to give them what they had both been starved for, but first she decided to make a slight detour. She straddled Draylen's pulsing body. Cherishing her swollen lips Quinn nibbled and teased them, before working her way down Draylen's delicate frame.

Tempting her, Quinn let the tips of her breast gently graze Draylen's wanton flesh, sending pings of desire radiating from her feminine core. Draylen trembled the moment she felt Quinn spread her legs. She raised her head catching a wicked grin on Quinn's face just before she seized the slick honeyed walls of her mound. Draylen pursed her lips tightly, moaning uncontrollably as Quinn teased her love bead, stroking it vigorously with the skill of her masterly tongue, awaking every nerve she possessed.

As the intensity heightened, Draylen searched for support to steady her unbridled spirit, gripping at the thick shag of the rug. As if on cue, Quinn locked her arms firmly around Draylen's thighs holding her prisoner to the delightful ravishment. She screamed out in reckless abandon, absorbed by the rippling waves of frenzy and splendor. She knew that she'd met her match when her soul ascended far beyond moon and constellations to worlds that only lovers were privy to and she wanted to exist there always. A chant of 'I love you' fell carelessly from her lips as she descended from the clouds and was restored to her lover's protective arms.

"That was amazing," Draylen said, nuzzling deep into Quinn's calming embrace as they lay beneath the discarded robe for warmth.

"I enjoyed it too," Quinn replied, satiated. "I missed you." She turned Draylen to face her when she noticed tiny droplets falling on to her arm. "Babe, are you crying?"

"I guess so," Draylen chuckled in between sniffles.

"Are you okay?" Quinn wiped away tears as they flowed. "I've never seen you do that."

"That's because I've never been this happy before. But thanks to you, now I am." Draylen smiled exposing her heart to Quinn. She was no longer guarded.

Quinn gave her a tender kiss on her lips. "I'm happy too, because of you."

"Quinn?"

"Hmm?"

"Why did you want to make love in the living room when there's a perfectly fine bed in the bedroom?"

"This is where we were when I told you that I loved you for the very first time. It's also where you confessed your love for me. I think this room is magical. It's where all of our truths were exposed." Together they stared up at the dimly lit chandelier hanging from the coffered ceiling. Tiny dangling crystals reflected above head like stars in the night sky.

"Well either we're going to bring the bed in here or we'll have to start telling our truths in the bedroom too. There's no reason why we can't have two magical rooms in this house, is there?"

"No there isn't," Quinn replied with a giggle. "In fact, if you want we can get started on making every room in the house magical, including the attic."

"Now you're talking."

"Draylen, I'm sorry for accusing you of sleeping with Dava. I was hurt because I thought that you didn't want me. Let's call it what it was—I was jealous."

"I'm as much to blame for letting Dava come between us. I should have communicated to you what was happening. I never meant to hurt you. I'm sorry for that." Draylen stroked Quinn's arm soothingly as it rested on her midsection.

"Do you think that you and Dava will ever work out your differences?"

"I don't know. Maybe in another three years." Draylen gave a hollow chuckle. "It would be great if we could get past this period in our relationship, because I do miss how we used to be, before we became lovers. I would like to get that back, but not at the expense of losing you."

"Give it some time then. Don't give up on her. Maybe your relationship won't be like it was before, but there is nothing wrong with wiping the slate clean and forging a new friendship."

"You're right. I'm going to wait a while and then try again. I only hope that she's receptive." Draylen faced Quinn and kissed her passionately on the lips before saying, "Tell me, should I be worried about this Sabrina you've been seeing?"

Quinn's brow quirked as she was trapped in Draylen's serious gaze. She thought that she had escaped any discussion about Sabrina, but Draylen's mind was sharp and rarely forget-ful. "Jerry and April thought that we'd make a good couple. Although we do share common interests, emotionally and phys-ically we aren't compatible. So we settled on being friends."

"I see. Does she know about me?" Draylen couldn't help her

jealousy from rearing its ugly head, but she needed to know if she had any competition.

"She knows about you and was hoping that we got back together. I couldn't seem to hide my love for you."

"Did you really go hiking?" Draylen asked scrunching her face.

"Yes," Quinn snickered. "And it was a lot of fun. You should come with us next time. Sabrina has organized a group of us and so far we've done three hikes. Will you come to the next hike with me?"

"I will go with you on two conditions. One, no more dates with anyone except me."

"Done. What's the second condition?"

"You have to say goodbye to your 'one date rule' forever."

"That rule was obsolete the moment I met you."

"Really?"

"Really. The rule had one major design flaw—I never took into consideration the possibility of falling in love at first sight, like I did with you. I love you, babe."

"I love you," Draylen slurred, seduced by her dizzying emotions.

Quinn mounted Draylen, stealing a mind numbing kiss even as she spread her legs apart, making a nest for herself, but was quickly spirited on to her back, overpowered by her lover's cunning tactics and quick hands.

"It's my turn," Draylen whispered into Quinn's ear, grinning victoriously as she nibbled at the sensitive spot just below her earlobe.

"Ahh," Quinn sighed. You don't play fair," She purred as Draylen continued to worry her spot.

"All's fair in love and war, don't you know that?" Draylen dipped her head and captured a turgid nipple and sucked greedily, bringing forth a howling cry of pleasure from Quinn's mouth.

"I've missed being with you like this," Draylen said as she latched onto Quinn's other breast, giving it the same attention. Then in one fell swoop she was on her back again, laid out on top of the thick rug and staring up into Quinn's devilish eyes.

"Babe, how could you?" Draylen whimpered, aghast by Quinn's guile.

"All's fair," Quinn reminded her before seeking entry into Draylen's luscious mouth, silencing any claims of foul play on her part. Draylen moaned deeply as their tongues spiraled joyfully together, giving her the greatest sustenance. When the kiss ended, Draylen lay outstretched in helpless surrender, brimming with an endless love for Quinn that rattled her soul.

"I'm yours. Have your way with me," Draylen pleaded staring intently at Quinn before closing her eyes to the intoxicating ecstasy that only she could provide.

Slow and purposeful, Quinn began to move against her moistened mound, fusing them with each writhing thrust of her hips. She bit down on her bottom lip as she fought to hold back her climax, with great difficulty. The absence of Draylen's love making had left her starved and now her body sought fulfillment. "No Dammit," Quinn groaned in frustration. She was losing control of her passions much too soon.

"I'm with you, Baby. Just let it happen. I'm with you," Draylen said assuredly, as she undulated meeting Quinn's masterful ebb and flow and together they rode out the tempest emerging fully renewed as they melted in each other's arms.

"ARE YOU SLEEPING?" DRAYLEN ASKED, PLANTING A KISS ON

Quinn's shoulder. It had been hours since they had succumbed to the wills of their burning hunger.

"No, I'm awake. I'm just enjoying being here with you." Quinn lay on her side in a fetal position, lulled by Draylen's shallow breathing. "I'm sorry about earlier. I couldn't control my need to have you."

"Babe, I needed you just as much. We've got a life time to make long earth-shattering love, okay?" Draylen said.

Quinn turned to face Draylen and gave her a quick love nibble on her full bottom lip, which did much to rekindle the smoldering embers that had not been doused by love's sated desire. "Draylen, there is something that we need to address in regards to our love making."

"What is that?" Draylen asked curiously.

"Two dominant women in the bedroom is gonna' make for a lot of fights in the future. We have to come up with a plan."

"Maybe we can take turns, one night you're on top and then the next night, me."

"And what about mornings and afternoons and impromptu moments when we've just got to have each other? How are we going to keep track?" Quinn asked.

"I don't know. Maybe we can devise a schedule or something," Draylen said chuckling.

"Are you kidding? Do you honestly think that in the throes of passion, we're going to be able to remember who did what when?"

"Quinn, it will be fine. We've managed to do okay, haven't we? True we do fight, but this is the kind of fight that I don't mind having with you. In fact it makes the sex even better, wouldn't you agree?"

"Yes, you've got a point." Quinn blushed.

"For now, let's just keep things as they are. We can revisit this discussion at a later date," Draylen said as she began to explore Quinn's breast.

Quinn quickly rose to her feet and held out her hand to Draylen. "Come on."

"Where are we going?" Draylen asked as she took hold of Quinn's hand and stood, following her from the room.

"We're going to the bedroom to make some magic."

34

Q uinn spent the better part of the morning sorting through stacks of memos, student papers and trade publications, deciding what to keep and what to discard as rubbish. Having taught so many years at Beacham University, it seemed as if one semester quickly rolled seamlessly into the next with very little fanfare.

This one would have been no different were it not for Draylen who walked into her classroom and into her heart, giving her life new meaning. She smiled as she remembered back to the very first day of class when Draylen raced into the room, seconds shy of having the door closed in her face. She shivered recalling the moment they first locked eyes and how she was unable to free herself from Draylen's warm caramel-colored stare, for what seemed like an eternity. Never could she have imagined that she would fall hopelessly in love with her, and yet she did—hard, fast and without warning. And if all went well, she would spend the rest of her life loving her.

"Gee, everywhere I look I see professors walking around with big smiles on their faces—and I see that you're no different. Is this what it's like at the end of every year?"

"Draylen, what are you doing here?" Quinn asked. "I just left you a few hours ago. I didn't know you were coming here."

"I know. I wanted to surprise you," Draylen said as she walked around the desk and kissed Quinn on the lips.

"Well I am definitely surprised. I've been doing my end of the year cleaning. It always amazes me how much one can accumulate in a year's time. Did you come to take me out to lunch?"

"Yes, but I also came by to speak with Jerry...No, I mean Dean Galloway. I get them confused at times." Draylen sat in the chair facing Quinn's desk, remembering what happened the last time that she was in her office. She shook her head to clear the images that ran rampant through her mind.

"What did you have to speak to Jerry about?" Quinn asked.

"Do you remember some months back when I dropped out of school?"

"Of course I do. It still remains one of my biggest regrets. If you and I never became involved then you would have finished your first semester here instead of leaving school."

"Well, I have decided to drop back in this fall semester."

"You're kidding. Are you serious?"

"Very."

"Oh Babe, I think that is just great!" Quinn's eyes grew misty while she beamed joyously. "This makes me so happy."

"I have decided to get my Master's in English."

"You're certain this time?"

"Quite certain. This time I'm going for me, not my parents and I won't let anyone discourage me this time either, not like I let Dava."

"But what about me? Is that going to be a problem for you, being in my class again?"

"No. That's what I wanted to talk to Dean Galloway about. I know that I would need to take your class in order to meet the academic requirements and since we are seeing each other, I wanted to see if there was an honest way around this situation."

"What did he have to say to that?" Quinn asked.

"He said that university will take my experience as a newly published or soon to be published author and apply it as credits earned, like an internship. That way I can avoid your class altogether."

"What a wonderful idea. The university does give credits for life experiences. It's a stretch, but if he's willing to do that for you, then I'm glad. I'm going to have to do something special for that old dude."

"Are you sure that you won't get tired of seeing me walking these halls in the mornings and then being with you outside of school in the evenings?"

"Not at all. I look forward to it," Quinn said smiling.

"I was thinking that since we're getting serious and all, that maybe it's time that you met my mom. We could have her over for lunch or something." Draylen studied Quinn's face.

"Are you ready for that?" Quinn asked, surprised at the suggestion. "The last time I asked you about meeting your mother, you didn't think that was a good idea."

"I have no qualms about it. I love you and I want you to know my family," Draylen replied.

"I can't wait for us to go to New York and have you meet my family. I know they're going to love you...Oh, by the way, what about your dad? I mean, what if he finds out that we're inviting your mom for lunch—won't he be livid?"

"Actually, no. My parents are back together, so I guess we'll need to invite them both. I suppose it still hasn't sunk in that they've reunited. I knew they were still mad about each other, they just needed time to realize it for themselves."

"Honey, I am so glad for you and for them." Quinn reached

into her satchel and pulled out an envelope, handing it to Draylen. "I was planning to give this to you later this evening."

Draylen was puzzled as she opened the envelope.

"What is this?" She asked as she slowly removed the contents and read them. "Plane tickets? To Paris!" Her hand trembled as she re-read the information on the tickets.

"I thought that we could go there this summer. I reserved two spots at a renowned writer's retreat. It's time for you to start working on your next book."

"My next book? I haven't even gotten my first book on the shelves yet."

"Yes, but it's only a matter of time. You can't rest on your laurels, Draylen Corliss. You're a writer, a soon to be published writer."

"But Paris? That's a bit extreme, isn't it?" Draylen asked, still in shock.

"I don't think so. You need to travel. How else are you going to get inspiration? I thought that I would also do some writing of my own. We can write by night and enjoy Paris by day—see the sights, eat delicious food, and immerse ourselves in the language of love. Think of it, two authors in the same household. Wouldn't that be great?" Quinn came to her feet and slowly walked around the desk and stood before Draylen, staring at her intently.

"The same household?" Draylen asked as her pulse began to race.

"Yes, the same household." Quinn reached inside the pocket of her slacks and extracted a small black cube-shaped box. Opening it, she presented the oval chocolate diamond ring surrounded by white diamond inlays on a platinum band. "Draylen, will you—"

"Yes!" Draylen interrupted. "A millions times, yes!" Draylen leaped from the chair and into Quinn's welcoming embrace, kissing her passionately.

"Draylen, I don't think I could be any happier than I am right now."

"Me either," Draylen said as she watched Quinn slip the ring on her finger. She marveled at its beauty as it sparkled in her tear-shimmering eyes.

"We should start making plans then."

"Quinn, I don't want to wait and I don't need a big wedding —unless it's what you want."

"I just want to be with you. We can get married before the writer's retreat and Paris can be our honeymoon as well, unless you don't want that. We can go anywhere you want."

"A honeymoon in Paris is perfectly fine by me. That sounds great. Of course, I'll have to tell Bradley that I'll be taking an extended vacation."

"About Bradley..."

"Yes, what about him," Draylen asked.

"I was thinking. I'm more than capable of taking care of both of us. Maybe you can hand in your resignation when we get back. That would give you more time to concentrate on school and your budding writing career." Quinn tugged at her bottom lip nervously, hoping that she hadn't asked for too much from Draylen too soon. She waited patiently as Draylen came to a decision.

"Quinn, I don't think that I can quit work at this time. I have plans for my future, I told you that. I need to see them through, regardless of the changes in my life."

"I realize that and since I'm going to be a part of your future, let me help you. I've worked hard all of my life and have been smart where my finances are concerned. Couldn't we share our dreams? Let me give you whatever you need for the properties you want to buy. I know you wanted to do it on your own , but I don't want you to work so hard at a job that doesn't fulfill you like writing does...Alright, if you must work, then take only a few assignments. I know that I'm asking a lot of you all at once. I only want to share in your world and I want what's best for you."

"I signed the papers this morning with the bank and..." Draylen pulled out two sets of keys from her pocket, "I am now a property owner. That was the other thing I did this morning. I went with my dad and made it official."

"I'm so proud of you, Babe." Quinn gave Draylen a long hot kiss that left them frazzled and breathless.

"I have an idea," Draylen said as she caressed Quinn's face. "What if I work part-time up until I get some tenants in both buildings, then I'll quit completely and do nothing else but go to school, write and make a home with you—not exactly in that order. It that agreeable?"

"I think that is more than agreeable. Let's make it a rule!"

ABOUT THE AUTHOR

TaKaylla Gordon is an author and avid reader of romance. *The One Date Rule* is her debut novel. A Chicago native from the South Side, Gordon enjoys experimenting with the many quirky angles of finding love despite all of its obstacles.

Gordon is the co-founder of Indie City Writers, a writing collective with a revolving focus that includes readings, expert author talks, critiquing, prompt writing and workshops. In her spare time, she enjoys being with family, hanging out in cafes with friends and watching a lot of YouTube. For more information, visit www.takayllagordon.com.

ACKNOWLEDGMENTS

There are so many people responsible for the making of this book. They have brought their love and kindness, their suggestions and critiques, keen eyes and warm hearts. This book is truly a labor of love and craziness. I have to name some very remarkable people who helped me on this literary journey. Roberta Littlejohn, the first person to read The One Date Rule and encourage me to move forward. K.B. Jensen for being my friend, confidant and ever-present teacher. I have fallen in love with the written word again. Thank you for introducing me to an awesome community of writers, Indie City Writers and Just Write Southside, that keep me on my toes. A huge thank you to Unoma Azuah for her brilliance. To my editors Yvonne Jeffries, S.E. Lauzen, Samantha Clark Rajala and Mary Howard, I thank each of you for what you added to these pages. I am grateful.

Where would I be without family? Nowhere. Thank you to my mom Delory Ann Gordon for being my constant cheerleader and prayer warrior, my sister Lintzia Gordon for being my backbone, and my nephews for making me feel like a rock star. Thank you to my Auntie Lenita Gordon for being in my corner and reading everything I've posted whether it was good or not.

To Gail and Arturo Terrell, thank you for lighting my fire. I thank all of my family for their belief in me as well as their patronage. Last but not least thank you to Sybil Wilkes my forever sister/friend for believing in me.

I dedicate this book to Kager and Nancy Lee Gordon, Lillian Gordon, Gerald Fisher, Antwan Terrell, Melvina Jackson and Darryl Dentley. Peace.

www.ingramcontent.com/pod-product-compliance
Lightning Source LLC
Chambersburg PA
CBHW031942240626
47153CB00003B/824